MY CHICANO HEART

THE NEW OESTE SERIES
León Salvatierra and Daniel A. Olivas, *Series Editors*

The New Oeste series celebrates the outpouring of creative expression by Latinx writers in the American West of the twenty-first century. In border-breaking literary arts informed by perspectives as distinctive as the American West, the authors in the series explore the artistic, cultural, and intellectual connections between the region's complicated past and its diverse future. With a commitment to the power of prose and poetry to unite, educate, and enrich, the series editors seek to support projects from unique voices that invite connection and inclusion within the American West. Currently, the editors seek fiction, poetry, and creative nonfiction that expand conceptions of the West and its people.

Preparatory Notes for Future Masterpieces: A Novel
Maceo Montoya

The World Doesn't Work That Way, but It Could
Yxta Maya Murray

How to Date a Flying Mexican: New and Collected Stories
Daniel A. Olivas

To the North/Al norte: Poems
León Salvatierra

*My Chicano Heart: New and Collected Stories
of Love and Other Transgressions*
Daniel A. Olivas

MY CHICANO HEART

NEW AND COLLECTED
STORIES OF LOVE AND
OTHER TRANSGRESSIONS

DANIEL A. OLIVAS

UNIVERSITY OF NEVADA PRESS | *Reno & Las Vegas*

University of Nevada Press | Reno, Nevada 89557 USA
www.unpress.nevada.edu
Manufactured in the United States of America

FIRST PRINTING

Cover design by TG Design

LIBRARY OF CONGRESS CATALOGING-IN-PUBLICATION DATA
ISBN 978-1-64779-134-6 (paper)
ISBN 978-1-64779-135-3 (ebook)
LCCN 2024003498

The paper used in this book meets the requirements of American National Standard for Information Sciences—Permanence of Paper for Printed Library Materials, ANSI/NISO Z39.48–1992 (R2002).

For my father,

Michael Augustine Olivas

(1932–2020)

Love is born into every human being;
it calls back the halves of our original nature together;
it tries to make one out of two and heal the wound of human nature.
—Plato, *The Symposium*

CONTENTS

ACKNoWLEDGMENTS

As I often have observed, giving thanks is fraught with peril because it is impossible to list every person—or institution—who played a role in the birthing of a book. But I hope that I have, over the years, personally thanked those who have been supportive of me and my strange vocation that we call the writing life. So, here are some thoughts on gratitude that will be inadequate and imperfect:

Mil gracias to those passionate, remarkable editors of the presses, literary journals, and anthologies that published many of these stories for the first time or included these stories in earlier volumes. I specifically and proudly acknowledge your publications, by name, at the end of this book.

I am again grateful to the wonderful people at the University of Nevada Press who—for a second time—saw fit to publish me. Your thoughtfulness, enthusiasm, and support are all any writer could want. And I lucked out again to have Robin DuBlanc assigned as my editor! Thank you for your close reading and smart edits.

I offer a big, virtual Chicano abrazo to the many extraordinary and devoted writers who have encouraged and inspired my literary life. And as I have done so on many occasions, I offer additional thanks to my fellow bloggers at the online literary site *La Bloga*.

As for my day job, I offer thanks to my friends at the California Department of Justice who have read my books and attended my various book readings. You continue to help me integrate my life as a lawyer with that of an author. And truth be told, you have inspired not a few of the stories I have written throughout the last twenty-five years.

I thank my parents, who always made certain that we were a family of books and that we each became proud holders of library cards. You taught your children to love and appreciate our Mexican culture and roots as well as art in all its forms. I offer a special acknowledgment to my late father, who had unfulfilled dreams of becoming a published writer. This is now my second book to be released since you were called back, and I miss that wonderful look on your face when you opened one of my new books for the first time. I miss you, Pop.

Last year also saw the passing of my younger brother, David J. Olivas. You wholeheartedly supported my creative writing life and often purchased my books for your friends and colleagues. You will always be with us.

Finally, I thank my wife, Susan Formaker, and our son, Benjamin Formaker-Olivas. As I have said many times before, I am nothing without you. You give me joy and you fill my life with so much happiness. I love you both with all of my Chicano heart. I hope that you enjoy my new book.

INTRODUCTION

In 2020, as my father was approaching the end of his physical life, I started to review well over a hundred short stories and novel chapters that I had written and published over the course of almost twenty-five years. From that exercise—perhaps one that admitted my own mortality—I chose some of my stranger stories to include with two newer pieces to produce a collection that was firmly footed in the magical realist, fabulist, and dystopian literary traditions. The result was *How to Date a Flying Mexican: New and Collected Stories* (University of Nevada Press, 2022). I observed in that volume's introduction that many of the stories confronted—either directly or obliquely—questions of morality, justice, and self-determination while being deeply steeped in Chicano and Mexican culture.

After that book was published, I realized that this survey of my prior fictions might produce another, somewhat different collection, but I wasn't quite certain what the theme would be. Also, as the pandemic dragged on even as we got vaccinated and boosted, I had started writing new stories, five of which were on the theme of love. Aha! Love. That was the thread that ran through many of the stories I had written over the last quarter century. This review of my previously published stories demonstrated that I often used fiction to address and explore love in its many forms: romantic, familial, platonic, and even narcissistic forms of self-love. Love can be beautiful, nurturing, fulfilling. Warped love—or what some perceive as love—can be controlling, destructive, spiteful. All of these aspects appeared in so many of my short stories. So, with this theme in mind, I had my task set for me.

The result is this volume of new and collected stories, thirty-one in all. Some of the tales are fantastical and filled with magic, others are more realistic, and some border on noir. But there are many ways to explore a theme. I have never allowed myself to be tied to one genre or another. They are all of equal merit to me. I am a storyteller who employs many tools because I see no reason to limit myself artistically.

While most of the stories previously appeared in my prior books, there are five new stories in this collection: "My Chicano Heart," "The Fairy Tale of the Man and the Woman," "An Interview with Love," "The Annotated Obituary of Alejandra López de la Calle," and "Nacho." In my opinion, these new stories represent some of my stranger tales, all told from either a magical, metafictional, or absurdist viewpoint. I am not quite sure what inspired me to go that artistic route. Perhaps the extraordinary pandemic era we have been suffering through is just too much reality for me at this time. Or perhaps the pandemic feels like a bad dream that can either be vanquished with magic or understood through an absurdist lens. No matter. For me, writing is a mystery that I care not to solve. Sometimes I fear that if I try too hard to analyze my creative process, I will lose altogether my facility to tell tales. In some ways, writing is like love itself: something to be acknowledged and appreciated, but not dissected and studied to death. I will leave vivisection to Doctor Moreau.

In any event, with these stories, I do not intend to exhaust every aspect of love; that would not be possible in one or even a hundred story collections. But I hope these tales will amuse you as well as offer food for thought on the most mystifying—but, I would argue, essential—of our human emotions.

MY CHICANO HEART

MY CHICANO HEART

Nacho sighs and then emits a whistle of exasperation through his teeth. He can't bring himself to look at his wife, Maricris, because he suspects that he will start to weep, and Nacho knows that he is an ugly cry. So Nacho forces his eyes to focus on the balustrade that runs along the perimeter of their porch. And this makes him wonder about the men—for surely only men did that type of work in 1927, the year their house was built—who shaped and sanded and painted the balusters and handrail. Had the women or men in their lives taken their hearts, too—in the same way Maricris had taken his—and had they fought with all of their essence to retrieve for themselves that most crucial of human organs? Nacho's thoughts wander further afield and he considers the state of their balustrade: it is sturdy and well crafted, but it could use a good sanding and a fresh coat of paint. But then Nacho's initial thought returns. He sighs, finally surrenders, and turns his eyes to his beautiful wife.

"Maricris," he whispers. "Por favor, give me back my heart. You have had it for ten years."

Maricris sits back in the porch swing that Nacho installed for his wife's thirty-fifth birthday five years earlier. Maricris cradles her mug of hot Nescafé—thick with half-and-half and three tablespoons of brown sugar—as if it were a baby chick or hamster or live grenade. And then she spits out an emphatic "No!" with her red lips forming such a perfect O that Nacho falls in love all over again. And then Maricris lets out a hearty "Ha!" because she sees that her husband has fallen for her once more. She then sips the hot coffee and savors both the rich flavor of her favorite beverage and her undeniable power over this man.

Nacho realizes that his wife is more beautiful at that moment than at any other, including their wedding day. And the inevitable moistness starts to well up in Nacho's big brown eyes—eyes he inherited from his mother and that resemble so many of the big brown eyes of the Mexicans from Jalisco—and he blinks, but the tears have turned Maricris into an expressionist painting and Nacho surrenders and allows the tears to drop freely from his big brown Jalisco eyes.

And then Maricris says it again, but this time in her own whisper: "No."

* * *

Nacho knows that he has no one to blame but himself. The day before they married, Maricris had asked him for his heart. Nacho could have said no, stood on principle—asserted his independence as an adult—and that would have been that.

But no. Nacho could not deny this woman anything.

So, as they lay in bed that long, luxurious day before their wedding, Nacho opened up his chest as Maricris greedily looked on, her mouth almost watering. He gingerly lifted his beating heart from its home and plopped it into Maricris's open palms. Nacho remembers Maricris's grunt of delight while she beheld his heart as it undulated and wriggled in her beautiful brown hands. She then scurried out of bed, in her naked splendor, and plopped Nacho's heart into a small hand-carved wooden box that sat on her dresser, a box Nacho had never noticed before. From his vantage point, Nacho could not see the box's top, which was adorned with a replica of a José Guadalupe Posada woodcut of nine rollicking skeletons riding old-time bicycles over a lone—and now doubly-dead—skeleton wearing armor. But over the years, Nacho would become quite familiar with the Posada calacas, memorizing each particular horrific grin of the vainglorious skeletons, and he would feel deep remorse for that lone skeleton whose life had been extinguished yet again even in death.

Nacho remembers in exquisite detail how Maricris then closed the box with a loud snap and hurried back into bed. She meticulously wiped Nacho's thick warm blood from her hands onto her immaculate white sheets, then snuggled into her man and gently examined with her fingertips the fleshy edges of the gaping hole on Nacho's chest that slowly closed until only a violently pink line ran like a deserted road from Nacho's throat down to his navel. Nacho could have said no, and Maricris would not have his heart today. But Nacho had little control when it came to Maricris's desires. And, of course, Nacho could see that Maricris knew this about her man, which only made Nacho love her more.

* * *

For twenty-two days after they married, Maricris kept Nacho's heart in the small hand-carved wooden box that sat on her dresser. Then one afternoon at 3:03 p.m., Maricris wandered into what was once her bedroom but was now theirs and happened upon Nacho standing before the dresser, arms akimbo, motionless, staring at the closed wooden box that held his beating heart. Maricris crept behind her husband and looked over his shoulder and down toward the box. Finally, after twelve long seconds, Maricris shouted: "Boo!"

Nacho did not start. Indeed, he did not react in any manner whatsoever. But his heart jumped so hard that it jostled loose the little brass latch on the box's lid and almost leapt from its splintery home.

The next day Maricris drove to the hardware store and returned twenty-three minutes later. Nacho watched from his seat at the dining room table as Maricris cleared the floor of their guest closet and set up a new twele-pound Stalwart Digital Safe that had been proclaimed a "best value" by a woman who hosted the *Security Nerd* blog and who proclaimed: "For its price point, this is one of the best home-safe options on the market. It has safety features such as an automatic lock after three incorrect entries on the keypad during any one-hour period, and the LED keypad gives an added layer of security. Plus, you can even make customizable codes for guests. There is also an override key if you forget your code or if the battery runs out."

After Maricris opened the safe and set the security lock, she marched to the bedroom and returned with the wooden box. Nacho could hear his heart beating woefully as Maricris set the box in the safe, closed and locked it.

"There," said Maricris. "No more temptation."

* * *

Nacho sometimes imagined that their life together was like a stage play with their dialogue written by an anonymous playwright and rehearsed over the course of six weeks until they were ready to act out their roles for an unseen audience. One occurrence felt particularly like a scene from a theatrical work-in-progress:

(*Scene: Present day.* MARICRIS *and* NACHO *sit at their breakfast table lingering over a lazy Sunday brunch. They are very old school so they each read a section of the* Los Angeles Times, *both lost in the printed words they read. After two beats,* NACHO *breaks the silence.*)

NACHO: (*newspaper up to his face, reading*) Mi amor . . .

MARICRIS: (MARICRIS *grunts, absorbed in reading her section of the newspaper*)

NACHO: (*lowers newspaper, looks at* MARICRIS) Mi amor . . .

MARICRIS: (*not moving newspaper from her face*) Sí, mi vida, sí . . . I am listening . . .

NACHO: (*skeptically, but pushing on*) It says here, mi amor . . .

MARICRIS: (*not moving newspaper from her face*) Sí, mi vida, sí . . .

NACHO: It says here that a new study shows that married men live longer than unmarried men.

MARICRIS: It only feels longer, mi vida.

NACHO: (*lifting newspaper back to his face, ignores* MARICRIS'*s joke and continues reading to his beloved wife*) And a 2009 study reported that men who married more educated women also enjoyed a lower death rate than men who married less educated women.

MARICRIS: (*putting newspaper down to look at* NACHO) Gracias a Dios that I got that master's degree.

NACHO: (*putting down newspaper*) Sí, mi amor. (*beat*) ¿Mi amor?

MARICRIS: (*lifting newspaper up in a vain attempt to end the conversation and continue reading in peace*) Sí, mi vida . . .

NACHO: (*beat*) May I have my heart back?

MARICRIS: (*not moving newspaper from her face, calmly, with little emotion*) No.

NACHO: (*imagining the perfect* O *that his wife's mouth just formed*) But why not?

MARICRIS: (*putting newspaper down*) Why should I? You gave it to me.

NACHO: I miss it.

MARICRIS: You do?

NACHO: Sí. Very much.

MARICRIS: But you knew what you were getting into when you fell in love with me.

NACHO: I did?

MARICRIS: No hay rosa sin espinas.

NACHO: (*considers his beloved wife's observation for a beat*) Ni modo. I ask again: May I have my heart back?

MARICRIS: (*beat*) Okay.

NACHO: (*surprised, elated*) Okay? You will give me back my heart?

MARICRIS: I didn't say that. Listen to my words.

NACHO: (*crestfallen, confused*) What?

MARICRIS: I will let you visit your heart, once a week.

NACHO: (*seeing an opportunity*) Oh?

MARICRIS: (*suspicious of her beloved*) But they will be supervised visits.

NACHO: Supervised? By whom?

MARICRIS: By me, of course. By me.

(MARICRIS *stares at* NACHO *with these last words. After three beats,* NACHO *grows uncomfortable, clears his throat, lifts the newspaper to his face to block* MARICRIS's *gaze.*)

NACHO: (*resigned*) Sí, mi amor. That will be fine.

MARICRIS: (*lifting newspaper up to her face*) And I will look into a Ph.D. program. Maybe I can add a few more years to your life.

(*End of scene, curtain*)

* * *

The supervised visitations with his heart proved to be more difficult for Nacho than he had expected. At first he derived great comfort—and maybe a little relief—from their new weekly ritual. Maricris and Nacho would finish their Friday night traditional dinner of chilaquiles that Nacho took great pride in cooking, using his late father's recipe. And then, after one or two cups of Nescafé and perhaps flan, tamales dulces, or tres leches cake, Nacho would clear the table while Maricris went to the guest closet, unlocked the safe (the keypad's beeping sound would inevitably make Nacho's scalp tingle in anticipation), and brought the wooden box to the now-cleared dining room table. And inevitably, Nacho would reach over to the latch, but Maricris would gently pat her husband's hand away with a soft *ah, ah, ah* (as she would to her child if she had one), and proceed to open the box herself. And Nacho would sit back, sigh, and take in the view of his beating, veined, ruddy heart. After three minutes of visitation in which the sounds of the married couple's breathing fell into a call-and-response rhythm with the *lub-dub, lub-dub, lub-dub* of Nacho's heart, Maricris would close the box, fasten its latch, and take it back to the safe. With four beeps of the keypad as Maricris locked away Nacho's heart, the ritual would end.

After six weeks of these supervised visits with his heart, Nacho grew restless. The comfort and relief he had once felt were replaced by trepidation and extreme dread. He needed to develop a plan to rescue his heart once and for all. Unbeknownst to Maricris, Nacho had tried several potential combinations on the safe's keypad, but to no avail. He went through the usual numbers: their birthdays, wedding anniversary, first date, but they all resulted in an unpleasant beep emitted by the keypad that mocked Nacho, sounding like it yelped *Loser!* each time he tried and failed.

But then Nacho's luck changed.

In the middle of one summer night, Nacho extricates himself from his beautiful wife—who snores softly and soundly—puts on a robe, and pads downstairs to try his hand again at the safe's keypad. He opens the guest closet and aims his Rayovac flashlight at the safe. And what he sees makes him jump. What? This can't be. The safe's door is ajar! Maricris must have failed to push it closed after the last supervised visitation two days before. Nacho squats and slowly opens the safe. And there it sits: the wooden box! The gentle *lub-dub, lub-dub, lub-dub* of Nacho's heart begins to quicken. Nacho lifts the box from the safe and slowly opens it. Oh, joy! His heart beats faster and louder and Nacho lets out a little *Ha!* but then realizes that he needs to be stealthy, so he closes the box, shuts the safe, and stands. Nacho steps warily from the closet, closes it with a soft *click,* and hugs the box to his chest.

What next?

In the garage Nacho keeps an ancient pair of Levi's, a Lila Downs T-shirt, and battered Chuck Taylors that he wears for yard work. He listens to the soft snoring of his beautiful Maricris upstairs, hesitates, but then creeps through the kitchen to the back door, which leads to their garage. Nacho enters the garage but leaves the light off since the moon is riotously bright and fills the space with a translucent, undulating glow through the row of rectangular windows that line the top of the door. He tenderly sets the box down on the workbench and opens a plastic bin that holds his clothes and shoes. Nacho strips off his perspiration-drenched pajamas and robe and stands for a moment, nude, in the moonlight. He reaches up with his right hand to the long scar that runs from his throat to his navel, gently fingering the ridged road of flesh. And Nacho smiles. After a few moments, he dresses, lifts the box from the workbench, opens the side door of the garage, and walks out to the side yard.

It is a warm Los Angeles night—almost eighty degrees—and the moon is even more dazzling than Nacho expects. He closes his eyes, breathes deeply, steels himself. *You can do this,* he says to himself. *You can do this.*

Nacho walks through the side yard to the sidewalk in front of their house. He looks to his left, then to his right, and then to his left again. He makes a decision to go left because it seems like the appropriate course of action. Nacho first takes one step, then another, finds himself trotting, and then, after a few moments, he is running, faster and faster and faster, clutching the beating box to his chest. And with each step his heart beats harder and louder. As Nacho runs along the deserted sidewalk, the moon glows brighter and brighter and his heart beats louder and louder until Nacho can no longer distinguish his heart from his breathing from the magnificent glow of the moon. And as he runs, Nacho feels moisture on his face. Is it raining? No, the sky is clear, not a cloud to be seen. No, it is not rain that covers his face, but tears pouring from Nacho's eyes, tears so big they could be dollops of honey or hand balm or hot blood from a gaping wound. Tears so big that Nacho can no longer see anything but a blur. And as he runs down the sidewalk clutching the beating box tightly to his chest, Nacho no longer knows what he feels and no longer knows what he is doing and no longer understands anything at all.

After twenty-eight minutes of running through neighborhoods

he no longer recognizes, Nacho finally lets out a loud "Oh!" and then stops running, staggers to a standstill, out of breath, his heart beating hard within the wooden box. And Nacho again lets out a loud "Oh!" He looks up at the moon, which now appears larger than it has ever been, and he feels as though the moon will swallow him up in all its lurid magnificence. It is, indeed, the most stunning, frightening moon he has ever witnessed. And in the silence of the night—a silence punctuated only by his beating heart and heavy breathing—Nacho sighs, shivers, and finally whispers: "Oh."

RES JUDICATA

The summer Romero died I'd just made partner at Walker, Elswick, and Harkin, one of the premier law firms in Los Angeles. Romero and I met almost eight years ago when I was finishing my last year at UCLA Law School. I used to study at this little French bakery in Westwood Village. My routine was to hit my classes and then take the bus into the Village—my tattered backpack heavy with law books—and settle into the corner of the bakery with a warm almond croissant and a large cup of cappuccino. Every so often an undergraduate would try to hit on me, but once he got an eyeful of what I was studying he'd move on, feeling a little intimidated by this cute little thing who wanted to be a lawyer. But Romero was different.

"Wow," he said. "Law. Cool."

I remember looking up, expecting to see some skinny white kid in a Bruin sweatshirt, hands in his back pockets, trying to look in control. Instead there was Romero: dark skinned, black hair, and sharp angular features that reminded me of my cousins in Mexico. He wore jeans, white T-shirt, and a paisley vest. Those were his pre-goatee days. I liked him better that way. His face gleamed, without a blemish, smooth like Indian pottery. I could smell his cologne, Chaps, a good clean smell. Romero carried his books loose on his right hip so he leaned to the left to keep balance.

"It's all right," I answered, trying to look composed.

He plopped his books down on the table, shaking my coffee cup almost off its saucer, and pulled up a metal chair with a loud squeak on the tile. "Mind?"

"No." I didn't, really, though I was surprised by his blatant attempt to start something. But I had been reading the same sentence, over and over, for the last twenty minutes or so. Something about the First Amendment and the three-part *Lemon* test. I was

11

feeling restless, a typical third-year syndrome, anxious to finish my last exams and focus on the bar. Then my real life could begin. My job as a first-year associate at the Walker firm sat in the near future like the Holy Grail, years of busting my rear end finally paying off. Not bad for a poor girl from the Pico-Union neighborhood.

"I don't have the discipline to do what you're doing," Romero laughed. I looked at his books: *Great Latin American Novellas, Art of the Short Story, The Norton Anthology of English Literature,* among others.

"I couldn't do what you do," I said. I realized that my voice shook a bit and my heart beat hard.

He kept his large brown eyes trained on mine as he laughed again. "Aren't lawyers supposed to be great fiction writers?"

Ah! So he had a good sense of humor on top of his great looks. I offered a weak *Touché* and closed my book with a snap. And that's how it started. Simply and with a good lawyer joke.

* * *

"Aguántate tantito y la fruta caidrá en tu mano," Papá said. We sat together on the rickety swinging bench that he had set up many years ago on our large cement porch. We could see everything in our neighborhood from that perch. Ardmore Avenue is not such an exciting street, mind you, unless you count the gang activity, as Mamá used to put it, that bubbles over from time to time.

"What?" I asked. My Spanish was so-so but I had special problems understanding Papá's dichos, those little aphorisms that amount to bite-sized bits of Mexican wisdom.

"You know, mija," he said as he reached over for his coffee. "Wait a little while and the fruit will fall into your hand."

I looked at him. Still so handsome even though he'd just turned sixty-five. Papá always reminded me of a darker version of Kirk Douglas. Years working construction had done nothing to destroy those looks.

"But I'm talking about love, Papá," I said. "We've been together for almost three years. With our schedules we barely see each other. This is our solution."

He furrowed his brow. I could see his pain as he tried not to boss his adult attorney daughter who had just told him that she planned to move in with a man without the benefit of marriage.

"I loved your mother too, and we waited until we were married."

Mamá had been gone for three years. I have no idea how scared he must have felt, left with three daughters to raise alone. Luckily the youngest, Lucia, was fourteen when Mamá died, so everyone was pretty self-sufficient. It was this other stuff, his daughters' dating life, that offered the most heartbreak. He was lost at sea when it came to this.

"Well, Papá, it's res judicata, as we say in the law."

"¿Cómo?"

"The thing has been decided, Papá."

He looked down at his cup of coffee and sighed. It was a beautiful Saturday morning and the sun shone brightly onto the porch. The only bothersome thing was Mrs. Reynoso's music that blasted from her living room, windows wide open so the entire neighborhood could enjoy a rousing cumbia at 9:00 a.m. at the beginning of the weekend. Papá looked deflated, and I know he felt like a failure.

"I love you, Papá," was all I could offer.

He let out another sigh and then looked at me. "I love you, too, mija, with all mi corazón."

Romero and I found a nice apartment in Silverlake the next weekend.

* * *

We had carved out a nice little life for ourselves. I worked horrible hours, as most of the young associates did, doing legal research, summarizing depositions, preparing witnesses, arguing a motion here and there, but never taking the lead on the appellate arguments or trials. That was for the partners. But I'd get there eventually. In the meantime I had to do the grunt work, but that was okay. That's part of the game and I knew the rules.

Romero was the happiest I'd ever seen him. He worked during the day at Starbucks to earn a few dollars and then he wrote in his free time. He eventually co-founded a literary journal on the Web. They called it *Palabras* and it featured fiction, poetry, and essays in both English and Spanish. They made no money, of course, but it was beautiful and it meant so much to him.

We scraped together whatever time we could to enjoy each other. We slept very little back then, but things seemed right, like someone else had planned it all for us and all we had to do was play our parts. The topic of marriage was the only sore point. It was like a scab that we kept picking. One conversation in particular sticks in my memory. We lay in bed after making love. Romero rested his head on my chest, listening to my heartbeat. He said it calmed him like nothing else, but this time I could tell that his mind could not be calmed.

"So, mi amor," he whispered.

"So?" I ran two fingers through his hair. He had grown it so long; it shimmered, limp and silky, and smelled like lemons.

"I love you."

"I love you too."

After a minute, he said, "Well, Yolanda, don't you think it's time then?"

"We just finished making love."

He laughed, which was the response I had intended. Romero had gotten so serious it made me nervous, so I went into joke mode.

He got up on one elbow and looked down at me. "You know what I mean, mi amor. Marriage. It's time, don't you think?"

We'd had this conversation on several occasions in the last two years. Usually Romero started it, and I always had an answer: wait until I get closer to partnership, wait until you finish your first novel. But these responses no longer worked. I was firmly on partnership track—was, in fact, one of the stars in the firm. Romero had finished his first novel and, after six months of looking for an agent, found one who really believed in his work. Things were great.

"Well, we're not even engaged," I ventured.

This surprised him. He had expected one of my many excuses. Romero's eyebrows arched and he grinned this silly grin. He jumped up and ran to the kitchen.

"What are you doing?" I called.

"Wait!"

After a minute or so, he strolled back into the bedroom, naked as can be, holding one hand behind his back, trying to keep a straight face. He came close to my side of the bed and got down on one knee. "Yolanda María Miramontes, will you marry me?" Romero held out his hand. Between his index finger and thumb, he held a ring made out of aluminum foil. The idiot made me cry. "Is that a 'yes'?" he asked, still holding the ring aloft in front of me. I nodded as I wiped my tears with the edge of our bedsheet. "I thought so, mi amor," he laughed and put the ring on my finger. "I thought so."

* * *

"Melanoma."

As the word left Romero's lips, our seven years together collapsed like so much shrink-wrap. He stood, tall and handsome, in the doorway of our study. The only blemish on this beautiful man was a dark spot on his left eyelid. We had both thought it was a sty, but when it got too painful, I sent Romero to his doctor. I was bone-tired after a six-week jury trial in Orange County, not to mention my numerous middle-of-the-night panic attacks because a decision on my partnership was only six months away. A cold December shower made our house seem safe and faraway from everything. But not after Romero uttered that word.

I stood and walked over to him. I couldn't breathe. "Surgery," was all I could choke out.

"Yes."

"Even chemo, dammit!"

"Yes." Romero reached out and pulled me close. "Yes," he said again. But the way he said the word made me shiver. He would go through it all, but he knew as well as I that melanoma was an evil cancer. It moved fast and usually evaded the scalpel with great cunning. "We will do everything that we have to," he said and pulled me even tighter to his body. I wanted him to squeeze me until I passed out.

* * *

The smell now made me nauseated. I figured that I'd get used to visiting Romero at Cedars-Sinai. But with each visit my physical reaction grew stronger. He had to be there. We tried to have him stay home until the end, but when his face hemorrhaged last month, we knew that I couldn't handle it. Now he was back at the hospital, the left side of his face, swollen six inches deep with eight tumors, wrapped in gauze. The next hemorrhage would probably be his last, Dr. Choi had warned us. The goal now was to make him "comfortable."

I sat in the metal chair next to him and held his hand. "So," I said trying to be matter-of-fact. "The bastards finally made me partner. I'm one of them now."

Romero squeezed my hand and tried to smile, but it hurt too much. "I'm proud, mi amor," he whispered.

Nine days later Romero simply bled to death. There was nothing left to remove, no way to close off the blood vessels. He was twenty-eight.

Now that I'm a partner, I can pull back a bit with my hours. I have young, eager associates working for me and they can stay all night at the office the way I used to. I now have a new goal. I will get Romero's novel published. It will be done. I have no choice. The thing has been decided.

QUACK

During an unseasonably warm morning in December 1967, Constance Barbosa was dubbed "Quack" by her husband, though she did not practice medicine nor did she resemble a duck in any way. Constance was a woman who did things in the 1950s and '60s that few women in the United States did. An engineer by education and training, she invented and patented many useful though slightly insignificant items that you and I take for granted but that, by the time she retired at the age of forty in 1967, transformed Constance into a millionaire several times over. The year she decided to pack it all up and enjoy her riches, she had designed and built a six-bedroom, split-level house in the Malibu hills that she shared with an energetic son, a brilliant daughter, a handsome, successful husband, and three lively black terriers.

Her nickname came from the manner by which her pets followed her in a perfect row: first Mamie, then Eleanor, and finally Lady Bird, each with plaintive eyes transfixed on their mistress, little sprigs of tongues dipping up and down from their pink mouths. Constance would putter around her magnificent garden, a droopy, deep-pocketed sweater hanging on her fine English bones—regardless of the weather—while her three terriers mutely stuck close to her heels. That warm day in December, Constance's husband, Rudolfo (or Rudy, as she called him) laughed and said she looked like a mother duck being trailed by her ducklings. "I will call you 'Quack' from now on," he had said in his beautiful baritone, laughing a bit too loudly as he wandered back into the house to have his second martini despite it being only 10:37 on a Monday morning.

At dinner that night, Rudy served up his famous chicken enchiladas. Because of the main dish's richness, it had to be served with a salad of cabbage, tomatoes, and celery. The large leafy mound sat in an old trustworthy wooden bowl with croutons the size of champagne corks strewn about haphazardly. Rudy doused the salad with his famous spicy dressing, a cross between an ordinary Caesar and a tangy hot sauce.

Constance had fallen hard for this man, ten years her senior, when he owned the five-star Hollywood restaurant that bore his name. Rudy had come from Mexico City as a young boy of thirteen, all alone and primed with a natural ability to do what he needed to become a success by any standard. Settling in Los Angeles during the Great Depression, he started as a dishwasher, then became a cook and then the manager of a small reputable eatery on Fairfax. Each night, rather than drink and chase girls, he studied English by reading newspapers and comic books, listening to the radio (he loved *The Jack Benny Show* and *Gunsmoke*), and going to the movie houses, alone. Rudy stashed every penny he could, sometimes going hungry just to increase his savings, until at the age of twenty he purchased an elegant but failing restaurant on La Cienega from a desperate Benjamin Coulter—so desperate that he did not care that he was selling Café Coulter to a "goddamn wetback"—for a pittance. Rudy renamed it "Rudolfo's" and designed a Californian/Mexican menu that was a hit with the executives from the studios, not to mention such Hollywood denizens as William Holden, Rod Steiger, and Bette Davis.

Constance and Rudy were the unlikeliest of couples who met in the unlikeliest of ways. In May 1948, to celebrate their dazzling, intelligent daughter's twenty-first birthday and last year at USC, Constance's mother and father, the Whitcombs formerly of Buckinghamshire, England, now of Pacific Palisades, took her to Rudolfo's for a fine dinner. The Whitcombs were not keen on Mexican cuisine but they tried to fit in, whenever possible, without lowering their standards too much. Besides, Rudolfo's had received a very good review from Edward Whitcomb's business partner, Charles Owens, who was known to be rather hard to please when it came to his second favorite endeavor, eating. (His *favorite* endeavor was embezzling large amounts of cash from his partner's share of Whitcomb-Owens, an exclusive and lucrative purveyor of fine men's shoes and belts on Wilshire Boulevard near La Brea.)

Constance never would have met her future husband had it not been for her very picky father who, in a fit of British indignation, demanded to see the owner of the establishment when an overworked waiter accidentally dripped a bit of Chablis on Mrs. Whitcomb, though she told her husband that it was nothing, really, nothing at all to get upset about. The waiter complied and within one minute Rudolfo Barbosa, majestic in a white double-breasted jacket, coal-black trousers, and shoes that shone like Rudy's perfect parted hair, approached their table with hands held together as if in prayer.

And Constance's gray eyes widened and blood ran to her cheeks. *This* was a man, she thought. So unlike her father, Edward Whitcomb, who was sturdy enough but who carried himself as though he were eighty despite being only forty-two. As Rudy apologized and offered the offended guest a complimentary bottle of champagne—which Mr. Whitcomb thought most wise, befitting a good businessman—his eyes caught Constance's: only for a moment, but they both knew right then that something more would happen between them. Indeed, they were married one year later.

The Whitcombs had a difficult time of it at first, but what could they do? Constance made good money as a new engineer and Rudy did quite well. It was America, after all, so they had to set aside the old British ways if they were to remain sane. To their friends back home in England, they referred to Rudy as a "Spaniard" (rather than "Mexican") who had quite a good business sense about him and who (Mrs. Whitcomb would add) was very handsome in a darker, exotic sort of way, you see. Of course their daughter fell in love with him. What woman *could* resist?

Several years after Constance and Rudy were married, the Whitcombs died in an automobile accident on Sunset Boulevard one cold wet evening in February. Mr. Whitcomb had been intoxicated but he assured his wife that he was in perfect condition to drive. The boulevard glistened, slick and winding, not more than a mile from UCLA. Mr. Whitcomb lost control just as he reached over to give Mrs. Whitcomb's knee a rare playful squeeze. Their Buick wrapped around an oak like so much tin foil and the bodies were thrown forty yards into the front hedge of the Harrises' beautiful Spanish-style mansion. Mr. Harris, wearing his favorite blue terry cloth robe, strode out of his house with hands on hips and a furrowed brow. "Jesus Christ!" he exclaimed. "Not again!" And he stalked back into his home to call the police, realizing that, by the looks of their bodies (arms, legs, and necks bent in unnatural ways), the Whitcombs did not need medical attention. "I hate this goddamn street!" was the only benediction Mr. Harris offered as he disappeared into his home.

Sixteen years later, Rudy served a fine Mexican dinner to his newly retired wife and their children, Alejandro and Ariana. "Children," smiled Rudy as he scooped large piles of salad onto their plates. "Do you know what I saw in the backyard this morning?" His diction was perfect despite his having consumed six martinis since the morning.

Alejandro, ten years old with bright, shiny brown eyes like his father's, bounced in his chair and giggled in anticipation. Ariana, quite controlled and proper at thirteen, shot a serious and knowing glance at her mother, who sat looking down at her wineglass, her eyes transfixed on the scarlet reflection performing a St. Vitus' dance on the glistening white tablecloth.

"Well?" asked Rudy. "What do you children think?"

The enchiladas sat in a flat Pyrex baking dish that was perched on a trivet in the middle of their long teak dining table. The melted cheese and red sauce still bubbled, making the sliced black olives look like so many sacrificial virgins thrown into the midst of a voracious live volcano. Rudy finished serving the salad and moved to his masterpiece, wielding a stainless steel spatula like a paintbrush. He eyed the enchiladas and, with great care and meticulous maneuvering, lifted two of the moist rolled tortillas and laid them gently on Alejandro's plate. Then, as if the floodgates had been irrevocably thrown open, Rudy rapidly though no less neatly served Ariana, Constance, and finally himself. Setting the spatula down on the edge of the trivet, Rudy refilled his wineglass (Constance's was still full and quite untouched) and sat down at the head of the table triumphantly. "Well, children, can you believe it? A large mother duck and three obedient ducklings following her every move right there in our own backyard!"

Alejandro laughed but Ariana sat silently, staring at her mother. Constance sighed and finally lifted her glass. Before taking a drink, she looked at her husband. Rudy dug his fork into the steaming enchiladas and chuckled. He was still just as handsome as the day she'd met him, though he had less hair and a slight paunch. Rudy continued his habit of dressing elegantly, even for dinner at home. This evening he wore a gleaming white shirt and brown woolen slacks. He spent less and less time at the restaurant, especially now that his wife had made them quite rich. Besides, the place ran itself, though it no longer was the place of movie stars and moguls. Rather, CBS Studios supplied most of the clientele these days. Not as fashionable, but nonetheless lucrative.

Their marriage had been a success, even during the period of Constance's grief caused by the untimely and gruesome death of her parents. But since the birth of Ariana thirteen years ago, Rudy had started to make little biting jokes at Constance's expense. They still made love and he often expressed a gentle affection for her, usually in the morning before his first drink, but things were certainly different than they had been in the first few years of their marriage.

Now Rudy continued, smiling as he dug into his salad, "The duck was about this tall," and he held out his free hand slightly higher than his head.

Alejandro's eyes popped wider than before and he noisily took in a deep breath through his nostrils. "Hadn't you seen it before?" he giggled, his mouth full.

"Oh, yes! Many times before. But I never really *looked* at this duck before. I sort of took it for granted."

Constance coughed and took a drink. Ariana turned to her father. She wanted to say something but did not.

"Wait," Rudy said. "Before I continue, we need a little music. No? What's a nice dinner without music?" He stood up and walked over to the RCA stereo, squatting beside it with the ease of a young man. Over a hundred LPs were lined up beneath the turntable in alphabetical order. Rudy ran his index finger slowly along the spines of the record covers until he let out an "Ah!" and pulled an album out. He examined the gleaming black vinyl (like a jeweler eyeing a brilliant new diamond) before blowing a bit of dust away and placing it gently on the turntable. As he walked back to his seat, Astrud Gilberto's girlish voice filled the room with a Brazilian tempo. Rudy sat down with a smile. "Now that's música."

Ariana finally spoke: "Papá, we know there's no big duck in the backyard. You're just making fun of Mamá and the dogs. That's all." Her voice shook.

Rudy looked at Ariana and then at Constance and back again. Both so much the same. Blood filled his cheeks and his eyes watered just a bit. "Yes, Ariana. You're correct. Papá is making a little joke."

Constance smiled a little. But Rudy's embarrassment quickly passed and he added, "But you know, I think your mother would enjoy a nickname. She doesn't have one, does she?"

Constance's smile fell from her face and she looked at her plate. "What do you suggest, Rudy?" she almost whispered.

Rudy's eyes widened and he leaned forward. "Why, 'Quack,' of course."

Alejandro let out a yelp of delight. Ariana stood up and threw her napkin on her food. "That's a stupid nickname!" she shouted, and stomped upstairs to her bedroom.

"What's wrong with our hija?" Rudy asked in genuine amazement. Constance did not answer. She simply took a long drink of her wine.

Alejandro, who had ignored his sister's outburst, asked, "And what should we call you, Papá?"

Constance put her wineglass down and looked at Rudy. "What, indeed?" she said. "What, indeed?"

* * *

Retirement did not seem such a good idea after all. Constance felt isolated and missed her former employees. She had left her first job after only two years to found her own company. Constance built it from the ground up, as they say, and grew fond of her "team." Aside from her secretary (who also doubled as the office manager), Constance's other three employees were her contemporaries—indeed, former classmates. There was Rachel Goldman, a serious and handsome woman who kept her engineering designs honest and to the point; unfortunately, her numerous boyfriends had been rather dishonest and meandering until five years ago, when Rachel fell in love and married a sturdy, reliable fifth grade teacher who wrote science fiction in his spare time.

Harold Bennett, the shyest member of the team, was thorough and clever, though rather insecure despite his great skill. He had an abundance of straw-yellow hair (cut once a month by his wife, Kathy, a lovely and intelligent woman) and wore eyeglasses with thick black frames. Freckles covered his face and arms like a Jackson Pollock painting.

The last member of the team was Patrick Ward, whose mother was Greek (he had recommended the name "Ariana" to Constance and Rudy), thus giving him an olive complexion that did not fit his name. Patrick could look handsome in certain lights, usually at dusk, with thick eyebrows and sharp, well-carved features that betrayed his mixed heritage. Constance liked his eyes: cloudless blue and almost translucent, they accented his darker features in an unusual but pleasing way. Constance missed Patrick the most when she retired. He had an easy manner, sitting at the conference table, leaning back, looking at the ceiling fan, a narrow black pipe jutting from the side of his mouth, absorbing his colleagues' discussions. He always waited until the others had spoken their piece before offering his own simple, one-sentence observation of the problem at hand. *Efficient* was Constance's assessment of Patrick. Efficient, even when being charming and flirtatious. Not a word or movement wasted. Like his designs: smooth and aerodynamic. Constance missed Patrick. And the others as well.

Rudy cleared the dishes (it was the maid's night off), placing Ariana's untouched dinner in the right-hand corner of the refrigerator's top shelf. He knew full well that his daughter would come downstairs within the hour because, though quite thin, she could eat as heartily as the next teenage girl. Rudy sculpted Reynolds aluminum foil around the plate and taped a note on it that said in very elegant cursive: *Mi hija, I still love you, I hope you know.*

Constance sat in her favorite chair, an old leather creature that hugged her thin contours like a second epidermis. Rudy hated that chair. It did not belong in their sleek, Danish-style home, furnished with matching modern teak furniture. He said it looked like a wart on a beautiful woman's cheek. But it stayed put. As Constance nestled deeper into the well-worn leather, Mamie, Eleanor, and Lady Bird tumbled in slow motion at her feet in the vain and shared hope of being the mistress's favorite. Constance noisily browsed through the *Los Angeles Times*. The headline heralded, "Medical Triumph: First Human Heart Transplanted." Constance focused on the picture of Denise Darvall, a twenty-five-year-old South African bank accounting machine operator who had died in an automobile accident. Her heart went into Louis Washkansky, a middle-aged wholesale grocer. A lucky ten-year-old, Jonathan Van Wyk, received Miss Darvall's kidneys.

"Quack!"

Constance jumped. She looked up and saw Rudy smiling, standing in the kitchen doorway, drying a plate as though it were a delicate heirloom. He looked so handsome! Rudy's teeth shown as white as his shirt, and his chestnut skin was still as smooth as the day she first met him at the restaurant.

"You startled me," she said.

"I can see that," Rudy laughed. "I was just trying out your new nickname, that's all."

"I don't think I quite like it, Rudy. Rather odd, you know."

"Yes, mi amor. But that's the beauty of it, yes?"

"Rudy?"

"Yes?"

Constance coughed and put the newspaper down on the coffee table. "I think that I'm going to visit the old gang tomorrow. For lunch, you know. You won't mind terribly if you're alone in this big house for a few hours, will you?"

Rudy's smile disappeared and he walked back to the kitchen. Constance sighed. She stood, ever so slowly, and followed Rudy. Mamie, Eleanor, and Lady Bird jumped to their feet and padded behind her.

Rudy was standing by the sink, looking down into the sudsy water. "I was going to go to the restaurant tomorrow anyway, mi amor. New cook. Need to see how he's doing."

Constance came close behind Rudy and touched his shoulder. She could feel his muscles tighten. "I'm not yet used to this thing called 'retirement,'" she said.

"Yes," said Rudy and he turned to Constance. "Yes, mi amor. It must be hard. Please, have fun with them. Tell them I say hello." As he said this, he put his arms around Constance's waist and pulled her close so that their noses almost touched, though at a rather sharp angle.

"I love you, Rudy."

He smiled. "My little Quack. I love you too."

Mamie, Eleanor, and Lady Bird sat on the cold tiled floor, their heads cocked slightly at different angles as they stared silently up at their mistress. Eleanor suddenly yawned with a snap of her black and pink lips.

Rudy looked down. "Your ducklings adore you," he said.

"Yes," said Constance. "They do, don't they?"

"Oh, by the way. Where are you going to eat lunch?"

"Why?"

"I need some fruit. There's a new salad we're trying at the restaurant and I want to make it myself. Try it on my family."

"Oh, guinea pigs, eh?"

Rudy laughed. "If you're going to eat near Farmer's Market, you could pick up some ingredients for me. I'll make a list."

"Yes, my love. Of course." She rested her head on Rudy's chest, feeling his heart beat against her cheek. "Of course."

* * *

Constance pulled into the spot she had always liked, far in the southeast corner of the lot, far from the other cars. Unlike yesterday, a few dark clouds traveled slowly in the otherwise bright blue sky, but the thermometer almost hit seventy-two degrees. Three weeks before Christmas and she could wander about as if it were spring! She hopped out of the car, feeling invigorated just by being here. The office building gleamed, all glass and metal, in the sunlight, a tight and perfect rectangle, four floors high, the home of various businesses including Biz-Tech, Constance's former company. Her father had criticized the "boring" architecture of America, and this building was the prime example of lazy, unimaginative architects. "And the palm trees planted everywhere! They look like used toothpicks! Only Americans would call those blasted things trees!" But Constance disagreed. This building, with four palms lining each side, was pure function. No nonsense. It served its purpose without being majestic, regal, or anything like the English structures her father had worshipped. And just then, as a cool breeze blew across the parking lot, making her eyes water just a bit so she had to blink, it looked beautiful to her.

"Constance, darling!"

Constance jumped, startled, and before she knew it, Sally Mejia, Biz-Tech's secretary and office manager, had her arms around her old boss. "Sally!"

Unlike her father, Constance never treated Sally like "the help." She was a colleague, an important part of the team. And she had always made Constance feel at ease, with her quick laugh and ability to get things done. She squeezed Sally, who was built like Constance, petite and almost fragile. Sally was ten years her junior.

"You're early," Sally said as she pulled back while keeping her hands on Constance's hips. "And skinnier too! That won't do!"

Constance laughed. "Look who's talking!" She looked into Sally's brown eyes, which sparkled with genuine delight. "Let's go in, Sally. I'm dying to see everyone." They turned, arms around each other's waists, and almost marched toward the building.

"When we heard you were coming, we thought we'd do something for old times' sake. Go over to Farmer's Market, get our old booth at Du-Par's, drink a lot of coffee. How's that sound?"

"Perfect! Rudy needs a few things from the market. So, is the whole gang here?"

Sally's smile fell from her face and she tilted her head to the left, away from Constance. "Well, Rachel and Harold will definitely be coming." Sally coughed a bit, but it sounded forced.

Constance stopped. They were but ten yards from the building's front doors. "And Patrick? Will he be there? He said he would."

Sally focused her gaze on Constance's shiny black pumps. "Well, he said something came up. Maybe he'd try to get there for pie."

Constance smiled. "Well, he'll be missing all the fun, won't he?"

Sally looked up and returned the smile, deep dimples descending into her bronze cheeks. "Yes, darling, he will."

* * *

"Pass the salt," said Harold.

"No," said Rachel. "You haven't even tasted your Salisbury steak. How do you know it needs salt?"

Harold pushed his eyeglasses back up the narrow bridge of his nose. He cleared his throat and spoke slowly: "You are not my wife. Now, please, pass the salt."

Rachel put down her egg salad sandwich and turned to Constance. "See, you're gone a short while, and Harold gets assertive." She pushed the glass saltshaker toward Harold, who offered a stiff smile in thanks. "No longer a shmendrick."

"Lucky for you I don't know any Yiddish," he said as he snowed his plate with salt. "Except for that one word. What is it?"

"Putz," said Rachel.

Harold's face lit up. "Yeah, that's it! Putz. It means . . ."

"We know what it means," interrupted Sally. "No need to spread your knowledge during lunch."

"Oh, yeah," Harold laughed. "Sorry. Mixed company and all that."

Rachel reached across the table and put her hand on Harold's shoulder. "You're a luftmensch, but a great engineer ..."

"Thank you, Rachel, but what does that ..."

"Almost as good as me!" She pulled her hand away and sat back, laughing.

"They've been at it since you left," said Sally.

Constance wiped her left eye with her thumb. She had been laughing rather hard. "They've always been that way! It's essential to their creative partnership, don't you see?"

"It's a pain in the ass!" said Sally.

"Tuchus," offered Rachel. "'Ass' sounds so harsh, so ... crass."

"Rhymes with 'ass'!" laughed Sally. "In Spanish, we say, 'nalgas.' Talk about crude!"

"Doesn't anyone speak plain English around here?" said Harold.

"Well, what you Americans call English we call ... well, I'd rather not say," laughed Constance. "You know I don't talk like that! Let's just say that it isn't the King's English, that's for sure."

"Of course, we kicked your royal rear ends out of here two hundred years ago."

Everyone turned to the head of the table. Patrick stood there, grinning, pipe tucked tightly into the left side of his mouth, hands shoved hard into his blue blazer's pockets. "You know I'm right," Patrick continued. "We needed our own language, different from the oppressors'."

"You're Greek, though," countered Harold.

"Only half," said Constance in a measured tone. "Half."

Sally looked at Constance and then back at Patrick. "Sit, Pat, sit," Sally said after a moment, and she stood up so that Patrick could sit near Constance. Patrick paused for a second or two and then slid into the booth. Constance admired his fluid, graceful movements. He reminded her of Cary Grant in *North by Northwest*. She scooted a bit to make room for him. Sally hopped back into the booth and closed it off like a cork.

After about a half minute of silence, Rachel said, "So, the whole team is back together again!"

Everyone laughed. Harold let out a snort and Rachel neighed. Patrick kept his pipe tightly clenched between his frosty white teeth as he uttered a staccato "Heh, heh, heh." Sally mimed a chuckle. Constance giggled just a bit.

Lunch went on for about an hour and it was, indeed, as if Constance had never left. She participated in every discussion, particularly of the new designs. All of them looked so wonderful to her. Why didn't they socialize more? She glanced at her watch during a lull. "Oh, dear! I must go!" she said.

"We're just gettin' goin' here," said Harold.

"Yes, do stay," said Sally. "Come by the office. Visit."

Rachel looked very serious. "Stay, please. Patrick, convince her to stay. She always listened to you."

Constance looked down at her lap. She could feel the heat from Patrick's thigh through her woolen skirt. "No, I can't. Sorry. We must just do this often, right?"

Patrick turned to Sally. "You heard your old boss. Let's let her go."

Sally slowly slid out of the booth. Patrick followed. Constance pulled several bills from her purse as she moved out of the booth. "This should more than cover it," she said.

"Care to be escorted to your car?" said Patrick.

"Oh, no. I'm fine. Besides, I'm going to buy some fruit. For Rudy."

After hugs and good-byes and promises to keep in touch more, Constance walked out the back of Du-Par's and into the Farmer's Market. The aisles teemed with giddy Christmas shoppers. She headed toward her favorite fruit stand near the middle of the market. The one owned by Mrs. Horowitz. As she dodged people, Constance thought about Denise Darvall, the young woman whose heart now beat in the chest of a middle-aged man. The picture in the *Times* showed her to be quite pretty, with dark hair and Elizabeth Taylor eyebrows. So young, so young. Not even thirty. Is this what the future holds? Interchangeable hearts? Other body parts? An engineer's dream! Lose an arm, get a new one. We need never die, need we?

Constance realized that she had reached the stand. Vibrant apples, glorious oranges, and steadfast pears greeted her with a grand, sweet fragrance. And Mrs. Horowitz, survivor of Auschwitz, widow for two years, stood in the middle of it all tending to her customers like the grandmother she was. The old woman's eyes sparkled when she spotted Constance. She smiled at her old customer. Constance reached into her purse for the list Rudy had given her. She rummaged around for it, but couldn't find the small slip of yellow paper.

"Mrs. Horowitz, hello! I had a list, but I've forgotten it at home."

As she handed change to a young man, Mrs. Horowitz smiled. "Not to worry. This is not such a big problem. Let's talk about what you need."

"Well, it's really what Rudy needs."

"Same thing. Not a problem."

"Yes," said Constance. "Let's talk about what I need."

* * *

"The fruits you chose were wonderful, mi amor. Did you like the results?"

Constance sat in her favorite chair, legs tucked up beneath her, drinking a cognac. Rudy poked at the logs in the fireplace. They crackled with each nudge.

"Yes, dear. Delicious. It will be a hit at the restaurant."

Rudy put the poker down and reached for his cup of coffee. He patted his stomach. "I'm on a little diet. No booze. Just juice and coffee."

Constance looked up at him. The light from the flames transformed him into a shadow with glowing edges.

"Well, if you lose too much weight, you'll have to fight the women off with a stick."

Rudy laughed. "Nothing to worry about. I have my one love."

Constance put her glass down and stood. Rudy came close and put his arms around her.

"Your little Quack," she laughed.

"Stupid nickname."

"No. I like it."

He kissed her hair. It smelled sweet, like the fruit he had sliced into a succulent salad. "Where are your ducklings?"

"In Ariana's room," she said softly. "They're sleeping at her feet."

Rudy hugged Constance closer. "Ah! A little competition."

"I want to check on her," Constance said, and she pulled away. "I'll be right back, my dear."

"Yes, but hurry back." Rudy watched her leave the room. The hardwood floor creaked just a bit with each small step of his wife. He smiled and reached for his coffee.

Constance tiptoed in her stocking feet up the staircase to Ariana's room. She could discern the terriers piled together at Ariana's feet. Constance gently sat on the edge of the bed and looked at her daughter's face. Rudy was right: she looked so much like Constance. The eyes, the nose, the lips. But the eyebrows. So different from Constance's. She couldn't tell whose they were. Rudy's? Patrick's? It didn't matter. It shouldn't matter. Not anymore, at least. That was all over. Constance leaned down and kissed her forehead.

"Sleep well, my little one," she said. "Sleep well."

LAS DOS FRIDAS

From Tonyo's window at the Colón Misión Reforma, he can see the Hotel Imperial, which looks newer, more luxurious than his choice but he can't be certain. It's nothing more than a suspicion growing from disappointment with his room. Tonyo scrutinizes the other hotels across the street. To the left of the Hotel Imperial stands the shrouded frame of the Embassy Suites Hotel allegedly opening early next year. A rather realistic rendering of the completed hotel adorns the shroud so that if Tonyo squints just a bit, it looks as real as the surrounding buildings, betrayed only by the artist's rather optimistic deep-blue, cloud-dappled firmament. The actual midday sky bears no relation to the color blue but has more in common with the cement-gray of the sidewalk below. He could smell the rain getting ready for a humid afternoon appearance.

Tonyo rubs the stubble on his chin and turns away from the window. He's hungry but can't bear room service or a foray into the busy streets. He remembers fondly the two tortas de pollo he wolfed down yesterday at a bustling little stand during his day trip to Toluca. Tonyo knows that if he tries he could find the same almost anywhere in the Federal District along the streets not too far from his hotel. But he has a habit of romanticizing trifles, like meals or hotel accommodations, so that attempts to replicate the experience will inevitably fail. And such failures invariably evolve into something larger, less easy to ignore. He had filled his life with these small disappointments, and the hotel room had already moved with great ease into this category. The accommodations had been considered more than adequate, even elegant, ten years ago. Now they simply felt cramped, revealing signs of wear at the edges, just within view. Tonyo realizes he should have stayed someplace else, someplace he had never stayed before.

He can't remember what went into the equation that led to his decision to leave Pasadena and come back to Mexico. Visiting family was always a fine way to pass time. And his tío Gilberto never failed to entertain his favorite American nephew. But when Tonyo's divorce from Nellie became final, forcing the sale of their house, a trip far from home made perfect sense. Indeed, his life had been torn asunder—something he never admitted even to his therapist or his parents—and he had developed enough self-awareness to prescribe, if not a cure, something of a balm for the gaping wound: get out of L.A. Period. But he took one step further: he sold his law practice and went on inactive status with the California bar so that he could avoid taking any continuing education classes until he knew where he was going to land, both emotionally and physically.

Tonyo is certain of one thing: he and Nellie *had* loved and respected each other. But he still couldn't grasp this new reality of being a single man with a failed marriage. Trying to understand what happened became the constant undercurrent of his life. He had given her wide berth to kindle a writing career, and it had paid off. Indeed, Tonyo had grown quite proud of his wife's modest fame as a novelist and he easily tolerated seeing bits and pieces of their lives show up in her books. But when Nellie's fourth novel came out last year to the best reviews yet, he was stung by the antagonist's uncanny resemblance to him. Though Tonyo knew his faults quite well, here they were in full relief for all the world to see. Worse yet, the review in the *Los Angeles Times* actually wondered if Nellie had borrowed liberally from her own marriage to a lawyer to create—in the reviewer's words—"one of the most self-absorbed, pedantic, and out-and-out puerile fictional husbands in the last twenty years."

"Sweetie," Nellie had said when he finally confronted her about it. "It's fiction. You know I appropriate from my life. I always have. But it's pure fiction."

He'd wanted to believe her—and he did for a few weeks. But as their friends and family read the novel, they cooled to him and eyed him with apparent disdain. Even his own mother appeared to see him in a new and unflattering light. His twelve-year marriage started to fray as he withdrew, became sullen, while compulsively rereading the most damning chapters. He even shaved his mustache in the hope that by altering his appearance, he could distance himself from his fictional persona. But Tonyo's upper lip looked so naked he immediately allowed a new mustache to grow in again. Finally, Nellie told him that enough was enough and that she couldn't write if he acted this way. Tonyo's big mistake: he asked her to choose him or her writing. The moment the ultimatum left his lips, he knew what she would choose. And that was that.

Tonyo checks the time on the radio alarm clock by the bed: almost noon. In L.A. it'd be 10, two hours behind. He figures he should do something. Anything. So he finally shaves, showers, and goes down six flights for a quick lunch at the hotel restaurant. He asks for a table far from the group of about two dozen American tourists who are being briefed by their tour guide: twelve wonderful days exploring the magnificent Aztec and Mayan ruins and anthropological museums from Teotihuacan to Oaxaca, Palenque, Uxmal, Mérida, Chichén Itzá, and finally Tulum. Though mostly well behaved, the tourists are too obvious and Tonyo hopes he doesn't resemble them. He knows he's succeeded when the waiter brings the bill, nods toward the tourists, and whispers, "Americanos." And then he adds with a smile: "¡Ay Dios mio!"

Tonyo nods in agreement, pays, and wanders to the lobby. The two young men and one woman at the front desk are ridiculously young and good-looking. Tonyo asks for a taxi and the woman, who had checked him in two days ago, immediately hops to, leading him through the gleaming glass doors and down to the sidewalk, where a line of taxis wait their turn. Tonyo tips her 50 pesos and she smiles broadly, reminding him of Nellie. He grins, holds her eyes with his a beat too long, and jumps into a taxi.

"El Museo de Arte Moderno, por favor," he says to the driver, who immediately slides with ease into the wild stream of traffic. Once safely en route, the driver attempts a little chit-chat, but Tonyo's mind is elsewhere. The driver accepts this without malice and drives in silence. When they finally arrive Tonyo overtips as a penance, which the driver acknowledges with a smile.

Tonyo wanders the museum with no particular plan. He remembers prior happy visits when he was much younger and life was easier to navigate. The artwork by Orozco, Rivera, Siqueiros, and others used to sing. But today they seem impenetrable, foreign, cruel. Even Tamayo's sandias look like so many scarlet mocking grins rather than exuberant meaty slices of watermelon. But then he sees her. Actually, both of her. A painting he never understood now calls to him: *Las Dos Fridas*. Tonyo approaches Frida Kahlo's masterpiece of self-awareness. He walks slowly, as if any quick movement might scare the painting away. Tonyo stops in front of it, five feet away, and allows his eyes to slide over the image. On the left sits Frida number one, black hair pulled back and up in an elegant bun. She wears a white, high-necked, European-style gown; a large, jagged hole reveals her left breast and heart. An artery runs from the heart behind her right arm to her lap, where she clutches a surgeon's forceps at the end of the artery. But blood still escapes, creating red blotches on an otherwise virginal lap.

Tonyo's eyes ease over to the Frida on the right. This Frida wears a traditional Tehuana dress of blue, green, and yellow. Her heart is also exposed, but the dress is not torn. An artery runs from Frida number one's heart to number two's heart. Another artery playfully runs down Frida number two's left arm, wrapping its way down like a vine to an oval photo of young Diego Rivera, which Frida gingerly holds between her thumb and forefinger. No blood leaks here, the photo serving as a perfect clamp. The two Fridas hold hands and offer no expression. In all the years he has admired this painting, Tonyo had not, until now, noticed that dark rain clouds swirl behind the sitting women.

Tonyo laughs gently. Of all the great Mexican painters, Frida Kahlo more than any other relied on her life, marriage, and physical suffering to supply much of her artistic subject matter. And despite numerous violations of their vows, Frida and Diego stayed together, for the most part loving each other, encouraging the other in art and politics. Perhaps that is Tonyo's problem: he is not an artist while Nellie lives and breathes literature. Tonyo knows that he could not create anything of beauty or power. And he couldn't fathom what drove people to create something beyond what is needed to make a living and pay the bills.

Tonyo feels a tap on his shoulder. He turns and sees a security guard, who points in an exaggerated pantomime to his watch. Almost closing time. Closing time! Tonyo had stood in the same spot for three hours. He nods to the guard, who walks away to inform other patrons it is time to leave. Tonyo turns back to the two Fridas. They stare at him, inscrutable, linked by blood. How did she do it? he thinks. How did she love Diego through it all? But her two sets of eyes offer no answer. Finally, he turns and joins the others in the quiet exodus. They are a diverse group. He hears whispers in German and English and Japanese mixed in with Spanish. And Tonyo now hears the rain, coming down hard. He reaches for his pocket umbrella and opens it as he passes the guard, who holds the door open.

"Gracias," says Tonyo.

The guard smiles and nods.

Outside, Tonyo looks for a taxi and spots the driver who brought him to the museum standing by his car under a large black umbrella. The driver sees Tonyo and opens the door for him. He gets in, happy to see a familiar face.

"You like?" the driver asks in English as he pulls into the heavy traffic.

Tonyo realizes that the driver knew all along his passenger was American. "Yes," says Tonyo as he wipes rain from his sleeves. "I liked it very much."

* * *

The chef chops vegetables and flips shrimp on the sizzling grill built into the dining table. He clearly is not Japanese, but he has mastered the art, although he betrays his pride only with a crooked half-smile that creeps onto his face when he does something particularly brilliant. Though Tonyo would have preferred Mexican food, his tío Gilberto wanted to do something special for his nephew. The chef finishes his wonderful act and serves the two men. Gilberto delicately picks up a steaming shrimp with chopsticks, places it onto his tongue, and closes his eyes dramatically. One, two, three bites. Eyes pop open, a broad, closed-mouth smile appears. Gilberto nods with approval. The chef offers his half-smile and proceeds to clean up.

Despite having recently experienced a small heart attack, Gilberto looks fit, trim, and elegant in a blue blazer, tan slacks, red tie. Semi-retirement is obviously doing him some good. He retains a few patients, maintaining a little office at his old hospital, thereby supplementing his fat pension so he can keep the house in the Federal

District as well as buy a new one in Yxtapa right on the beach. Gilberto's children and grandchildren visit regularly. His wife is happy. Life is good.

"Eat, sobrino, eat," Gilberto prods. "It's the best Japanese food in the city."

Tonyo notices his uncle's beautiful hands as they move about the table effortlessly, as if the chopsticks were part of his anatomy. Not an age spot to be seen anywhere. The hands of a proud surgeon.

Tonyo fumbles with his chopsticks and eventually gets something into his mouth. "Perfect," he says, and he means it.

They eat in happy silence for a while. Gilberto orders two more bottles of Asahi. Tonyo can feel that his uncle is waiting for the right moment to say something about the divorce. And then it comes.

"So, sobrino, are you doing all right?" Gilberto's English is refined, perfect. Tonyo wishes that he could speak Spanish with such ease. "Yes, I'm fine."

Gilberto pats his nephew's arm. "Are you certain?"

"Yes, tío. Thank you."

Gilberto nods. "Do you need to meet a nice woman?"

Tonyo sits back and laughs, but his uncle's expression is serious, probing. "I'm fine, really, tío."

Gilberto leans close, squints, and whispers: "I know where there are beautiful women and they do not cost very much at all."

Tonyo can't say anything for a moment. Then he lies: "Tío, that's very kind of you, but I met a lovely woman today."

Gilberto sits straight, raises his left eyebrow, and almost yells: "Where?"

Tony takes a drink of his beer to give himself time to think. "At the museum," he finally says.

"Oh, there are many beautiful women who go to the museum," Gilberto says wisely. "Is she Mexican?"

"Yes. Mexican."

"Ah," he says, now in a softer voice. "Name?"

Tonyo takes another drink. He's beginning to feel the alcohol. His upper lip is beaded with perspiration and the back of his shirt sticks to his skin.

"Sobrino, what is her name?"

"Frida," says Tonyo. "Frida."

"Ah! Frida! Excellent." Gilberto taps his nephew's elbow with the bottom of the beer bottle. "To Frida," he says.

Tonyo lifts his bottle. "To Frida."

They each take a long drink.

"So, what is Frida's full name?"

Without missing a beat, Tonyo answers: "Frida Morán Ordoñez."

"A fine name," smiles Gilberto. "We have a Morán somewhere in the family."

"Yes, a very fine name, tío," says Tonyo. "A very fine name."

The chef serves the final morsels of shrimps and vegetables. Gilberto laughs: "My sobrino never needed help getting pretty women."

"Please, tío."

"I must meet this Frida."

"You will," smiles Tonyo. "In fact, you might have seen her at the museum before."

"Which museum?"

"Modern art."

Gilberto shakes his head. "I don't like that museum much. I prefer the anthropology museum. Magnificent!"

Tonyo picks up a shrimp. He's getting used to eating this way. "To each his own, eh, tío."

"Oh, yes, sobrino. That is an ancient truth."

* * *

Tonyo stands in front of *Las Dos Fridas* a second day in a row. He had been so full from last night's dinner, he skipped breakfast altogether instead grabbing a taxi straight to the museum. It's a little less crowded today but Tonyo doesn't really notice. He's there to commune with his new girlfriend. Both of them. Why he lied to his uncle he will never know. But Tonyo realizes that he's been offering little lies more than usual since the divorce. Nothing major, really. And nothing designed to cheat anyone of anything. Tonyo has simply found that it's an easy way to avoid conflict. Perhaps he will confess to his uncle and bring him here to meet Frida. And they will have a good laugh and then a fine meal. Or else Gilberto will begin to worry about Tonyo and suggest he get some help.

Tonyo notices that the clear morning light gives the painting a different feel, even a new texture, as compared to yesterday's cloudy afternoon sun. This is an advantage of beginning the day early. In this light, the two Fridas are not as solemn, not as entrenched in their respective turmoil. His mind jumps from Frida to the growing hollowness of his stomach back to Frida and then to Nellie. Nellie. Is she writing a new novel now that she is free of her burden? Will it be based on her divorce and her liberation from the deadweight of—what did that reviewer say?—a self-absorbed, pedantic, and out-and-out puerile husband? Tonyo chuckles: he should be entitled to more than half of Nellie's royalties since he proved to be such a successful muse, despite protests to the contrary.

"She is beautiful, isn't she?"

Tonyo comes abruptly out of his trance and looks to where the voice came from; he tries not to react to what he finds standing just to his right. But he knows he's unsuccessful.

The woman who spoke to him easily observes this fact and lets out a little chuckle. "I wish I were as beautiful as Frida," she says.

Tonyo recovers and turns back to the painting. "Few women are as beautiful as she," he offers diplomatically.

Tonyo suddenly realizes that the woman spoke to him in English but with a slight accent. She is young, perhaps mid-twenties, with a trim figure exaggerated by a tight black T-shirt tucked into black jeans. Her dark complexion and black eyebrows almost make her short bleached hair glow an ominous not-quite-white. But her hair is not what startled Tonyo. A port wine stain covers most of left cheek and descends down to her chin. The shape of Africa, Tonyo immediately thinks. What was this type of birthmark called? Tonyo closes his eyes to bring up the term. Mikhail Gorbachev had it. And Tonyo's cousin Olivia had one, too. Ah, yes! Nevus flammeus. That was it. Poor Olivia used a heavy pancake makeup to cover it. But Olivia's stain was only on her chin and couldn't compare to what Tonyo has just encountered.

"Deep in thought?" the woman asks.

Tonyo opens his eyes. "Sorry. I was just trying to remember something."

"Care to share?"

"No."

Tonyo doesn't like the familiar tone this woman is taking with him. And he had been enjoying a very nice private time with Frida.

So he decides the best course of action is to remain silent and keep his eyes on the painting. Perhaps the woman will get the message and leave without his having to be rude. But she crosses her arms, turns to Frida, and stands silently, admiring the painting. Tonyo's plan falls apart because now he feels out of place, an intruder. He remembers how his cousin grew her hair long so that she could hide behind it. This woman, however, appears to have not an ounce of self-consciousness about her stain. She almost flaunts it with that short haircut. Where does such a young person get the bravery to be herself? He can't help himself. He turns from Frida to the woman. She holds her chin up, lips pursed, eyes narrowed in concentration. And then Tonyo notices something else about this interloper: her hands and arms are dappled with what appears to be paint. Red, green, yellow, blue, and black. She's an artist. This explains much. Tonyo can now categorize her, make sense of the woman's bohemia, her impulse to accept the birthmark as merely an aesthetic element of her being.

"You are beautiful," says Tonyo. He doesn't know why these words come out and he feels ashamed.

The woman smiles but keeps her eyes focused on the painting.

"Sorry," fumbles Tonyo.

"For what?" she says, still not looking at him.

"For saying something so personal."

She laughs. "I've heard worse."

The woman still keeps her eyes on Frida. Tonyo suddenly feels more relaxed, though he doesn't know why. He turns to Frida. Tonyo and the woman now stand in united silent adoration. Is this woman flirting? he wonders. What a silly thought, considering that he has just told her that she is beautiful. She has the right to wonder if Tonyo is flirting. He smiles at what his uncle would think if he showed up with this unusual example of a woman. Gilberto would likely understand the attraction, but the doctor in him would lead to his lecturing on the marvels of medical lasers and how port wine birthmarks can be removed, leaving virtually no trace.

Tonyo turns to the woman. And he's as startled as when he first laid eyes on her: she had left silently while Tonyo was lost in thought. He scans the room as if he's searching the horizon for a rescue boat. Nowhere to be found. He feels a bit panicked. Tonyo had begun to feel comfortable with her presence. Tonyo finally shakes his head.

What a silly middle-aged man he is. No wonder he's alone. He knows that he'll think of this young woman for days, while she certainly will forget the encounter by dinner. He looks back to the two Fridas. She is still with him. All two of her. And that's all Tonyo really needs right then. But he doesn't know this. He simply stares at *Las Dos Fridas* and wonders if he will ever see the young woman again. Perhaps she will show up tomorrow, and they can share this spot again. Maybe she's being coy. Careful. And with this small thought, he smiles, derives some comfort. He will visit again tomorrow. That is his plan. It all makes perfect sense.

PAINTING

That pinche Alejandro . . . makes me take my pinche clothes off to paint me, my picture, me in the nude because he says mi cielo, that is how your soul comes out to touch me, fill me up, only with your naked skin. Some kind of pendejo jackass shit line he laid on me and because I was all fucked up on Coors I said, okay, you want to paint my naked ass, okay, here it is, and I take off my shirt, sweatpants, and everything and just kind of toss my shit up there on the fence and I hear a coyote scream like a woman in labor and the sun is coming up and Alejandro says, perfect! Perfect! You look so bonita, Ana, he says, and he holds up his pinche thumb like those old movies and closes one eye, one perfect brown eye with eyelashes out to here and then he starts to paint. And he paints. And he paints. And the sun begins to spit out reds, yellows, and oranges and I'm kind of cold but he says in a whisper, almost done, mi amor, almost done, don't move, I need to finish. And then I go all soft inside because he believes in his art, his painting, and in me. But then I begin to shiver and I say, fucking finish already, pendejo, and then he throws me this look like I fucking kicked my abuelita or something and he says, fuck you, bitch, fuck you. I say, wait, wait, I didn't mean it, mi cielito, I didn't fucking mean it, but he's already walking away muttering something. I don't know what to do so I cross my arms over my tits and walk to his canvas, all naked still, and take a peek at what he's been doing and it like totally takes my breath away, locks my breath up in a little box, because I'm beautiful in this painting. So beautiful. I pick it up and hold it, smelling the fresh oil paints, and then I walk it over to the fence, set it down, and step back. And the coyote is quiet now and the sun begins to warm me and I just stare at myself by the fence. Who is that? She's so beautiful. Totally beautiful. And I breathe in the morning and the paint and I can't stop looking at her. At me.

EIGHT

HOUR ONE

Here. Wear this at all times.

Espíritu Chijulla looks down at the laminated tag, her own face staring back at her. She doesn't like the way she looks: confused, guilty, too light, head blocky like a Diego Rivera painting. At *all* times? she asks, not daring to touch the tag.

Mr. Leonis lifts his moist brown eyes toward Espíritu without otherwise moving a muscle. At all times while you're *here,* he answers, making a little whistling sound through his narrow nostrils.

Espíritu is frightened by the neatness of this man, her new supervisor. Starched from head to toe. Crewcut. Mustache clipped short and tight against a stern upper lip. His desk is a perfect terrain of neat piles: manila folders, various containers for paper clips, Post-Its, scratch paper. She has an urge to push her lips against Mr. Leonis's and force her tongue into his tight crevice of a mouth just to see what he would do. But instead of kissing him, Espíritu picks up the tag and clips it to the pocket of her blouse.

Mr. Leonis lowers his eyes. Good, he says. Good.

Espíritu stands in front of Mr. Leonis's desk in silence.

Good, I said.

She nods and turns. As she walks from him, Espíritu holds her right hand against her chest and gives Mr. Leonis the finger. Have a nice day, she says as she leaves his office.

Have a nice day, Mr. Leonis answers as he swivels in his chair and reaches for his mouse. Bitch, he mouths. Bitch.

HOUR TWO

After receiving her assignment files from Ms. Edwards, a woman

42

who resembles Abraham Lincoln but without the beard, Espíritu finds her cubicle. Gray and blue everywhere. Her nameplate says ESPIRITA CHIJULA. Doubly wrong. She dumps her files on the gray expanse of clean desktop.

Hey, she hears. She jumps. A man's face peeks over the cubicle wall. Hey, the man says. I'm Simon.

Hi, Simon, Espíritu says.

Can I visit?

Sure, she says.

Simon walks around his cubicle and enters hers. Simon Redneb, he says. He sticks his hand out. Espíritu shakes it. It is very moist so she pulls back quickly.

Redneb? she asks. Unusual name.

It was Rednebsky at one point. Someone, my grandfather, I guess, wanted to be more American.

Redneb is more American? Espíritu asks as she dries her hand on her skirt. She notices that Simon could be handsome if he tried a little bit.

Simon looks down toward Espíritu's knees. You know, they were caught fucking right where your legs are right now, he says. Simon smiles, exposing too-perfect glistening teeth. Right there, he says, pointing, almost touching Espíritu's right knee.

Out of disgust, Espíritu pushes away and her chair glides back a few feet. No way, she says. No way.

Way, Simon laughs. Totally way. Right there. They thought everyone had gone for the day. But Mr. Leonis and that woman from accounting came back to get some files for a big meeting that got scheduled at the last minute. They caught them doing it doggy style.

Espíritu laughs. There isn't enough room down there to do it doggy style.

Simon stops smiling. A line of red spills upward from his brow toward his hairline. His eyes narrow. Oh? he says. How would you know?

Go, says Espíritu. I've got to work.

Simon stays put. He shoves his hands into his pants pockets. Espíritu sees that he's trying to hide a budding erection.

Go, she says again.

Simon leaves, slowly, making squeaking sounds on the industrial linoleum.

Espíritu peers under her desk. Hmmm, she says. Hmmm.

HOUR THREE

Espíritu completes inputting another file. She closes it, sets it to her left, reaches for a new file, and flicks it open. He fingers glide over the keyboard. The computer hums happily and she feels like this could be a good job. Simon tries to visit but Espíritu quickly learns that if she doesn't look up or say a word, he eventually slinks away. She smirks as she thinks about the one time she did it doggy style. Overrated, she thinks. Not worth the trouble.

HOUR FOUR

Simon tries to convince Espíritu to join him at Coco's. Great BLTs, he tempts. And the pies. Forget-about-it! The best!

But she says, No. I brought my lunch.

You old stick-in-the-mud, says Simon, as if this taunt could change her mind.

Bye, says Espíritu.

Simon starts to walk away and then stops. Don't forget the staff meeting after lunch, he says. Attendance is mandatory.

Thanks, says Espíritu. Have a nice one.

Thanks, says Simon. You too. He disappears with a squeak.

Espíritu reaches into her large black bag and pulls out her lunch. Tuna on wheat, a beautifully dappled banana, diet 7-Up, sharp little carrot sticks. She spreads it all out on her desktop, an unfolded paper napkin as her place mat. As she starts to eat the sandwich, she thinks of her sister, Mona, who died three years earlier. Mona was the cute one. The one everyone liked. The baby of the family. Espíritu wonders what Mona would be doing right now if she hadn't taken those pills two days before her senior prom. College? Or straight to a job, where she could wow everyone with her energy and perky good looks? The tuna feels pasty and odd in her mouth. Espíritu takes a long drink of 7-Up. The bubbles tickle her lips and then her tongue and finally her throat. As she puts the can down, she thinks, this is going to work. I like this place. This is good.

The entire "input team" sits around the blond wood conference table that is so shiny the overhead lighting makes it glow like a huge, oblong klieg light. The gray-blue room hums with co-workers' laughter and snide asides. Espíritu sits with eyes fixed on the lone object that rests at the far end of the table: a pink rectangular cake box. An elastic silver-colored string runs along all six sides of the box, and a red phoenix is emblazoned on the top. In black marker, the number 89 191355 is scrawled across the phoenix's angry face. A phone number? No. One digit too many. Wrong spacing.

Hi, someone says.

Espíritu turns to her right and faces a beautiful brown face.

I'm Bebel, the beautiful brown face says.

I'm Espíritu, says Espíritu. She likes this new face. Crinkly eyes. Short black hair as shiny as a new Mercedes. Young. This new face makes Espíritu think of a Mayan princess.

You remind me of a Mayan princess, says Espíritu.

Bebel looks down, blushes a deeper brown, and flashes solid white teeth. Thank you, she says. Espíritu breathes in deeply, trying to determine if Bebel is wearing perfume. She can't smell anything but fruit-scented shampoo.

The room suddenly becomes quiet. Bebel and Espíritu look up and see Mr. Leonis already standing at the end of the conference table near the cake box. He sits with a little grunt and interlaces his fingers like a corner of a log cabin. How old is he? wonders Espíritu. Fifty? Sixty? She looks at the pink cake box again. Must be someone's birthday, she figures. But where are the paper plates, forks, little napkins, cutting knife?

Mr. Leonis clears his throat, making a sound like a Siamese cat trying to dislodge a persistent hairball. Welcome, he says, moving his head around the table and nodding mechanically. There isn't much business today other than to note that I will be sending out a new memo which supersedes the one I sent out yesterday. Please shred the old memo and read the new one after our meeting.

What was yesterday's memo about? whispers Espíritu to Babel.

Recycling, Bebel whispers back, making the little hairs on Espíritu's forearms dance.

Now on to our little celebration, continues Mr. Leonis. We have a new employee in our midst. She just started today.

Espíritu's eyes jump and she feels her cheeks grow warm. Simon grins stupidly at her from across the table.

Espíritu Chijulla, says Mr. Leonis mispronouncing *Chijulla*, making it sound like CHI-JOO-LAH. Please stand so we can say hello, Espíritu.

Espíritu slowly rises. She thinks, CHEE-WHO-YAH, you dick. It's easy to pronounce if you goddamn tried. She can feel tears well up. Bebel smiles up at her. Simon's grin becomes a leer. The dozen employees of the input team offer a weak applause.

Say a little about yourself, says Mr. Leonis. He is not smiling.

Like what?

Where are you from? Mr. Leonis suggests.

Espíritu coughs. New Mexico. Taos.

Ah! says Mr. Leonis. Beautiful state. Beautiful city.

Espíritu looks at him. Been there? she asks.

Mr. Leonis looks down. No. Seen pictures. In a book. When I was a kid.

Espíritu appreciates Mr. Leonis's attempt at civility so she thinks about what else she can say about herself, like why she moved to Los Angeles, how she hasn't been married yet, her degree in art from the University of New Mexico, how her parents split up when she was twelve, and how her mother basically raised the two girls by herself, how there's only one girl now. But before she can do this, Mr. Leonis says, You may sit now, Espíritu. Thank you.

Espíritu sighs and sits.

I brought this lovely cake to welcome our New Mexican friend to the company, says Mr. Leonis, still not smiling. He reaches for the pink box, snaps off the elastic, shiny string, and flips the lid open. Coconut-lemon, announces Mr. Leonis. My favorite, he adds, now trying to smile.

Espíritu feels a wave of nausea come over her when she spies the mound of shredded coconut piled high on the white frosting. It reminds her of when she was ten and her parents stopped talking to each other. Worse than that, her father started coming home from work later and later, and her mother stopped doing his laundry and let the house go to pot. Toilets, showers, sinks, everything stank. One day Espíritu noticed a god-awful stench emanating from the oven.

She opened it slowly and peered in. At first all she could see was the vague outline of an aluminum cooking pan. Espíritu put her face closer while holding her nose. And then she saw them: hundreds of squirming maggots making a happy home in the moist rotting chicken carcass. She threw up on the oven door.

This coconut cake is too much for Espíritu to take. She stands up and rushes toward the door, hoping she can make it to the bathroom in time. Mr. Leonis says, Good, Espíritu. I forgot the utensils. They're on my desk. Do you mind grabbing them?

HOUR SIX

A migraine, Espíritu lies to Mr. Leonis. They come over me sometimes, just like that. Sorry.

Several co-workers observe as Mr. Leonis tries to sound compassionate. Maybe you should go lie down, put a cold compress on your forehead, he says, feeling watched. You can have your cake later, he says.

The very thought of the coconut-lemon cake makes Espíritu's stomach convulse. No, I'm allergic to coconut, she lies. And lemon, too.

Mr. Leonis scratches his chin. Odd allergies, he says.

I'll be fine, Espíritu says. Inputting will make me feel better.

Mr. Leonis appreciates this to no end. Okay, he says. But if you need to rest, just let me know. He turns and gives a look of triumph to the gathered co-workers. Show's over, he says.

Espíritu tries to sit straight. She swivels slowly to face her computer. The screen saver has kicked in: an aquarium scene. She lets her eyes follow a smiling angel fish. She does this for almost an hour.

HOUR SEVEN

The Mayan princess walks by. ¡Hola! she chirps.

Espíritu turns from her computer screen and lets her eyes rest on Bebel's face. She wishes Bebel would lean down and kiss her softly on her forehead, and then nose, and finally lips.

You doing okay? asks Bebel. You look pale.

Peachy, she answers.

Bebel reaches over and presses her palm to Espíritu's forehead. Espíritu smells hand cream, almond scented. She fills her lungs with the smell and closes her eyes. She feels safe under the pressure of this little smooth hand.

No fever, Bebel announces. Must have been a migraine, just as you thought, she adds. She lets her hand linger on Espíritu's forehead.

Yes, it was a typical migraine, Espíritu lies. Lying is easy here, she realizes. Bebel suddenly moves her hand away and Espíritu feels abandoned.

Don't go, she says to Bebel.

Have to. I'm behind in my inputting.

Espíritu deflates.

But let's have drinks after work, if you're feeling better. Okay? Do you like margaritas?

Espíritu inflates. Yes! I'm feeling better already.

In an hour, then, Bebel says as she floats away. But if alcohol might make you sick again, you will have a mocktail, understand? Bebel emits a proud, motherly chuckle as she disappears.

Can I come? asks Simon, eyes visible from above the cubicle wall.

Espíritu ignores him and turns to her computer. She smiles and touches her forehead, the scent of almonds still lingering. Simon's eyes eventually sink below the gray-blue horizon until he disappears altogether.

HOUR EIGHT

Here, Espíritu says. I finished everything but the García account.

Great, says Mr. Leonis. Great. Especially considering your migraine and all. I think this is going to work out well. He tries to smile but all he can manage is a slightly curved gash.

Yes, she answers. Yes. He doesn't respond. Espíritu stands in silence waiting for more.

Mr. Leonis looks down at his desk. Goodnight, he mumbles. The curved gash dissolves into a straight line.

Goodnight. Espíritu turns and gives Mr. Leonis a hidden finger.

Bitch, mouths Mr. Leonis. Bitch.

Bebel waits by the exit. A grin breaks out on her face when Espíritu comes into sight. Margarita time! she smiles.

Yes, says Espíritu. Margarita time.

Espíritu puts her arm around Bebel's shoulders and leads her out of the building. Margarita time, she repeats to the Mayan princess, who grins wildly, like a little girl blowing bubbles for the first time. Espíritu pulls Bebel closer. Margarita time, she says one more time.

WEATHERMAN

His face is a morphed blend of Emilio Estevez, John Updike, and Space Ghost. He plucks his eyebrows so he won't look so Cuban. "Because, after all," he likes to say, "I'm puro Chicano." Which is a little jab at me because even though my pop is Mexican, Mom is half Cuban.

That face could have adorned a wall at the post office as a one of the FBI's Most Wanted. Instead it adorned the TV screen each weeknight reporting the weather on the 11:00 Channel 4 news. He had the highest ratings in L.A, too. Rico Ramírez "On Top of the Weather" in Los Angeles.

Rico lived in Westwood, off Glendon near UCLA. He bought a condo for half a million in 1998, which was kind of stupid because the studio is in Burbank so he had to crawl in his new Lexus on the 405 to get to work. But Rico always believed that living in Westwood Village adjacent to the UCLA campus was phat living and he'd earned the right to live there with the white folks. He could date any UCLA coed he wanted, but he didn't. He was careful. He had worked way too hard scratching his way out of the Pico-Union area to throw it all away for a little UCLA blonde snatch. Rico imagined the headlines in the *Los Angeles Times:* "Channel 4 Weatherman Rapes UCLA Coed." Despite his wealth and success—or because of it—that's what the blonde's father would claim. He was still nothing but a Mexican. And a dark one at that. Forget all about those white chicks who threw themselves at him at Acapulco's happy hour. Nothing was going to destroy his little piece of American success.

When it came to women, Rico was scared. Of Chicanas, too. His Spanish was just so-so and because he was famous, beautiful smart Chicanas didn't want to see his cultural failings. And what about the ones who were climbers and saw Rico as a way up? Rico didn't blame them. He knew what it meant to want things. He knew that hunger could make you say things you don't mean, like "I love you." So he threw himself completely into his work, and in the end it paid off with high ratings and a great three-year contract. At night after the telecast he went home and drank several Dos Equis and beat off to the Playboy Channel and went to sleep listening to KNX News Radio set on a fifty-nine-minute timer. At twenty-eight, Rico had it all except a normal life.

"Man," I'd say after a couple of beers at Acapulco, wincing at my inner pain as yet another hot UCLA coed came by to ask for Rico's autograph, "if you're not going for them, throw a couple my way, man!"

"You're the goddamn lawyer, Guillermo. You could have anyone you want, too."

But that wasn't true and he knew it. Yes, I did well enough in grammar and high school to get into Loyola-Marymount University and then into a halfway decent law school up north. Yeah, I was successful, but I was built like my mom: low to the ground and chunky. In other words, no Jimmy Smits. And I was a government lawyer doing criminal appellate briefs—sometimes a jury trial when the district attorney's office conflicted out of a case—for a lousy 55K a year, driving a 1991 Honda Accord with a shitload of student loans left to pay off. So I'd tell Rico, "If you lose your job, all this will slip away and you're gonna kick your own brown ass for not doin' somethin' about it when you had the chance."

And Rico would smile this bizarre little smile that looked like a crack on a downtown sidewalk and say, "My time will come." That's all. At those moments, even though we'd hung together since first grade, I couldn't read his face.

Well, he was right. Rico's time would come. But not in the way he ever imagined. Brett Hendrickson. Sharp dresser with beautiful capped teeth and a face like a friendly and younger Clint Eastwood. A former hockey star who started doing sports in Toronto after he retired from the game and eventually moved to Newark and then Denver before getting a huge break in Dallas anchoring the local weekend evening news. An L.A. producer who happened to be spending time in Dallas with his brother discovered Brett. It was all in this long article in *Buzz Magazine* a few years ago before that mag went under. So Brett made the big time in L.A. with an anchor's seat doing the 11:00 Channel 4 news. Brett was actually hired as the co-anchor with this gorgeous, ethnically ambiguous woman named Debra something-or-other. The networks like doing that. Pairing an ethnic woman with a white guy. You seldom see the reverse except on weekends when there are fewer viewers, and that's just the gig Rico landed. Weekend anchor, and his ratings were solid. Maybe that's what threatened Brett. Maybe he figured it was only a matter of time before he'd be replaced by the guy doing the nightly weather report—my homeboy, Rico.

Rico's parents came from the state of Jalisco, and even though they spoke English with a very heavy accent, they decided to speak no Spanish around their son. The result was Rico felt insecure about his Spanish. Still, during his weather reports, Rico would pronounce certain So Cal cities with a beautiful accent. If he were talking about Santa Barbara he'd say, "The weather is looking beautiful, in the mid-eighties, from here to Sawn-taw Bahr-baw-rrrraaa." Or, instead of saying "Montebello," he'd pronounce it "Moan-tay-bay-yo." Shit like that. But he'd always pronounce "Los Angeles" as "Los Angeles." The Latino viewers ate it up, and the white folks and everyone else suddenly realized that "Santa Barbara" and "Montebello" were Spanish names.

Rico's selective Spanish pronunciation clearly got under Brett's skin. He thought Rico was trading on his ethnicity—which he was, but so what?—and that pissed Brett off, particularly because Rico was his rival. Brett also noticed that Rico's English was perfect, with not even a hint of an accent. And with that, Brett saw his opening. Brett was a lot of things, but stupid wasn't one of them, not when it when it came to watching out for his ass.

At 11:17 one Monday night, Brett introduced Rico. Rico was standing there looking cool in a great double-breasted blue pin-stripe number and smiling his I'm-the-Number-One-Weatherman -in-All-of-Goddamn-L.A. smile of his. Then they broke into a little small talk, which was required by their contracts. It made the news a "warm" show.

Brett said, "I hear it might actually sprinkle in Sawn-taw Moan-ni-kah."

Rico just stared at Brett, trying to understand what he'd just said.

Brett continued: "Well, Rico, is it going to rain in Sawn-taw Moan-ni-kah?"

I was sitting in front of the TV and almost spilled my diet Coke and Barcardi because I could see Rico's face just freeze up like those wax figures in that old Vincent Price horror movie. After a couple of seconds of deadly silence, Rico finally recovered and said, "Yes, Brett, there's going to be an 80 percent chance of showers in Santa Monica tomorrow."

And I yelled, "Shit!" at the TV because Rico said "Santa Monica" like any white guy off the street. But Rico is a trooper so he finished up his two minutes of weather and handed it back to Brett.

I stayed up late that night thinking that Rico would call me to talk about what had happened, but he didn't. Tomorrow, I thought. For sure he'd call me tomorrow. But he didn't. So I tuned in the next night and that asshole Brett did it again!

"So, Rico," Brett smiled at 11:17, "I was planning to drive to Moan-teh-rrrray Park for a little party. No rain there, I hope."

Poor Rico looked like some stranger had just run up to him and pulled on his dick. But he recovered, sort of, and said: "Monterey Park will be looking great tomorrow."

The next night Brett asked about "Sawn Maw-rrreee-no." And Thursday Brett mentioned "Kaw-law-baw-sawss," and Friday it was "Sawn Ferrr-nawn-doe." And Rico always responded by using the hard English pronunciation: "San Marino," "Calabasas," and "San Fernando." And each time he spoke, Rico looked like a little kid who had just gotten caught looking at *Penthouse* or the Victoria's Secrets catalogue. It was heartbreaking.

But Rico never called me. I watched each night assuming he'd need to talk, but he never picked up the phone. And I felt too embarrassed to call him. So I waited.

Finally, on Saturday evening, Rico called me and we went for drinks at Gladstone's, the one at CityWalk in Burbank, not the real one in Malibu. The day had been goddamn hot, but that night a cool breeze blew through the Valley. After ordering a couple of San Miguels and bullshitting about the beautiful women who walked by our table to gawk at Rico, I said, "What the fuck is Brett trying to do?"

Rico suddenly shrunk down, looking morose. He took a long swig of beer. I could see that he still had some of his TV makeup on. It made him look a little odd, not of this world. Rico finally said, "He's seen through me. It's over."

"What? That slimy son of a bitch hasn't done anything but made a fuckin' fool of himself!"

Rico put his hand up to stop my diatribe and said in a soft voice, "Look, Brett isn't a bad guy. He's just looking out for number one. He's good at what he does and he's paid his dues. Can you blame him for wanting to save his ass?"

I nodded. Rico was right.

"Besides," he continued, "his little pronunciation game showed me the truth."

"What truth?" It was getting hot in the restaurant and the crowd was almost unbearable.

"You know. Playing the ethnic boy for the crowd. For money."

"Goddamn good money, dude. Don't forget that."

Rico gave me a weak smile. "I'm just tired. That's all."

Over the next month, Brett kept up his shit and Rico just kept on taking it. The ratings at 11:17 started to slip as Rico lost his personality and the viewers sensed that something was wrong and switched to Channel 2 or 7. Rico and I stopped talking, partly because I was buried with six appellate briefs and one for the U.S. Supreme Court. Then he called one afternoon while I was trying to get a huge habeas filing out to federal court.

"Guillermo," he said in a cheerful voice, "I need some help this weekend."

"Well, 'hello' to you, too."

"Sorry. It's been a little crazy. A lot of changes."

I let there be a little silence. Then I said, "What's up?"

"I'm moving. Got a new place downtown. Actually pretty nice."

I stared at the receiver like they do on TV sitcoms. "What the fuck are you talkin' about?"

"Sold the condo in Westwood. Got a new one downtown. Closer to my parents. Closer to my new job."

"Slow down, homeboy. What new job?"

I could almost hear him smiling over the phone: "Teaching. In the Communications Department at USC."

Okay, he's my bud. But this? "Are you nuts? You gave up doing weather to teach?"

I'll never forget what Rico said next. He said very slowly, as if to help me understand, "Well, Guillermo, my time has come."

That was two years ago. We survived Y2K—the world didn't melt down, and neither did Rico. And Rico was right, I guess. His time had come. His class at USC is a huge draw and he's finally dating. I mean seriously dating. Sonia Montoya. She teaches Spanish. And she's Puerto Rican, which is really funny because she speaks Spanish soooo fast, not like Mexicans, so she's teaching Rico to speak like a Puerto Rican. But she's great. And she introduced me to Lisa, who's a public defender. Lisa Aronson. Nice Jewish girl, as they say. My parents like her but my mom, after having her over for dinner the first time, put her chubby little hand on Lisa's toned arm and said without a hint of malice, "Lisa, you're such a nice girl. It's a shame you're not going to heaven." My God! I almost—I don't know what. But Lisa simply smiled and said, "Thank you, Mrs. Fonseca. Your son is so wonderful. I hope that I can make him happy." And Mom cried and cried out of happiness because her baby, her "hijo," had a beautiful smart woman to take care of him. And I've lost fifteen pounds because I finally have a reason to look good.

Brett Hendrickson. Well, he was right to be worried about the demographics. He got bumped and now he's doing the Channel 13 news, which is a huge insult. His replacement is this big guy who did sports for a few years on Channel 5. You know the dude. Ex-football player for USC, a great place kicker, and handsome as hell. Wilfredo Torres. Talk about puro Mexicano! He was goddamn born in Mexico City and came up to the States when he was almost twelve. At least, that's what the Calendar section of the *Los Angeles Times* said. And everything he says is enveloped in this beautiful soft accent. Even when he says Los Angeles: Lohz Ahhhnng-heh-lezzz. And his ratings are great, too.

Hey, it's a numbers game. You know that.

THE FAIRY TALE OF THE
MAN AND THE WOMAN

Long ago there lived a Man who longed for nothing more than someone to love and to love him back. He lived in a neighborhood among strangers in a house that looked like all the surrounding houses. Some days when he drove home from his mundane job, the Man could not remember which house was his. In fact, one day (a Thursday, to be exact), he drove his Honda Civic into a driveway that he thought was his but in truth was two houses down from his own.

The Man parked his Honda Civic and dragged his tired body to the front door. His key did not fit—of course, because it was not the Man's front door—and this puzzled him. But the front door was not locked, so it opened when he tried to insert the key. The Man shrugged, figuring he must be a bit confused because he was tired, and entered the house.

Remarkably, the house that was not his was furnished as his own house was: he saw a flatscreen television above the brick fireplace, a brown couch in the middle of the living room facing the television, two standing lamps, a small end table with a lamp as well as magazines stacked three inches high, and a coffee table set between the fireplace and couch. So the Man had no reason not to feel quite at home in this house that was not, in fact, his.

The Man sighed from fatigue, loosened his necktie, threw his jacket and briefcase onto one end of the couch, and dropped his tired body onto the other end. A television remote control—that looked precisely like the Man's own remote control—sat on the coffee table. The Man reached for the remote control and turned on the flatscreen television. He switched it to HGTV and quickly became absorbed in the travails of a handsome though mismatched young couple with two rambunctious children who relocated to Ireland because the wife had gotten a wonderful job so the whole family had to leave New York City for the Emerald Isle. The Man had seen this episode before but this fact made him relax even more because there would be no surprises.

Unfortunately for the Man, seven minutes into the program—just as the real estate agent was waxing poetic about the large, American-like kitchen in one of the properties she was showing the young couple—the front door of the house that was not the Man's opened.

"Who are you?" asked the Man of the figure that stood in the shadows of the doorway.

"I have the same question for you," said the figure that stood in the shadows of the doorway.

"I live here," said the Man.

The figure moved into the light of the living room. The Man could now see that the figure was that of a woman, about his age, more or less.

"I live here," said the Woman.

At that moment, the Man realized that the brown couch he sat on was not his brown couch: it was much newer and made of nicer fabric and had a pattern of almost indecipherable flying birds. His couch did not have birds—or any fowl, flying or otherwise—in its pattern. Indeed, the Man's couch had no pattern whatsoever. A bit startled, the Man looked around and noticed that while the living room's furnishings were similar to his own, they were actually much newer and better made. And on the far wall by one of the standing lamps, he noticed for the first time a framed print of *The Two Fridas,* something that did not hang in his own house. He stared at Frida Kahlo's double image and realized that he owned no prints or paintings whatsoever.

"Oh," the Man finally said. "Lo siento," he then added, though he was not certain if the Woman spoke Spanish. "I thought I had come into my own house."

With that, the Man turned off the flatscreen television just as the wife in the episode was saying that even though she appreciated the large kitchen, she did not *love* the bedroom carpeting in the Irish flat (and, of course, the real estate agent said in a lilting Irish brogue, "That's an easy fix, my dear!"). The Man then stood, reached for his jacket and briefcase, and said: "I will leave now."

Because the Man looked quite harmless, the Woman said: "I assume it won't happen again, unless you want it to."

At this, the Man paused and thought. Then, after a few moments, he said, "If I do come into your house by accident again, I have a question."

"Yes?" said the woman.

"Do you have any food allergies or restrictions?"

"Gracias por preguntar," said the woman.

The Man smiled, pleased to learn that the Woman spoke at least rudimentary Spanish.

The Woman said, "I am allergic to shellfish, but other than that, I love everything."

The Man nodded, made a mental note, and left the house that was not his.

The next evening, as the Woman was settling in for a quiet evening reading a novel after a long day at work, she heard footsteps traveling up her walkway. After a few moments of silence, there was a gentle knock on the door. The Woman carefully placed a bookmark in her novel, stood, and slowly walked to the door. She peeped through the peephole, and sure enough, there stood the Man, carrying what looked like a casserole dish.

When the Woman opened the door, the Man smiled, held up the casserole dish, and said, "Zucchini pizza casserole!"

"Oh, my," said the Woman. "I've had zucchini, and I've had pizza, but never have I had both in one dish."

"Es una receta maravillosa," said the Man. "A true taste sensation! I found the recipe on the internet."

"Come in," said the Woman. The Man obliged and headed to the kitchen, which was exactly where his kitchen was situated two houses down.

To the Woman's surprise, the zucchini pizza casserole was indeed a taste sensation. She could not help proclaiming, "¡Eres un excelente cocinero!" At this the Man smiled because no one had praised his cooking before. Indeed, the Man had never received any praise whatsoever for anything that he did.

After dinner the Woman made coffee and defrosted in the microwave a frozen strawberry cheesecake that she had been saving for her birthday. After a few bites, the Man said, "Wonderful cheesecake!" And then he added, "Delicious coffee!"

After dessert the Woman and the Man moved from the dining room table to the couch and discussed many things. It was, in fact, the best conversation either of them had had in a very long time. Finally, when both began to feel a bit sleepy, they said goodnight, and the Man took his empty casserole dish with him as he left.

Two nights later the Man appeared at the Woman's doorstep and knocked. The Woman peeped through the peephole and saw the Man standing, smiling, holding a large bowl covered in aluminum foil. She opened the door, and the Man's smile broadened. He proclaimed, "One-pot creamy garlic chicken and rice!"

The Woman nodded, smiled, and let the Man pass. He marched straight to the kitchen and started opening cabinets and pulling out dishes. The Woman closed the door and stood for several moments in silence while the Man clanked about in the kitchen. The Woman weighed her options, considered the alternatives, pondered the possibilities. Finally, the Woman's reverie was broken by the Man announcing, "The food is almost ready for serving!" The Woman took a deep breath, thought for a moment longer, and then went to meet the Man in the kitchen.

And so it was, over the course of twenty years: three or four times a week the Man would appear, unannounced, on the Woman's doorstep holding some kind of dish (Italian, Mexican, Thai, or some unusual concoction the Man had discovered on the internet), they would eat their dinner while discussing this and that and then this again, finish with coffee and dessert, and then adjourn to the couch to chat a bit more. Then, when both began to yawn, the Man would gather up the casserole dish or bowl or platter or Pyrex and say goodnight.

One evening the Man showed up with a big pot of albóndigas and a pile of fresh homemade corn tortillas.

"This is my favorite dish," said the Woman as she tasted the delicious soup.

"Oh," said the Man. "I didn't know."

"You never asked," said the Woman.

The Man made a mental note of this new information.

They settled in and enjoyed their dinner, then coffee and dessert, before retiring to the couch. They both moved much slower now—twenty years can do that to a body—and they spoke slower, too. But they were basically the same people they were twenty years ago. After a while they fell into thoughtful silence. Finally the Man decided to ask a question, but at first he hesitated.

"How blue is the sky in April?" the Man finally asked.

The Woman thought for a moment. She had not expected this question. She then responded, "It depends on where you stand when you look at that sky in April."

The Man nodded. "Yes, that is true."

"Why do you ask?" said the Woman.

"I asked you that question because I am too afraid to ask you the question I really want to ask you," said the Man.

"Oh," said the Woman. "I think I understand."

"Pues," said the Man, "some questions are better left unasked."

"Es la verdad," said the Woman. "But then again, sometimes a question should be asked."

The Man pondered this, and then said, "What if I am afraid of what the answer may be?"

The Woman did not answer. They sat in silence for seven minutes. Then, with a sigh, the Man stood, gathered up the empty bowl, nodded, and left.

The next evening the Man did not show up with dinner.

And the evening after that the Man again did not show up with dinner.

One evening, after three weeks of the Man not showing up with dinner, the Woman realized that she was not saddened by the Man's absence. In fact, the Woman felt somewhat elated, lighthearted, giddy. She did not attempt to understand why she felt this way because there was no reason to question her feelings.

One evening, in the fourth week of not having dinner with the Man, the Woman enjoyed a delicious cheddar and mushroom omelet smothered in a spicy salsa that she bought from Trader Joe's. Just as the Woman was finishing her dinner, she heard a knock on the door. She stood and peeped out the peephole, and sure enough, there stood the Man, holding a large pot of something.

The Woman stepped back and stared at the door in silence. The Man then knocked again, this time louder. The Woman took another step back, then turned and walked into the kitchen. As she heard the

Man knock again, the Woman made coffee, placed three Oreo cookies onto a plate, and settled in at the small kitchen table. The Man knocked again. And again. Finally, all grew silent save for the crunch of the Oreos in the Woman's mouth. She then heard the Man's footsteps move along the walkway to the sidewalk and then stop. She listened to the silence. Then, after no more than six seconds, the footsteps continued down the sidewalk away from the Woman's house.

And in the silence of her kitchen, with nothing more than the sound of the clock ticking and tocking, alone with her coffee and remaining Oreo cookie, the Woman let out a little chortle. And then, slowly, a smile formed on the Woman's face.

"Finalmente," said the Woman. "Finalmente."

MATEO'S WALK

Though he just celebrated his fiftieth birthday, Mateo refuses to give up his search. He knows that Isabel lives someplace near downtown Los Angeles, no doubt on a street Mateo has walked maybe a thousand times. And though it has been more than twenty years since they last saw each other, Mateo trusts his sharp eyes, eyes he inherited from his mother, eyes that could spot a jackrabbit in the hilly scrub near their small village in Mexico, his home from long ago. So six mornings a week, Mateo puts on his baseball cap, slings a backpack onto his round shoulders, and walks ten blocks to work in the toy district, where he unpacks boxes, sweeps the floor, and sometimes acts as the cashier when Mrs. Kim needs to get lunch or take care of other business. This job is safe, simple, and keeps Mateo free to walk and search and dream. Today he takes a different route to work, different from the route he took yesterday and different from the day before. Mateo knows he must alternate his trips so that he can increase the odds of finding Isabel. The morning is hot already, almost eighty degrees, the Santa Anas—the Devil Winds—spreading their evil. It is not a lucky day. But Mateo remains hopeful, trudging along Spring Street, perspiration covering his face like a thin veil, wishing he had left his jacket at home today. He turns left on Fourth Street. A man steps out of Bar 107 hugging a sheaf of papers to his chest, gives Mateo a nod, a smile. Mateo nods and smiles and continues. The people are so nice here in downtown, he thinks. Suddenly, for some reason, Mateo stops in front of a café and looks through the plate glass window. Why he stops here he does not know. He squints and eventually lets his gaze rest upon an empty table, a newspaper spread across it. Mateo wonders if Isabel had been sitting at that table, looking at the want ads or maybe looking for sales, and then perhaps she had just stood up for a second to use the restroom. He waits. One minute. Two, three. But no one comes back to the table. Not Isabel, not anyone else. Mateo exhales loudly. He turns and looks down Fourth Street. It is time to get to work, he thinks. Mateo takes a step and then another, picking up speed as he walks without thinking. He decides to take Third Street tomorrow. Yes, Mateo hasn't walked that street in a few days. Maybe tomorrow he will be lucky.

WILLIE

Wilfredo likes to dress to get Papá all riled up. You know, Willie wears those short-shorts that you see on the ladies who walk up and down that bad street near the Shell station that Mamá says no self-respecting good Catholic would wander by unless your car died and you needed to get some help from Manny who works there. Mamá says those putas have no right to mess up our nice neighborhood. But the neighborhood don't look so nice, and I figure some pretty ladies walking up and down a street can only make things look nicer, right?

So Willie likes to put on these short-shorts that are so tiny that his nalgas are hanging out and then he pops in these blue contacts so that his eyes look like he's out of some scary space movie where only one person knows that the aliens are taking over people's bodies and no one, not even your father, believes you when you say they're going to take us over, too. I hate those movies. They make my stomach hurt.

Anyway, today Willie comes down the stairs looking so pretty with his long legs showing and his eyes not looking scary this time for some reason but shining a blue that looks like Uncle Chucho's restored Mustang instead of a space alien's eyes. And I think to myself that even Willie's cheeks look special, kind of red like a flower, like the blush Mamá finally let me buy from Sav-On even though I'm only twelve but she says, mija, you're a good girl so it's okay. I think Willie likes to take a little of my blush every so often because I see fingerprints in it that are bigger than mine but that's okay because I think he looks prettier than me anyway so he should use it. So this morning here comes Willie looking really extra pretty and Papá is reading *La Opinión* at the breakfast table, drinking his hot black coffee after finishing a nice big bowl of menudo, which is his special treat on Sunday mornings.

Willie sits down at the table without saying nothing. Mamá is busy at the stove, cleaning something up, I don't know what. I'm on the floor watching a *Power Puff Girls* video on the small TV that sits on the kitchen counter near all the Coke cans for recycling. I look up and smile at Willie. Willie reaches across the table and grabs a piece of pan dulce, and these little gold chains that hang from his wrist just jingle-jangle and they remind me of Christmas, which is a mile away. Willie gives me a wink and I smile and look at Papá who is now looking up at Willie but Papá isn't smiling and so my smile falls from my face like a dirty sock. I don't like Papá's eyes right now. They're all squinted up and his big black eyebrows come down in a mean "v" and he puts his coffee cup down on the green place mat and some of it spills over the sides of the cup but Papá doesn't seem to care.

Finally Papá says, "¿Qué es esto?"

"What's what?" Willie says through a mouthful of pan dulce.

I turn to look at my video again but not for long. Mamá screams and my head swivels like a chair and I see Papá holding Willie against the wall and something doesn't look right because Willie is looking down at Papá even though Willie is shorter by about six inches and then I see that Willie's feet aren't touching the floor no more, they're just dangling there like a doll's feet and I notice for the first time that he's wearing these pretty clear-plastic sandals. And I don't know what to do so I just sit there with tears coming down my face like someone just turned on the backyard hose and Mamá isn't moving either but now she isn't screaming, just standing in the kitchen, hands pulling at the dishrag, mouth open like an empty can of tuna and eyes owl-wide.

And Papá starts to yell something in Spanish so fast I don't know what he's saying. And then I see Willie's pretty fake blue eyes flicker toward me. And he smiles. Not a big smile. Just enough so that I know he's smiling at me. And suddenly my tears turn off. Just like that. And the house seems so quiet now, like we're suddenly under water, but I see Papá's lips moving fast like a cat. And Willie just hangs there against the wall, smiling at me. Looking pretty.

THE JEW OF DOS CUENTOS

Though I don't want to appear immodest, when I moved to Dos Cuentos I became the pueblo's most sophisticated resident. I don't say this as an insult to the other inhabitants. No, not at all. They are hardworking men and women. But the facts are these: though I was born in Cuernavaca, Mexico, for much of my adult life I had lived in New York where I wrote—in English—two books of poetry, one of literary criticism, and a novella. One of the Hollywood studios optioned the novella and asked me to write the first draft of the screenplay. Several East Coast and New England universities included my poetry and criticism in their curricula. My publisher was happy with the good reviews and respectable sales, considering that I had never written a full-length novel. That would come in time, they were certain.

In short, my then wife, Himilce, and I lived a most remarkable life for Mexican expatriates. We were even invited to—and happily attended—President Kennedy's inauguration. As Mexican Catholics, we were so proud of the young elegant man with his beautiful vision of a wife. They proved to the world that followers of the pope included people who enjoyed the latest fashions, fine food, classical literature, and modern poetry. It was a magical time for us all.

But a year after the assassination, a year after that most horrible of national nightmares, our little world started to fray, slowly at first, then quickly, without hesitation. Oh, I blame myself. It was I who cared more for the alcohol-soaked parties and my young, willing female fans than I did for poor Himilce. So the year Congress rewarded LBJ with the Tonkin Bay resolution and Cassius Clay defeated the legendary Sonny Liston, Himilce obtained an annulment. She moved back to Mexico City to lick her wounds at her mother's home and I moved to this little town to drink myself to death. Hollywood eventually canceled my contract. All was lost.

But for reasons I cannot fathom, this tiny town that I inadvertently stumbled upon, this mere trifle of a community, proved to be the salve my soul needed. No one knew me and the few who learned that I was a published author were no more impressed than if they had discovered I possessed brown hair or all my teeth. I lived a simple life off the small but continual stream of book royalties, no one asked questions, and I simply became known as the quiet writer who wrote no more. This, however, was not quite true. I owned the international rights to all my books so I spent my days translating my work from English into Spanish under a contract with a small but well-respected Mexican publishing house.

One morning as I drank my morning café con leche while reading a telegram from Himilce to inform me—with no intended malice, I believe—that she had just married a stable and successful surgeon in the Federal District, I heard a rather loud rapping on my front door. I seldom received visitors save for a delivery boy from the mercado twice a week so I was a bit startled. I wiped my mustache with a napkin and answered the door.

Some people believe that first impressions are the most important and that one should always meet a new person with this in mind. I believed then as I do now that the gentleman who stood on my modest porch adhered to this belief. Before me stood a trim, finely groomed man in his mid-thirties, though he could have been older. I recognized his suit to be of the subtle yet elegant quality often worn by the men who attended the New York soirées of my past life. Whereas my hair had already grown thin, this man's head sported a glorious thatch of thick, wavy red locks that seemed to pulsate with life. He held a gray fedora in his left hand, a small package in his right. The man smiled but his eyes betrayed something other than joy, something faraway and melancholy.

"Sir," he said. "I am Samuel Schifrin." His Spanish was, not surprisingly, impeccable though I detected a hint of something European in his diction. Before I could introduce myself, he said my name and that it was an honor to meet me after years of enjoying my writing. Though I felt as though my privacy had been compromised, there was also a twinge of relief to learn that someone in this pueblo had read my books.

And then we stood in silence, he in elegant attire, I still in my dressing gown. Finally I invited Mr. Schifrin to wait in my small study while I made myself more presentable. When I returned to the study, he stood with his arms locked tightly behind his back, perusing the many books that lined the far wall. I could detect a small click of his tongue. He turned and smiled.

"Such a wonderful collection," said Mr. Schifrin. "A fine, full collection."

I offered him café but he declined. He gestured toward a chair and I nodded, giving him permission to sit. He slowly lowered himself into the chair, crossed his legs, retrieved a silver case from his vest pocket, and offered me a cigarette. I happily accepted and we sat for a few moments enjoying this common yet exquisite pleasure. I decided to be bold.

"Are you a publisher?" I asked.

Mr. Schifrin laughed. "Oh, no, sir, not at all. I am merely a new resident of this fine pueblo."

I joined him in his mirth more out of embarrassment than anything else. How could I be so arrogant? But he didn't seem to mock me.

"What brings you to such a humble community?"

Mr. Schifrin's smile evaporated. "Perhaps the same reason you left New York to settle in Dos Cuentos."

"Oh?" I said.

"You came here to escape, did you not?"

It was then that I grew uncomfortable. Though several American newspapers had reported on the annulment, the press of my homeland had not taken much notice, something I appreciated. But I decided not to allow myself to become defensive. Here was a gentleman who had read my books. Of course he knew something of my personal life. This could be no surprise. But I wanted to be the person asking questions. It was at this moment that I spied the small package that Mr. Schifrin had brought with him. He had set it on the corner of my desk.

"A present?" I asked as I motioned with my cigarette to the package.

"Perhaps," he smiled.

He stood and retrieved the package and handed it to me. His sleeve rode up his arm, revealing something that gave me a shiver: a tattoo in faded black ink of six carefully squared numerals.

"Please," he almost whispered, "if you don't mind."

I reached for the package and realized that it was the size of a manuscript. As I removed the brown paper, I saw that the "present" consisted of approximately two hundred neatly typed pages.

"Your book?" I asked, now intrigued.

"No," said Mr. Schifrin as he sat again. "I merely did the translation. From the German to Spanish."

The first page indicated the simple title: "My Life." Just below the title were the words: "By Ruth Schifrin." I glanced at his left hand and noticed for the first time a faint indentation on his finger indicating a wedding band now gone.

"My late wife," he answered before the question could leave my lips.

And without prompting he proceeded to tell me his story and why he had sought me out. Mr. Schifrin and his late wife had been friends since childhood, both being of well-established families in Berlin before the Nazis took everything. They ended up in the camps when they were both fourteen years of age. Miraculously, though their parents and siblings did not survive, they had and eventually reunited after the war. They married and settled first in New York and then Los Angeles, where Mr. Schifrin opened a bookstore and his bride made a nice home. This is where he learned Spanish. He had been introduced to it by a customer, Mr. Osvaldo Zamora. Oh, Mr. Schifrin fell in love with the language! In his spare time, he studied and practiced with his new friend. He found that he had a facility for language which, combined with his enthusiasm, led in twenty-four months to a proficiency that would have taken a person of normal skill many more years to acquire.

In this time, however, Ruth Schifrin had grown thin, frail. Her years of near starvation in the camps had set in motion a lifetime of ills that would not only prevent her from conceiving a child but also lead to an early death.

At this point of his story, Mr. Schifrin grew quiet. I let him sit silently with his thoughts. I couldn't imagine his loss. Finally, he looked directly into my eyes. "My Ruth was an educated woman, a woman of deep thoughts," he said softly but with great conviction.

"She knew that she would not live long so she vowed to tell her story so that no one would forget."

"Forget?" I ventured.

"What happened," he said. "In the camps."

As these words hung between us, I looked down at the manuscript in my hands. I asked: "And how can I be of assistance?"

With these words, he allowed a grin to appear on his face. "Ah," he said. "Yes, you can help, if you wish."

"But how?"

Mr. Schifrin moved to the edge of his chair and rested his elbows on his knees, again revealing the tattoo. "As I said, I've completed the translation from the German into Spanish. I think it is a pretty fair job. But it was exhausting."

"Yes," I nodded. "I can't imagine how difficult it must have been."

He let out a sigh. "I'd like it translated into English as well. But I haven't the energy to do such a thing."

"Why do you need an English translation?"

"A California publisher is interested," he said as he settled back in his chair. "But they want to publish it in Spanish *and* English. And, as you know, the Spanish portion is done."

Silence became our other companion again. I had no choice, not really. "I will translate it," I said.

Mr. Schifrin lowered his eyes. "Are you certain?"

"Of course," I said cheerfully, as if I were accepting an invitation to attend a dinner party. "It will be an exciting new project. I'm getting tired of looking at my own words."

That was two months ago. The pueblo has now grown so accustomed to Mr. Schifrin that it finally granted him the honor of an epithet: the Jew of Dos Cuentos. There is no malice in this, merely a statement of fact. Indeed, the longer he stays in our pueblo, the more friends he makes. He is, in the end, a charming and thoughtful neighbor.

As for me, I've been absorbed in the life of this remarkable woman Ruth Schifrin. Her widower visits every day to read what I've done and to offer suggestions, which are usually quite insightful. And as I translate each page, I learn more and more of Ruth's strength as well as of the hideous nature of hate. I learn strange names like Sachsenhausen, Belzec, and Uckermark, places Ruth knew too well.

But I have now come to a particular chapter, somewhere near the middle of the manuscript, where I need to stop. It is chapter 7 and I have read it three, maybe four, times. I have roughed out a fairly decent translation but I keep coming back to a paragraph that has, for some reason, ignited something in me that I cannot define. This is how I have translated the passage:

> I have always possessed a facility for drawing, even when I was very young. Before the camps I had earned many art awards in school as well as praise from my teachers, parents, and friends. In the camps I hungered not only for food and my family but also for the feel of a pencil in my hand and beautiful rough paper upon which I could draw trees, flowers, and birds. One morning I shared these feelings with one of the older girls, Sarah. That evening she handed me a small piece of charcoal. I knew better than to ask where she had gotten it. I hugged her tightly. The next morning, just as the sun crept up the unusually clear sky, I was compelled to use my charcoal. While the others slept in our crowded barracks (which the guards called a "dormitory" that housed fifteen three-tiered bunks), I found a smooth patch of floor just under my bed. Sunlight came at a perfect angle from the far window and illuminated my makeshift canvas with a soft glow. It is here that I sketched a small nature scene of a river that ran between two large trees. I drew slowly, savoring each stroke. When I finished, I leaned back, just a bit, to view my drawing. It was not as good as the artwork I had done before the camps, but I smiled nonetheless. It took me a while to know what I was feeling. And then it came to me: I felt human again.

Though I will never fully understand how so many people could perpetrate such evil, I feel as though I am finally grasping the potency of love, the vigor of hope. I am also wrestling with those questions that have confounded the human race from the beginning of time. What separates us from animals? Why do we create? What compels some to destroy? Ruth has made me ponder these ideas. She has planted something in me that is beginning to take root. And for that, I will be forever grateful to her.

BLUE

ONE

All I want is to remember her smell. That's all. It's her smell that
I miss most. I can't forget anything else, though. The labor pains,
the nurse wiping my forehead with a damp cloth and calling me
sweetie and reminding me to breathe. And then the doctor saying
she saw her head peeking out. And then, almost like magic, the sight
of her wet, squirming new body. But I can't remember her smell.
That smell from the next day. After her first bath. She had trouble feeding. Didn't want to take my milk. The nurse said, sweetie,
that happens sometimes. Keep trying for a while before giving up.
But she knew it didn't matter. Still, I tried to coax her. I directed
her little mouth to my nipple, cooing to her: drink, baby girl. You
gotta drink to get strong and meet the world. And I'd put my lips
on her hair and breathe in her freshly washed smell. Baby smell. My
baby's smell. But it's been too long since that time. And all I want
is to remember her smell.

TWO

My old man said it was for the best. She'd have a better chance with a
family that could feed her, give her a good home, a proper upbring-
ing. My old man said that when he and Mom got married, they were
out of high school. And he had a good job. That's the way you're supposed to do it, said my old man. Finish school. Then get married. To
a man with a good job. Why couldn't you wait, mija? I never could
answer my old man. I was in love, though. That's something. Right?
That's something, all right. No one can tell me different.

THREE

Little Green. That's what Richard called me. Because when he first saw me sitting in Mr. Bruno's biology class, I was wearing this green T-shirt and a green skirt. All green. And it wasn't even St. Patrick's Day. So I was Little Green to Richard from then on.

FOUR

Carey. That's what I would have named her. There's no Careys in my family. One of the reasons I like the name. And it's a strong name, too. Because a girl needs to be strong. Right? Stronger than a guy. That's what I think. I wonder what they called her? Wouldn't it be amazing if they named her Carey? And I used to think that one day we'd meet and I'd tell her I would've called her Carey, too. And she'd know that we always had a connection, like magic, like we always were together. But I don't think that anymore. No reason to.

FIVE

Blue is what they call people who get sad. It's weird, though. Blue makes me happy. And there are all kinds of blue. The sky in the morning. The sky in the afternoon. Richard's eyes. How he got blue eyes no one ever figured out. Those eyes made me fall for him. A blue so clear they made you blink and wonder if they were contacts or something. But no. They were real. Blue like you've never seen. Blue that can't be described. Blue that isn't sad at all.

SIX

California became home for my family. San Diego, L.A., Bakersfield, even Sacramento. Up and down the state. Mom's family came from Mexico and settled in L.A. about forty years ago. But Pop's family—when they crossed the border, they scattered. They're the ones in those other cities. Pop jokes that the Moreno blood must be in my veins because I'm not afraid to wander. Nine cities in seven years. But I always call home. They always know where I am. I'm not running away. I'm just seeing California. That's all.

SEVEN

This flight tonight to Vegas wasn't too expensive. Mom and Pop helped me with it, anyway. I just couldn't drive. Too tired. But I had to go. Wouldn't you? I got the call last week. They had tried my parents first. And then Pop called me where I'm living now. Oakland. He was gentle. With the news. I don't know why they wanted me to know. Maybe they knew that I've been trying to remember what she smelled like. Maybe they knew I always thought of her. I don't know. It doesn't matter. At least they called.

EIGHT

River? That's a river? That's what I said to Pop when he first pointed out the L.A. River to me. I guess I was fourteen. A year before the baby. We were on the freeway driving to Tía Rachel's house in Canoga Park and he pointed and said that's the L.A. River. But it looked like a big v of cement with bushes and some trees growing in it. Not too much water, either. Nothing like the rivers I'd seen in my geography books. You know, like the Amazon. River? I said. That's a river?

NINE

A case of you is like a case of the flu. That's what Mom liked to say. But she hasn't said it a lot recently. Now she just says how much she wishes I'd stay put. Near home. I look down from the plane and see only clouds. Mom is down there someplace. And soon I'll be near my baby. But she's not a baby anymore. She's a girl. Or was. But at least I'll be able to see her. And her parents. And I'll thank them for giving her a good home. That's what I'll say. Because it's true. I'm sure.

TEN

The last time I saw Richard was at high school graduation. He didn't come to my house for the party. But he came up to me right after the ceremony while I was trying to find my parents in the crowd. It was so hot and all I wanted to do was get out of the robe and stupid cap and drink something cold. But he came up to me and said, happy graduation, Little Green. And I said, happy graduation. He touched my arm and gave me his blue eyes. Said he was leaving the next day. For Tulsa. I said, there's no Mexicans in Tulsa. He laughed and his eyes got bluer. But I guess he's a wanderer, too. Don't know if he's still in Tulsa. I wish I could tell him, though. About my trip to Vegas. To see my girl. Our girl. They told Pop about it. About the pool gate opening when it shouldn't. How it happened during the party and no one noticed until hours later when people were beginning to leave. But it was a night party so it was kind of dark. And they told Pop about how they tried to make her breathe again. But I know she had a good home. With lots of love. Lots of toys. Thank you, I'll say. Thank you for taking care of my baby.

LA GUACA

There was a man who owned the finest restaurant in the pueblo. Though no name adorned the establishment, the villagers dubbed it La Guaca. The man, as well, had no name, at least none that the villagers knew. He was a complete mystery, a man apparently with no family, no origin, no history. So they called him El Huérfano.

One evening, as the villagers gorged themselves on enchiladas, tamales, pollo en mole, and other delectable dishes, El Huérfano rose from his usual seat at the corner table and cleared his throat. The room fell into silence.

"I plan to take a bride," said El Huérfano to the startled villagers. "But," he cautioned, raising an elegant finger, "she must be perfect in every way."

Most of the families had at least one unmarried daughter because the Revolution had taken from this earth most of the pueblo's eligible young men. So this announcement raised great hope in the hearts of the parents and their hijas.

"I invite all of the pueblo's señoritas to feast here tomorrow night," said El Huérfano. "No one else may come. And I will choose my wife from among the guests."

"How will you choose?" an older woman asked. But El Huérfano turned and disappeared through a back door. A great cheer filled the void because this mysterious but wealthy man would make someone's perfect daughter his bride.

The next evening all of the pueblo's single women swarmed La Guaca dressed in all their finery. Though El Huérfano was not the handsomest of men, times were hard and there was little chance of living a comfortable life without a marriage of convenience. Remarkably, all of the women found seats in La Guaca and they waited. The tables sighed with great platters of food and bottles of fine brandy. Finally, after what seemed an eternity, El Huérfano appeared.

"As you know," he began, "I search for the perfect wife."

The room murmured in anticipation.

"Before you sits a great feast," he continued noticing one particular beauty who sat motionless amidst the others. "But it is poisoned."

A horrified gasp rose from the young women.

"The poison is so potent, it will kill in a matter of minutes." El Huérfano now whispered: "But it will not harm a perfect woman. If you wish to leave, please do. Otherwise, enjoy your dinner."

Only one woman stood and left. The others slowly served themselves and commenced eating, each believing that she would survive. After a few minutes, the first victim fell. And then there was another and yet another. Finally, only the most beautiful woman was left. She stood and walked to El Huérfano.

"You shall be my wife," he said as he touched his lips to hers.

She leaned forward and they kissed. El Huérfano could taste the wonderful feast from the beauty's lips. But then his eyes bulged and he fell back.

"¡No!" he sputtered as he dropped to the floor.

"Sí, mi amor," said the beautiful woman. "Sí."

VOIR DIRE

It's only the third day of jury duty and we're all going a bit stir crazy. Except for some of the older folks who are retired and have been on a zillion juries before and are proud of it. I can tell they just love jury selection and what they call voir dire—you know, when the judge and attorneys get to ask the potential jurors all sorts of questions to see if they have some kind of hidden bias against the plaintiff, defendant, or the American justice system in general. But it's all really a crapshoot in the end. Sure, sometimes a person's bias is as clear as the L.A. sky isn't, but no question can really get to a person's hidden agendas. Some unmarried lawyers wear wedding rings during trial because the jury will trust them more. You know, people see a young, good-looking woman like me (yeah, I'm good-looking and I know it), and figure that even though I'm a lawyer and not home with six kids, I must be normal with a nice husband and maybe a baby or two in my future. But I don't bother with that bullshit. I came out of the closet in law school and I fought too hard to go back in, even if it might win my case for me. I mean, I remember how I sat Mamá and Papá down at their big oval table, the one I used to scamper under with my cousin Eddie, and told them I had something important to say.

"Mija," said Mamá. "You can tell us anything. Really." But I didn't believe her.

"Yes," said Papá. "Anything."

I looked at them for such a long time before I told them. Mamá sat plump and solid in her chair like a panda. Her eyes looked so scared. And Papá, with his smooth angular face and black wavy hair (just like Victor Mature, he immodestly reminded us), tried to look cool and in control but his lower lip twitched just a little. What was I going to tell them? I was dropping out of law school?

77

Pregnant? Eloped in Vegas and just flew into LAX with a new husband who was a Republican? My heart ached; my whole body ached, actually. I wanted to vomit. But I breathed deeply and took a sip of my Sprite and just said it.

"I'm a lesbian."

It was May, just before finals, and goddamn hot. Their old house had no air-conditioning so they kept the windows open to let what little breeze there was in. The crickets were so loud I thought that maybe Mamá and Papá kept a few thousand in the kitchen for pets.

"Eh?" finally wandered from Mamá's little lips. "Eh?"

Papá sucked all the air out of the room and fell back in his chair. The crickets got even louder and I felt like I was in some bad Vincent Price movie. Papá finally posed a strange question: "How long have you been thinking of this?"

"Thinking?" I asked, not understanding. "Thinking?"

"Yes, Sylvia. How long?" He trained his large brown eyes on me like tractor beams. Maybe he could will the truth out of me.

"It's not something you really think about, at least not at first."

"What do you mean?"

"I mean, first you kind of feel it and then you start thinking about it." I felt some comfort because we were talking and no one was screaming. Yet.

"So," Papá slowly began again. "When did you make this decision?"

I don't remember what Mamá was doing at this moment because I was mesmerized by Papá's line of questioning. I focused on a lone beautiful and unruly curl that fell down onto his preternaturally smooth forehead.

"Papá, it's not a decision to make. It either is or it isn't."

"Don't give me that lawyer talk, Sylvia," Papá said in a low controlled rumble.

I wished then that he'd simply yell at me. This slow burn scared the crap out of me. But what did I do? Acted like the smart ass that I am. "But, Papá, I'm not a lawyer yet."

His eyes widened and Mamá pulled back because she saw something coming and Papá lifted his wide hand and slammed it so hard on the table that I swear my chair and all the furniture in the room jumped like a 4.8 earthquake had hit our house. "Do you think I'm a stupid man?" Now he was yelling.

"No," was all I could muster. There I was: an adult, twenty-three years old, and my papá made me feel like a five-year-old who got caught shoplifting a Kit Kat bar. And Mamá started to cry.

"Again, how long have you been thinking of this?" Papá asked, but this time in a softer voice.

"Ten years, I guess, in terms of thinking about it."

Mamá stopped crying. "Since you were thirteen?" she gasped. "You knew you were ... were ..." She couldn't say the word. But I felt I had to answer.

"Well, actually, in terms of how I felt, since I was nine or ten."

Mamá started to cry again. But I was being truthful. I remember staying with Grandma when I was nine and becoming mesmerized by these three little ceramic mermaids she had hanging from her bathroom wall. They were gorgeous. Delicate little girls with fish tails and little seashells on their tiny breasts. They played some kind of water volleyball with two ceramic bubbles. And all I knew was that I wanted to be with them forever. They made my heart beat so hard and I wore a goofy grin as I imagined what was under those little seashell bras. I think I knew right then. Not intellectually, mind you. But in the deep recesses of my soul.

Anyway, Papá sat silently staring at his hand that still remained flat, palm down, on the table. It looked like a fat spider that had fallen ten stories to its death. Papá took another deep breath. "Ten years is not long enough."

What did that mean? "Long enough? How long is long enough?"

"I don't know," he said. "But ten years is not."

Then Mamá perked up suddenly. "But, mija, what about Edmundo? You know, that nice boy you dated in college. What about him? You liked him, didn't you?"

She sounded so desperate. I didn't have the heart to tell them that Edmundo was now happily married to a brilliant architect and living in a beautiful condo on the Big Island of Hawai'i and that the brilliant architect was named James.

"I never felt that way for Edmundo."

"Is there somebody?" ventured my father. "I mean, is there a woman?"

Good question, I thought. Actually, there were two women, one assistant professor and one first-year student, but that information would have exploded their heads right there and then and I didn't have the energy to scrape their gray matter from the ceiling and walls. So I lied. "No one special."

And then the whopper. The one from left field. The one only my papá could come up with. "Need any money?"

My jaw dropped. Need any money? Where did that come from? I'd just told them that I was a lesbian, not that I was shopping for a new Honda Accord.

"No, Papá. Thank you. But my scholarship and loans are covering everything. Remember, UCLA is way cheaper than Stanford was."

That was six years ago, and we try not to talk about my various loves unless it's serious. Anyway, regarding juries, I'm not really cynical or jaded—too young for that. I know our system is probably better than most. I'm just a true believer in the complexity of the human psyche. So jury selection is not a science. The only good thing about jury duty, though, is that I don't have to wear a suit or nylons or heels. That's a particular joy when it's hot in the Valley like today. About ninety or so. And I guess I get points somewhere for being a good citizen. Other than that, it's a pain in the ass. I mean, there aren't even any potential dates in the jury lounge. They're either way too old like Mother Teresa (before she died, of course), or young and cute but trying to catch the eye of some guy. So I have two friggin' weeks stuck in the Van Nuys courthouse going nuts, trying to take care of my own caseload by phone during my breaks and answering emails from home at night so I can avoid going to my office after hours when this Nazi of a court clerk decides to let us go home for the day. But going home isn't so hot since Angela left. I mean, after I kicked her out. That's a different story.

The jury "lounge" is the pits but at least the air-conditioning works well. The room is decked out in typical 1960s government bland, with mucous-green industrial carpeting that almost matches the lumpy fabric that covers the very boring, though semi-comfortable, wood-framed chairs. A sickly coat of ancient yellowed white paint covers the walls, and row upon row of sadistic fluorescent lights cover the entire ceiling. There's a ban on *Jerry Springer* so the TV is perpetually tuned to a local station that plays nothing but reruns of shows like *Who's the Boss, Full House,* and *The Partridge Family.* I actually like watching *TPF*—as I call it—because that teenage Susan Dey is so goddamn cute and perky. So on that third day of jury duty, I put down my draft summary judgment motion and gaze upon the pouty face of Susan, daydreaming about how she must sound when she comes. I know I'm bad but I haven't had sex in about three months, since I've been single, and I gotta keep from going crazy bored. What's the harm in it?

It's kind of funny that I daydream about Susan Dey because people have been telling me forever that I look like her except that my hair is as black as a judge's robes. It curls every which way into my face and down my back and it's crazy beautiful in its own way, if I do say so myself. And my skin is darker than Susan's but I have the same baby lips, perky little nose, sad eyes, and a dimple on my chin. I could have been a fuckin' Partridge. I daydream that I'm a long-lost cousin from Mexico who plays a mean tambourine because I have no musical talent whatsoever. And then Susan Dey and I could have little running gags about guys and maybe we'd have a slumber party, just the two of us, and then at night, when she got real sleepy, I'd say that I was cold and ask if I could cuddle with her to keep warm. Shit! I need a date so bad.

Sometimes I wonder how things would be if I were straight and I got married to a nice yuppie Chicano—a "Chuppie"—and I have two kids, a boy named Quetzalcoatl and a girl named Nahua, just to show that we remember our Aztec roots even though we can barely speak Spanish and we make a very nice combined income—and Mamá and Papá would visit and hug their little nieto and nieta and pat my handsome husband on the back and give me smiles that could warm the coldest winter. I think about that. And then Susan Dey's face creeps into my mind and that other imagined life slips away like soapy shower water into a drain.

My father always likes to say, "No le busques tres picos al toro." Literally, it means, don't look for three horns on the bull. In other words, don't make things more complicated than they are. Pretty good advice. It certainly applies to jury duty. It is what it is. Just gotta get through it. And I guess it applies to me, too. Somehow. He also says, "Nadie sabe lo que tiene el costal, nomás el que la carga." No one knows what the sack holds except the person who carries it. I guess that applies to me, too, because my sack feels pretty heavy sometimes. But it's mine. I've earned it. And I have no intention of trading it in for another.

SIGHT

Alfredo sits across from his best friend, Alfredo, who goes by "Al." Alfredo looks down at the opened package that sits on his antique mahogany dining table.

"Best fucking birthday gift you'll ever get," says Al as he drinks from his bottle of San Miguel. "The best, mi amigo. No shit."

Alfredo stands and his chair makes a squeaking sound on the hardwood floor. He then, very carefully, reaches into the box and pulls out the gift. "Heavy," he whispers. "Heavier than it looks."

Al smiles. "Yes, hombre. Pinche heavy."

Alfredo lifts the gift, a pewter plate, large and muted in the afternoon sunlight that invades through the bay window. "Looks like a plate," he says.

"Uno nunca debe confiarse en las apariencias," says Al.

Alfredo holds the plate higher and the sunlight glints off its side. "Appearances are deceiving?" he asks.

"Perhaps."

"What do I do with it?" asks Alfredo.

Al laughs. "The question is: what will it do with you?"

* * *

"Mi amor, what is this?" asks María as she runs her index finger along the rim of the plate. It feels cool and smooth to her touch.

"A gift," says Alfredo. "From Al."

"Really?"

"Really."

"Since when did Al acquire taste?"

"Now, now. Be nice."

* * *

María bounds out of their bedroom wearing blue UCLA shorts and a little T-shirt that says DON'T ASK. Alfredo looks up from his *Time* and admires her figure. "Gym?"

"Yes, mi amor," she says. "How else can I keep you interested in me unless I have buns of steel?"

"Not fair," says Alfredo. "You're beautiful *and* brilliant. You keep that nonprofit afloat."

"Yeah, making a lousy $75K a year."

"More than I make."

"That's different," laughs María. "You're a writer."

"Have a good workout."

"I will," she says as the heavy oak door groans open.

"I love you."

María blows a kiss to Alfredo and leaves.

* * *

A half hour after María leaves for the gym, Alfredo hears a sound coming from the plate. It sits solidly in the middle of the dining table like a shrine. Alfredo walks over to it. He hears voices emanating from the plate's murky silver center.

"Oh, that feels good," he hears. It sounds like María's voice. He looks into the plate and sees her, lying on a massage table at her gym. She has no clothes on and lies on her stomach. A young woman in white shorts and matching T-shirt massages the back of María's thighs. Her white hands look like reverse shadows on María's cinnamon skin. Alfredo wants to blink but he cannot. He leans closer.

"How about this?" the young woman asks María. She works her small strong hands up deep into María's buttocks and down towards her crotch. The young woman closes her eyes and bites her lower lip with straight white teeth.

"Mmmmmmm," is all María says. "Mmmmmmmm."

The plate suddenly goes blank and the voices stop.

Alfredo says, "Oh, shit."

* * *

An hour later, María comes home. She has showered and her ebony hair glistens with moisture. "Hola, mi amor," she says.

Alfredo sits on the couch. His brow is furrowed deep with lines.

"Everything okay?" asks María.

Alfredo sits silently. Then, as María walks over to him, he asks, "Good workout?"

"Oh, yes, mi amor. I really needed it."

"Get a massage?"

María almost jumps. She coughs and runs her fingers through her hair. "Why, yes. Before working out. A quick one."

Alfredo sighs. "Hope it felt good."

María coughs again. "Yes, it did." She looks over to the dining room table. The plate is not there and the table looks barren like a desert. "Where's the gift?"

Alfredo looks at her.

"Mi amor, what happened to the plate?"

"I decided that it didn't belong here anymore."

"What?"

"It just didn't belong."

María shrugs. She kisses Alfredo on the forehead and heads toward the staircase. "Gonna go online for awhile," she says.

Alfredo sits looking at the gleaming, polished expanse of the dining room table. It looks like a dark ocean to him.

"It just didn't belong," he finally says with a little laugh. "Just didn't belong."

TABULA RASA

"I shaved my mother's head yesterday."

Yesterday. That was Sunday. Elena let her words just hang there between us as I watched her clear the desk of extraneous matter—black Sharpie markers, Scotch tape, rulers—so she could make room for the new posters that we just picked up from Kinkos. I observed her small brown hands maneuver quickly, without a wasted movement, intent on a purpose. I wanted to grab her hands, stop them, squeeze them, and make her look at me while she told me what she did yesterday. But I didn't because she'd pull away, tell me not to be so macho, a typical male. A typical *Mexican* male. And then I'd say, No, I'm Chicano and almost done with college. I'm no Neanderthal. So, instead of getting into a stupid fight, I stood silently and let her finish cleaning the desk.

When she put the last desk-thing away (a plastic paper clip holder), she leaned back and rested tight fists on her narrow hips. Elena wore her favorite baggy khakis with a skintight black t-shirt; the words CHICANO MUSIC AWARDS hovered over her left breast. An unruly black curl bobbed happily across her forehead and I again had to keep my hands to myself, not reach over, fix it. I think Elena knew it bothered me and let another curl find its way down. She stared down at her handiwork. Now every nick, scratch, and ink stain sat exposed on what was once an expensive piece of mahogany furniture that probably graced some high-priced lawyer's office back in the '60s.

"There," she finally said. "Bring the posters over so we can take a good look at them."

I obeyed. I walked over to her neatly made bed and grabbed posters. I laid the pile of light green cardboard on the desk. Elena tilted her head to the left, and then to the right. "Beautiful," she said.

I nodded. We stood in silence for about a minute.

"Mom had been warned that the chemotherapy would probably do this. You know, her hair," Elena continued as she flipped through the posters to see if there were any misprints.

"Yeah," I said. "I know." I couldn't read her expression and this bothered me. We've been together since freshman year and I figured I could decipher every look that crossed her beautiful face.

"I was cooking breakfast and I heard her scream. I ran upstairs, to her room, and I found her in bed, sitting up, with a clump of white hair clutched in her hand."

"Damn," was all I could offer.

Elena pulled a reject out of the pile and handed it to me. "I just ran and put my arms around her." She continued to thumb through the pile. "I calmed her down, finally, and decided to make it nice. As nice as I could."

I put the rejected poster back on her bed. I figured we could go back to Kinkos and get a refund for each one that didn't come out right. "What did you do?" I asked.

She let out a sigh and looked at me. "I ran a hot tub, helped her in, and then very slowly clipped her hair with scissors." Elena's eyes flickered down toward the posters and she quickly pulled out another reject.

"And?"

"Then I lathered her head real gently and shaved it, slowly, while humming a little song she used to sing to me when I was little."

I didn't know what to think. First, the image of Elena shaving Mrs. Montes's head was almost too much for me. Second, I couldn't figure out why Elena was even here today. The posters didn't have to go up until closer to the demonstration against the Townsend project. A huge luxury housing development got city approval despite serious environmental concerns. Basically, the Townsend Corporation was going to clear-cut over a thousand acres of trees, shrubs, and tall grass to supply homes to the wealthy. We were willing to get arrested before our foothills were destroyed. We had almost eighty students and faculty ready to converge at the site this Friday. So we could have waited until tomorrow to put up the posters.

"The rest of these look fine," Elena announced. She straightened them out. "Where's the staple gun?"

"I saw it in Thien's room," I said as I started toward the door. Elena shared this small but very functional three-bedroom house with two other female students.

"What were you doing in Thien's room?"

I stopped in my tracks but didn't turn around. "She needed some help in calculus."

Elena let out a little cough. "She has her eyes on you."

I didn't hear a hint of a laugh in her voice. "Mi amor, I'm a one-woman man," I said and started walking again.

"And don't you forget it," she answered in an almost whisper. "My love for you is pure."

I stopped again and laughed at this overly formal pronouncement, but Elena stood there without even a shadow of a smile on her face. We stood there, frozen, for a few moments.

"So is mine," I finally answered.

"Are you sure?" she said, still not showing any sign of levity.

"Of course," I snorted. "I might not be perfect, but I'm sure of *that*."

"Es mejor mancha en la frente que manchita en el corazón," Elena said, this time with the left corner of her mouth rising up in a half smile. One of her favorite dichos: It's better to have a stain on one's forehead than a stain on one's heart.

I now felt that I could go and get the staple gun without looking like a jerk. Just as I left, she raised her voice: "Thien's room is a pigsty! How can you find anything in there?"

Elena was right but I knew where to look and went right to it. Walking back, all I could think of was Elena humming softly as she used a razor to make clean rows of smooth skin down the back of her mother's head, and in her heart wishing that with each gentle stroke, a bit of the cancer was being stripped away.

* * *

The sun shone brightly through the oaks. More people showed up for the demonstration than we had expected. The TV camera crews set up across from the bulldozers and we stood on the other side, behind the chain link fence. My roommate, Darius, had already cut a large flap in the fence but he held it down until I gave the signal. Elena breathed heavily by my side. She carried a sign that said, TREES, NOT HOUSES! Someone blasted an old Bob Dylan song on a boom box. Several men and women in dark suits milled about. I didn't know who they were, but they scared me just a bit. The Townsend work crew hadn't shown up yet so the bulldozers sat motionless. It was noisy, like a carnival but without the rides and cotton candy. I finally gave the signal by yelling, of all things, *Charge!* and Darius lifted the flap of chain link to let us in. And in we came, chanting, screaming, singing, clapping. The camera operators went into action. Within seconds, we had swarmed the bulldozers like insects in search of sustenance.

The cops finally arrived—six patrol cars in all—and surrounded the area. I lost sight of Elena but I figured she'd be safe. Our plan was to cover each of the five bulldozers with bodies and there were more than enough of us to do this. One of the officers got on a bullhorn and told us to leave the premises because we were trespassing. We just cheered, almost in unison, and packed in closer to the bulldozers.

Then it happened. Someone, I don't know who, threw something. It flew over the fence and hit the hood of a patrol car with a metal thump so loud we all suddenly became quiet. We heard one loud *Disperse!* come from the bullhorn. Then one of the officers tossed a small metal canister over the fence. Smoke! That little can let out so much of the stuff I couldn't believe it. And then another can came sailing over and then another. Finally, we were engulfed in stinging white thick haze. Our group became frantic, people started to push, and fall, and run toward the flap. I heard screams. I tried to find Elena. Where was she?

"Clear the area!" the officer yelled through the bullhorn.

Though my eyes stung, I finally spotted Elena. She had climbed to the very top of one of the bulldozers. She had wrapped her nose and mouth in a red bandanna. I could hear her screaming, see her fist pulsating in rhythmic jabs into the smoky air. I froze. I didn't recognize the look in her eyes: wild, angry, like an animal. At that moment I was no longer a part of her. Elena became a different person, speaking a different language, seeing a different world. I heard her voice pierce the chaos. She chanted, "A life for a tree, a life for a tree!" A strong wind blew the smoke higher so that for a moment I couldn't see her at all. But I could hear a voice: "A life for a tree, a life for a tree!" But I didn't know the voice anymore. I just stood there, not knowing what to do next. Not understanding what was happening.

SAN DIEGO

I have no reason to be nervous. We had planned this dinner long ago, after a few false starts. But now my famous lengua smothered in thick mole sits in the middle of the dinner table looking as elegant as sliced cow tongue in a dark red sauce can, anchored by a large bowl of steaming Spanish rice at one end and at the other a bowl of refried beans. The table looks perfect with three place settings—my husband safely at the St. Francis in San Francisco for his annual law firm retreat—perfectly chilled bottles of Dos Equis waiting patiently in the fridge, and Susana Baca crooning on the Yamaha with other nice choices sitting in their cradles. But no Papá. And no Papá's new girlfriend. Shit.

I know what you want to say to me: *Of course you're nervous. Your mom has been dead five years and your dad suddenly decides to find a new woman after swearing there could be no one after Leticia. It's perfectly normal. Just let the night happen. Everyone is entitled to a second chance.* And I'd say: You presumptuous little dumb-fuck. How can you even pretend to know my papá? Or me, for that matter? And there ain't no way you could even fathom my late mother. And then I'd kick your pitiful fat ass.

Okay, even with a low six-figure joint income, I'm still a little rough around the edges. You can take the girl out of La Puente, but . . . And sorry about the hostility but you don't know Papá. He's an idiot. Not the classic nitwit who sits in his own feces drooling kind of idiot. No. He's made a pretty good living all his life running a little business here, another one there. Nothing fancy. But he goddamn put food on the table, kept a small but decent roof over our heads, sent me and my brother to college, and kept Mamá moderately contented with no more than three, maybe four, affairs with customers. Nothing Mamá couldn't handle. But when it came

89

to choosing a suitable mate, what did Papá know? I mean, he never should have married Mamá. She was a bitch on wheels and it's no wonder he cheated a few times. If she'd had big tits and a face to die for, maybe I'd understand why he chose her. But Mamá's chest was as small as Michael Jackson's nose and she was homely as a stick. Thank God I take after Papá, who is pretty handsome, if you ask me. But he hung in that marriage for thirty years. He said he loved her. *Love.* Fuck. He *believes* in love. So, you see, he's an idiot. And I have a bad feeling about this new woman he's hooked up with. Connie. Connie García. That's her name. I almost choke on it and I haven't met her yet.

Ah! The doorbell. I get up, straighten my skirt, examine my teeth in my reflection in the hall window, and open the door. And there he is: glistening gray hair combed back, clean-shaven, grinning like a schoolboy, wearing that perfect-fitting blue blazer I bought him last Christmas. On his arm is his date. Connie García. Okay, let me stop here. I have an announcement: I am *not* a racist. I might be a bitch (I blame genetics on that), I might be a pain in the ass, I might drive an SUV, but I do *not* dislike people based on race, ethnicity, religious persuasion, or whether they can afford a Coach purse. But why, oh *why* did I expect Connie to be Mexican like us? Her last name perhaps? Duh.

"Mija, this is Connie," chirps Papá.

Silence. My mouth hangs open like a used condom. Papá and Connie just stand there smiling. Connie sticks her hand out to me. Somehow I gain enough control to take it. It's very small, her hand. Tiny. A diminutive sack of bird bones. I try not to hurt her as I shake it slowly.

"Hi," says Connie.

"Hi," I manage to get out. "I'm Sonia."

More silence. Suddenly I feel like a schmuck—a word my husband picked up at the firm—and I motion them into the house. So we have progress. They are now standing in my home. I close the door. Papá hands me a bottle of white wine, which is all wrong. He knows better because I told him that I was cooking lengua. Unless of course it's Connie's stupid idea to bring *white* wine for a Mexican meal.

"For you, mija."

It's a warm night so Connie doesn't have a wrap or anything to hand me. And then I notice that she has a very nice figure. She's wearing this simple little summer dress—must be a size 2, for God's sake—a floral print that shows off very young-looking thin arms and a very nice non-surgically-enhanced neck. She reminds me of Mrs. Tanaka, my fifth grade teacher. Pretty, petite, with perfect skin. But Connie must be at least sixty, based on what Papá has told me about her.

"Connie," I say. "Connie *García?*" I can be blunt.

"Yes," she laughs. She covers her mouth with her teeny-tiny hand when she titters. Just like Mrs. Tanaka did.

But I need more information. "*García?*" I emphasize again.

And she laughs again and now Papá joins in with a chuckle. "My late husband was García," she says through her hand. "I was Fujiwara before that."

So she has a thing for Latin men. Sick. Totally sick.

"Oh," I say, not smiling. "That's interesting."

More silence.

"So," says Papá. "Are we just going to stand here or what?"

Connie laughs again.

I come to. "Lo siento," I say, falling into Spanish for reasons beyond me. "Sorry. Come on. The food's ready so let's get started." My chones are all in a twist now, but I better pull my shit together.

Connie smiles broadly. Nice teeth. "Good," she says as we walk toward the dining room. "I'm famished."

The size 2 is famished. Yeah, right.

"Then you'll love my lengua," I say.

As Papá pulls a chair out for Connie, she says, "Lengua?"

"Let me put this wine in the fridge," I say, ignoring her question. "Beer goes better with Mexican food."

As I walk to the kitchen, I hear Papá whisper, "We'll have the wine later." Bingo. I was right. It was Connie's idea to bring white wine. Chardonnay, to be exact. Nice label, actually. Napa. Something nice for me to drink when they're gone. I grab three bottles of Dos Equis and bring them to my guests. And then he does it. Papá opens Connie's beer and pours it into her glass. He never did this for Mamá. *Never.*

"Thank you, Al," she says.

Al. *Al.* Who the fuck is Al?

"Al?" I say.

Connie goddamn laughs again. "'Alfonso' is such a mouthful."

Papá just opens his beer, dispenses with the glass, and takes a gulp while keeping his eyes on me. His eyes say, *Please don't do this.*

"Al," I say. "Al. I like it. It's so new. So modern. So La Jolla." You see, after Mamá died, Papá followed me down to La Jolla. He sold all his little businesses, the house, almost everything, and bought a neat little condo down here a couple of miles from me and Carlos. He didn't want to live in Los Angeles anymore. "Anywhere but L.A.," he'd said after the funeral.

"Mija," Papá says. "I like it. I know it's different from what Mamá called me."

"You mean 'pendejo'?" I say as I open my beer, which lets out a defiant hiss. I also bypass the glass and take a long, cool gulp. Damn, it tastes good.

Papá almost chokes. But Connie laughs. Again.

"Danny used to use that word," she offers. "My late husband. Danny. He liked to say, and I quote, 'The whole pinche world is filled with pendejos.'"

Papá lets out a bellow of a laugh. "I would have liked Danny," he's able to get out.

Well, you can imagine how sick I felt at that moment. That bitch had Papá tied up in knots. Everything she says and does seems charming to Papá. She must be good in bed or something, the little cunt. Shit! My Papá in bed that that size 2. I felt like puking. But I'm hungry so I serve dinner.

As I serve, Papá falls into small talk. "So, you see, my Sonia here runs the entire computer system for the San Diego Superior Court," beams Papá. "She has a huge staff."

"Yes," says Connie as she admires the food. "You told me she won this big award for her work."

Oh, so this is her game. Get on Sonia's good side with flattery. Well, it won't work.

"So, how long has Danny been dead?" I ask as I pile my plate high with rice.

Papá's eyes widen like the huge inner tubes floating in my pool.

But Connie is unfazed. "Three years," she smiles. And then, after taking a bite of lengua, "Oh, so tender!"

"Yes," I say, "you have to cook tongue a good long time to get it that tender."

"Like butter on *my* tongue," she jokes, not bothered by what she's eating. Papá likes this joke and chuckles, casting adoring eyes on Connie.

I need a different avenue of attack. "So, Connie, Papá tells me you're retired."

She nods, chewing away happily. I pass her the basket of steaming corn tortillas. She takes one with a smile.

"From what?"

She puts the tortilla down and takes a delicate sip of beer. "Teaching. Special ed."

Oh, so she's fucking Mother Teresa now. Think. Think. Ah! "How can you afford to retire?" Gotcha! If she's fishing for a new paycheck in Papá, this will come out.

Connie pauses, looks lovingly at Papá and sighs. "Well, Danny did very well as an engineer. Good pension. Very large life insurance. And we could never have kids."

At this, Papá consoles Connie with a little pat on her arm. I offer a kind nod, though the kids thing kind of hits home because of my fertility problems and all. But I must keep focused. "How much did Danny leave you?" I ask.

Papá's head snaps up like some sort of toy on a spring. "Sonia! Such a question!"

Connie stays cool. "No problem, Al." She turns to me. "Danny was very wise about the insurance. One million. I've invested it in an annuity." She wipes her mouth as daintily as a southern belle. "God bless him."

The Yamaha switches to the next CD, a Stan Getz bossa nova collection.

At this point, I would have liked to tell you that dinner was a disaster, with my every pointed question ripping a new hole in the shroud of Connie's secrecy to reveal to Papá the she-devil that she is. But no. Dinner goes just fine, if you like uneventful meals. No matter what I say, Connie charmingly relates it to her past life with Danny and Papá laughs. We finish dinner, enjoy dessert, have nice coffee.

"How about that wine?" asks Papá after we finish. "We can sit by the pool. It's so beautiful out tonight. ¿Verdad?"

"Al," coos Connie, "why don't you take the wine outside while Sonia and I clean up a little?"

Papá smiles in agreement, almost skips to the kitchen, gathers up the wine and three glasses, and disappears through the back door.

Connie and I stand and silently bring plates into the kitchen. Then it happens. As I rinse a plate, Connie comes up close to me, right under my chin because she's so short, and grabs my arm. She pinches me, not in a sweet, motherly way, but in a vicious, I-want-you-to-listen-up-now-bitch way. She narrows her eyes and I can't move. She hypnotizes me. And then she says it to me very slowly so I can understand every word.

"If you fuck this up," she begins, "I will hunt you down. Got it? He's mine. End of story. ¿Me comprende Usted bien?"

At least she uses the formal tense.

"I understand," I answer. All this time, she's pinching my arm harder and harder. Finally I let out a little yelp and pull away.

"Good," she smiles. This time she doesn't cover her mouth. I see that her teeth are indeed perfect. Too perfect. A mouth full of dentures.

"Hey, you girls," my father yells from the backyard. "The wine is poured."

Connie pats my arm. We walk out in silence. Papá hands us each a glass. He looks so handsome standing there. Trim and dapper. And happy.

"A toast," he says as he slips his arm around Connie's tiny waist.

We raise our glasses. I'm still in shock.

"To my two girls," says Papá.

We clink our glasses. Connie narrows her eyes at me again. And smiles broadly.

"Yes," I finally say. "Your two girls."

We sip our wine as the crickets chirp wildly and the well-lit pool fills the backyard with glistening blue-green reflections. Our lemon trees infuse the air with a clean, spicy scent. Stan Getz's smoky, sexy sax serenades us through the outdoor speakers. It is a beautiful night.

"Nice wine," I say.

"Yes," says Connie. "Napa Valley."

"Yes," I say. "Delicious."

Papá grins like an idiot as he savors the moment.

"My two girls," he almost whispers. "My two girls."

LA DIABLA AT THE FARM

Ah, mis amigos. I have missed you so much! But you see, I needed some downtime, as my gabacho friends say. I needed to "recharge" myself. Partake in a little sopa de pollo para el alma. But I have returned, refreshed. My ch'i is back in balance, I have corrected the bad feng shui in my life, and I thank the powers-that-be that my house was not built facing a fork in the road, a dead end, or a valley. In short, all is well and I am ready to tell cuentos again.

¿Cómo? You think I joke? Oh, I would never joke of such things. One must be in balance or else one cannot function as fully as one must. As my papá was fond of saying: El campo fértil no descansado, se tornará estéril. You know: The fertile field that is not given rest will become barren. Well, I was under great threat of becoming barren, spiritually speaking, of course. This is true of all living things. Even for the Devil. Yes, El Diablo. Or, as I've told you many, many times before, if you're in certain neighborhoods in Los Angeles, it's La Diabla. Because the Devil is legion, the Devil resides in most towns and cities and may be a man or a woman or both. It all depends on what is needed. So, apropos of my cuento for today, in some of the upscale areas of my beloved City of Angels, the Devil is very much female.

Well, one day back at the end of the 1970s, when disco was still king and just before the Reagan years, things weren't going so well for La Diabla. Yes, she resided in a beautiful beachfront home in Malibu, which should make any soul feel refreshed each day. But remember that she had gone through all that loco shit with Don de la Cruz, not to mention that crazy Quetzalcoatl. ¡Ay Dios mío! That was some crazy-ass crap, wasn't it? My cabeza starts to swim just thinking about it all! And though she's a bit modest, if push came to shove, La Diabla would admit to having something to do with some of the best evil that befell the world in the late '70s: Jim Jones and his little escapade in Guyana, the oil spill from the *Amoco Cadiz* off Brittany's coast, the rise of the Ayatollah Ruhollah Khomeini and Donald Trump, and the untimely death of Elvis. Legion always tapped her for the big jobs, even if it took her out of Los Angeles. Anyway, brilliant work, if you think about it.

But spawning evil day in and day out can knock the stuffing out of anyone. ¿No? La Diabla couldn't get away from her work, even living in beautiful Malibu. I mean, think about it: her neighbors were film and music people who could give her a run for her money when it came to committing depraved and degenerate acts. It all made her feel so weary. Even her boy toy, Eduardo, an "actor" who made his real living as a very fine waiter at the Good Earth restaurant in Westwood, began to bore her. Besides, he slept with her not because she was beautiful. Oh, no. As you know, any man who fucks La Diabla suffers horrible pain. Eduardo did the dirty deed because La Diabla had promised him great future success as an actor. Anyway, La Diabla needed to get away for a while and re-create in the truest sense of the term. But where to go? What to do?

La Diabla had already traveled throughout the world, from Paris, Texas, to Paris, France. She had enjoyed all climates, innumerable foreign delicacies, every conceivable carnal delight. But those were working vacations, really. She toiled wherever she went, never resting even while taking great joy in spreading her spleen. One day, feeling particularly fed up with it all, La Diabla sat in her study, closed her eyes, and let the rhythmic crash of the waves work on her subconscious. Where could she go? What would be different? New? Relaxing and refreshing? And then it came to her in a burst, just like that. Palo Alto! She had of course been to San Francisco and Oakland and even Sunnyvale, but La Diabla had missed Palo Alto despite a very fine recommendation from one of her favorite disciples. This gentleman (let's call him "Simón") attended one of Stanford University's graduate programs (I won't divulge which one for obvious reasons) and in his spare time was a staff artist for Stanford's admirable and well-established humor magazine, the *Chaparral*. Simón's particular talent was embedding subliminal messages in his illustrations. These messages were not innocent ones to encourage the student body to drink Coke or buy Nike shoes. Oh, no. *His* subliminal messages encouraged Stanford's young folk to cheat on tests, haze neophyte fraternity brothers, listen to Boz Scaggs records, and buy additional copies of the *Chaparral* for loved ones.

In any event, Simón had always waxed eloquent when it came to life on "the Farm," as this fine university is called by all who love it. And he had nothing but praise for the surrounding communities of Palo Alto, Mountain View, Menlo Park, et cetera. All-meat pizzas at Fargos, sirloin steak burgers from Kirk's, TOGO's six-foot-long submarine sandwiches, a cool mug of beer at the Oasis. As you can see, Simón's life on the Farm revolved around food and drink. But he also sang the praises of the incomparable LSJUMB (those crazy pendejos make the football games so loco!), evening strolls along the Quad, visits to Hoover's last erection (Hoover Tower to you), and chatting about current events over a frothy latte at the campus coffee shop. It all seemed so relaxing to La Diabla. Why not stay near the Farm?

So La Diabla contacted a broker and located a wonderful house for lease on Cowper. Perfect setting: not too far from campus, nestled among other fine homes in Palo Alto, with trees lining every street. And a bargain, too, though she really didn't need to worry about money. Who could ask for more? With a phone call, it was all set. La Diabla would finally have a vacation, come back refreshed, and be ready to do battle with good once more. ¡Híjole! She was going to come back swinging like a drunken puta! She leased her Malibu abode to a record executive who had been kicked out of his Pacific Palisades mansion by his third wife, packed up a few things, and flew up north.

Settling into the quaint Palo Alto home took little effort. It fit La Diabla like the knitted leg warmers she was fond of wearing during the cool beach winters. The hardwood floors gleamed with new polish, and the Shaker furniture proved to be functional, comfortable, and oddly calming. Ah! The only thing that gave La Diabla the willies was St. Anne's Church, which was no more than three blocks away down her street. But she decided not to let the competition bother her. Two full months of no work, just relaxation. Right? Of course, right!

So time passed. One week, then two, now three. And with each day of doing nothing but strolling the finely manicured neighborhood plus a few jaunts onto campus, La Diabla grew more and more relaxed. The worry lines on her beautiful brow began to recede, her frown softened sometimes into a small smile, her neck and shoulders loosened. Why hadn't she done this before? She knew the answer: La Diabla was a classic type A. No doubt about it.

Well, I wouldn't be telling you this cuento, mis amigos, if La Diabla's little vacation continued to go swimmingly. No, that wouldn't be a story at all. So let's get down to it. ¿No? So I ask you: what would ruin such a perfect and well-deserved sabbatical from evildoing? Think hard. Remember my other tales of La Diabla? ¡Ándale! Got it? ¡Sí! Sex! La Diabla was missing *it* so bad! You know, she loved to have *it* in her all the time. Call *it* what you will: hueso, pistola, pinga, picha, bastón, camote, elote, bastardo, pito, chorizo, lechero, pirinola. Or, as you simple English speakers would say, dick. Nothing made her happier than to have one pulsating and thrusting in her nido, concha, tamal, pepa, mondongo, mamey, paloma, et cetera, et cetera, et cetera. She even daydreamed of her insipid young man back in Malibu. La Diabla needed a fuck right away. But all she seemed to appreciate were these Stanford undergraduates. Should she mess with such youthful specimens of budding manhood? It would be wrong, wouldn't it? Ah! So it would. Which is precisely why it would be so right for La Diabla. She is so evil and horny! A powerful combination. So one morning as La Diabla tossed about in her lonely clean sheets, she reached up and grabbed her own chichis and swore that she would get laid that very night! Oh, the horror of it all! I'm so relieved that my son went to Berkeley!

Because La Diabla didn't go to college she hadn't realized how easy it would be for a woman of her beauty to land an undergraduate male, especially one attending the Farm. She could have her pick, as they say, particularly if La Diabla attended a fraternity rush party. But she was ignorant of such things. She needed help figuring how to proceed. This could not end in failure or she would surely explode! La Diabla called her friend Simón, who luckily had not yet left his apartment for class.

"Simón," she purred into the receiver. "I need your assistance."

"Yes, mi amor," he purred back. "Anything. Except, you know."

And she knew what "you know" meant. Sex. You see, several years ago, after having a bit too much vino, Simón—who is a mortal—and La Diabla went for it. And as you might remember, when a mortal has sex with the Devil, it ain't pretty. Oh, the pain! It is indescribable. So I won't even try. Even the booze couldn't numb poor, unsuspecting

Simón. Thus, despite La Diabla's extraordinary pulchritude, Simón didn't want to hit *that* again. And La Diabla understood completely.

"Well, Simón," she continued. "I do need to have sex but I won't burden you with the deed."

Relieved, he said: "Ah, but you want me to set you up, right?"

"Any sexy friends?" she ventured as she let her left hand slide between her legs.

"Friends?" he said. "You don't need any of my friends. There are dozens of young men on campus who would kill to get some off you."

La Diabla loved the flattery. "So how do I meet one?" Her fingers explored the wet folds of her womanhood.

"Meet me at the coffee shop at 7 tonight."

"Really?"

"Really."

"Oh, yes!" she said as she climaxed.

Simón shook his head. "I won't disappoint you."

La Diabla couldn't answer. She dropped the receiver in its cradle with a *clack* and closed her eyes to dream away the morning in delicious anticipation.

She awoke at noon and spent her dear time bathing, dressing, and putting on makeup (or war paint, as she liked to joke). La Diabla felt like a young girl again. It was all so exciting! What wonderful man would she have tonight? Who would suffer the exquisite torture of sex with La Diabla? The mystery made her dizzy with anticipation. To burn off some nervous energy, she put on Michael Jackson's *Off the Wall* album and danced around the house, holding the album cover out in front of her like a partner. Oh, Mr. Jackson looked so handsome to La Diabla. Maybe she could find a man like him tonight! (Please do not be shocked . . . this was many years ago, remember?) She worked up such a sweat shaking her booty that she had to shower again. But no matter. All would be wonderful soon. Simón virtually guaranteed it!

La Diabla got to the Stanford coffee shop a bit early, giddy as a young girl, and ordered a glass of Chablis. She found an empty booth and perused the bustling room. Such good-looking young men everywhere! ¡Ay! Who would be in her tonight?

"Hey, chica, stop drooling," said a familiar voice.

La Diabla looked up and rested her eyes on Simón's tanned angular face. She laughed. "Oh, Simón, we could skip this hunt and go back to my house," she purred.

Simón held up a finger: "Un momento. Let me grab a beer."

When he came back, he took a long drink of his Anchor Steam and let out a tiny burp.

"You're so sexy when you're rude," whispered La Diabla as she reached for his knee, which made Simón jump.

"Mi cielo," said Simón as he stopped La Diabla's migrating hand, "let us stick with our plan."

"Sí, mi amor," she said, feeling a bit chastened. "Who do you have for me?"

Simón nodded backward. "Over there, by the painting of the old man."

La Diabla lifted her exquisite chin and narrowed her fiery eyes. In the corner sat a young man with dark curly hair, a mustache, and a muscular build. Before him sat a coffee mug and a large textbook in which he was brushing back and forth with a yellow highlighter.

"Ah!" said La Diabla. "Muscles and brains. Not bad, mi amor, not bad at all."

Simón acknowledged the compliment with a self-satisfied grin.

"But how do I approach a college student?" she asked. "This is new to me, mi amor."

Simón leaned forward and whispered conspiratorially: "Easy. Take your wineglass and ask if he minds company."

La Diabla frowned. "Don't play with me. I'm so horny I could behead someone right now."

Simón knew she wasn't exaggerating because he had seen La Diabla kill for less. So he patted her hand and said, "I'm not joking. And then to break the ice, ask him what he's studying."

"Oh?"

"I guarantee you will be fucking him within the hour."

"Really?"

"Yes."

La Diabla asked: "Do you know him?"

Simón laughed. "No, not really. Not well. His name is Andy. Met him once at a party in Flo Mo. He's a junior, pre-med, and currently single. Broke up three weeks ago with a cute little sophomore from Casa Zapata."

Oh, mis amigos, such words made La Diabla squirm with sexual energy! A future doctor with the body and face of an actor who probably hadn't enjoyed any sex for a few weeks. How could she lose? Not possible. She squeezed Simón's knee in thanks, grabbed her wineglass, and made her way to Andy's table.

After a few moments he realized someone was standing over him. Andy looked up, a bit annoyed, but then his eyes widened as he took in La Diabla's beauty.

"Mind a little company?" she asked, her heart beating so hard it seemed to be traveling up her chest into her throat.

Andy offered a crooked smile. La Diabla loved crooked smiles. He stood, gave a slight bow, and pulled a chair out for her. She sat and crossed her long smooth brown legs.

"And who might you be?" he asked as he took his seat again.

Now this was a tough one. La Diabla had enjoyed many aliases throughout her centuries-long life. But she wanted something special for tonight. Something cheap, dirty, fuckable. Who should she be? She glanced around the room searching for an idea. Just then a young woman walked by carrying several books, including *Nicholas Nickleby*.

"Nicki," said La Diabla turning back to Andy. "With two *i*'s."

"Nicki with two *i*'s, I am Andrew," he smiled, "but call me Andy."

They sat in silence for a few moments, basking in each other's admiration. Simón observed them from across the room feeling quite proud of himself.

La Diabla was ready to make her move: "So, what's your major?"

Andy grinned. "Hum bio. I'm pre-med."

La Diabla had no idea what hum bio was, but she certainly knew the meaning of pre-med. This pretty boy had brains.

"Well, you know what they say," she purred.

"What?"

"All study and no fucking makes Andy a boring boy."

Can you believe it, mis amigos? Such audacity! No woman has ever said such a thing to me, and I'm not chopped liver! I've had a few chicas in my day. But this is loco! And what do you think Andy did? Well, he fell back in his chair, shook his head, and tried to respond. But not a sound came from his lips. La Diabla knew she had hooked him. So she played a bit with this poor boy.

"How about it?" she said and slid her foot up Andy's poor unsuspecting right leg. He quivered at her touch.

Andy sputtered: "But I have a roommate."

La Diabla whispered: "I have a house in Palo Alto all to myself."

Oh, magic words indeed to a Stanford man! Better than "I have a single in Serra." Andy became woozy with anticipation and the possibilities!

"Let's go!" he yelped, like an excited puppy. And then he whispered: "I assume you have a car."

Of course La Diabla had wheels! And only the best: a cream-colored 1979 (then only a year old!) Mercedes convertible 450 SL with tobacco interior. A joy to ride with the top down on your way to get laid! ¡Chingao! So they sped to La Diabla's rented house on Cowper, and, and, and . . . Well, this is where my little cuento gets a bit strange. I'm not quite certain if this old hombre has the palabras to express precisely what happened next. Let me take a swig of my cerveza. Ah! That's better. Now a copita of Presidente. A reverse chaser! Okay, my lengua is loose, my mind is agile, and I think the words will now come.

This is what happened: they screwed in the hallway, they did it in the closet, they humped up the staircase, they did the fandango in all three bedrooms! For hours and hours they did not stop! La Diabla couldn't believe her luck to have hooked up with such a campus stud! And after a full twenty-four hours of this craziness, she had to rest, take a nap, to get ready for the next round. This is where it gets strange, mis amigos. La Diabla fell into the deepest sleep of her existence, and she dreamed! You see, she hardly ever slept and she certainly never dreamed. In her dream she strolled alone on the Stanford campus, peering into empty classrooms, gazing down deserted paths, listening to the complete silence of an abandoned university. This brought a chill to La Diabla's spine, something that was as alien to her as righteousness and piety. And in her dream she felt the anguish of solitude as complete and total as can be. So horrible was this feeling that a tear appeared at the corner of La Diabla's left eye and made its way, slowly at first, down her cheek and then sped off her face and splashed to the ground.

Then she woke! At first she forgot where she was. Then La Diabla heard Andy moving around in the bathroom. Oh, this Andy. What was he doing to her? He was different from the rest. He didn't feel the horrific pain when he put his manhood into La Diabla. Why not? What was different about him? But after a moment, it came to her. Andy merely lusted after La Diabla—for the beautiful woman she appeared to be—and he didn't know that she was the Princess of Evil. In other words, mis amigos, Andy didn't try to please La Diabla to get something in return such as great wealth or tremendous fame. No. His was an honest, heartfelt desire to fuck La Diabla.

And as the nickel dropped (to coin a phrase, pun intended), Andy opened the bathroom door, grinned a lascivious grin at La Diabla, and bounded back into bed. As La Diabla let this young man enter again, she shed another tear. For you see, she was falling in love. And we all know that La Diabla cannot allow herself to do such a thing. It would ruin her without a doubt, creating that one true weakness in her being that would make her almost human. So once they finished, she knew what she had to do to this mortal. There was no choice.

As Andy came for what would be his last time, he said, "Nicki, I love you."

"Yes, mi cielo," La Diabla whispered. "Te amo mucho."

Oh, such sadness, such romance . . . like a Juan Gabriel song. I'm getting a bit choked up just thinking of that poor lad, now long dead. I'm not quite certain that I have a moral for this little story. But I'm reminded of a dicho my abuelito was fond of: "El amor es el último que resiste morir." You, know: Love is the last thing that dies. Perhaps it is. Perhaps it isn't. Ni modo. But for one poor Stanford pendejo—who should have known that this woman's offer was too good to be true—it doesn't much matter.

Mis amigos, that is the end of my cuento. There you have it. Sex. Love. Death. Stanford. What more is there? Nada más.

REAL TIME

CAMERA ONE

Diana saw it. So did her two roommates, Avram and Raquel. And it saw them. For but a second, maybe two, their six human eyes widened and locked onto its wild but somehow controlled eyes. The gray sky muted the colors of the trees, grass, birds—everything—so that they weren't quite certain they were seeing what they were seeing. The three humans squinted in unison. *It* seemed to squint back at them.

"Oh, my God," said Diana. She held the platter of steaming Spanish rice in front of her like a mispositioned shield. Her nose itched but she dared not put the platter down.

"Let's get closer to it," said Raquel.

Without moving his head, Avram shifted his gaze over to Raquel. "No," he whispered.

Realizing what they were looking at, Diana said, almost as an apology, "I thought it was a possum or raccoon or something."

With this last utterance, its ears perked, and its taut golden body froze in mid-stride. The family of quail that only a moment ago scurried nearby was nowhere to be found. Raquel shifted her left foot toward the low metal fence that separated nature from their trimmed conquered backyard, but Avram grabbed her shoulder before she could move her other foot. He could feel Raquel's toned muscles through her thick Gap Oxford shirt. Before Avram could offer a verbal warning, it turned its head from them and, with nonchalance so palatable that it seemed to mock the humans, the creature disappeared into the hilly shrub. Within moments it was out of sight. A fat noisy crow dove down from their roof and perched on the fence, feeling brave now that the predator had moved on.

"A mountain lion," whispered Avram, still holding Raquel's shoulder.

"Let go," growled Raquel, but he didn't.

"In Los Angeles?" Diana murmured. "How can that be?"

"West Valley," corrected Raquel. They all kept their eyes locked onto the spot where the animal had stood. "People haven't completely destroyed the natural habitat up in these hills."

"Well, you're enjoying this beautiful house so how can you complain?" laughed Avram.

"I'm only renting, like you," said Raquel as she shrugged Avram's hand off her shoulder. They all finally looked at each other.

Avram laughed again and reached for the large, blue plastic bowl of Doritos that sat on the overburdened card table. Popping a crispy triangle of fried fake tortilla into his mouth with a crunch, he said, "Oh, *that* makes a difference. I must have missed that class taught by your favorite Commie professor. Velasco? Right? Professor Jaime Velasco?"

"No se hizo la miel para la boca del asno," whispered Raquel. She turned quickly and went into the house. The crow let out an impossibly loud squawk and flew off into the gray sky.

"Nice job," said Diana.

"What did she say to me?"

Diana sighed. "She said that you were the biggest jerk to get into UCLA Law School." She put the platter down for emphasis. The plastic forks and knives rattled, and the lemonade in the perspiring pitcher rocked back and forth in little waves.

"No she didn't."

Diana's nostrils flared. "The chicken is burning. Go apologize to Raquel."

"No." Avram crossed his arms across his broad chest. He stood almost a full foot taller than both his roommates.

"Go, and I'll pull the chicken from the barbecue before it's totally ruined."

They stood in silence for six seconds. Avram uncrossed his arms. Now he could smell something burning. "Okay, okay. I'll say sorry to my little Communist roommate."

"Good. And cut that 'Commie' crap out. It's beginning to bug me."

Avram went into the house. Beads of perspiration formed on his upper lip and he was angry at himself because he could feel his groin grow warm. The slight chance of being alone with Raquel still sent a thrill through his body even though they'd known each since their first year of law school and he knew deep down nothing would ever happen between them. Avram walked across the beautiful hardwood floor, past the kitchen, dining room, living room, and toward the staircase. Renting this gorgeous four-bedroom home was the smartest thing he ever thought of. This was their last year of law school, he argued during one of their last study sessions last year, and they should make the most of it, live in a real house together, not separately in identical seven-hundred-square-foot Westwood bachelor flats for $1,000 per month, roaches included. Sure, the commute on the 101 and then, God, the 405, would be a pain, but imagine studying constitutional law or preparing for interviews up in the hills with a view of the Valley and a pool thrown in for good measure. Only $3,000, including utilities, split three ways. Imagine!

"A pool?" Raquel had asked in disbelief. "An actual swimming pool?"

Avram offered a smile, hoping that he looked handsome to her. "Yep, a swimming pool." He imagined what it would be like to sit back and watch Raquel in a tiny one-piece swimsuit just lounging in the sun.

"How could it be so cheap?" said Diana, rubbing her nose with a closed yellow highlighter.

"The guy doesn't want to sell yet," said Avram, trying not to sound too enthusiastic. "But he wants to move to a smaller place. His wife died a couple of years ago and his kids are out on their own. He's rattling around that place and just wants to make enough on a lease to maintain his puny mortgage payments."

Raquel turned to Diana. "A pool, Di. A pool." So that sunny afternoon in May of last year, Avram convinced Raquel and Diana that his idea was nothing short of brilliant.

He reached the staircase and started up but then froze. He heard something. And it scared him. The hair on his neck and arms rose in some kind of primal alarm. Avram cocked his head to the left and then to the right, holding his breath to be as quiet as possible, and he listened. At first it didn't sound human. It reminded him of something he had heard in a nature documentary: a high-pitched whine, like an animal in pain. What was it?

"Raquel?" he called out. And the noise stopped suddenly. He then heard footsteps, Raquel's bedroom door open, more footsteps, and then the smaller bathroom door shut. The noise started again. In slow motion, Avram walked backward, down the steps, and reached the landing. The sound had come from Raquel. "My God," he whispered. "My God."

CAMERA TWO

"No se hizo la miel para la boca del asno," whispered Raquel. She turned quickly and went into the house. Early Eric Clapton blasted on the stereo (Avram's choice), which propelled her faster through the house toward the staircase. *Why did he grab me like that?* she thought. That innocent gesture opened something in her and she couldn't stop the feeling. Raquel tried unsuccessfully to catch her breath as she grabbed the fine-grained banister with both hands. *Why did he grab me like that?* She hadn't slept much the last four or five days. She was at wit's end interviewing for jobs on campus. Raquel pulled herself up the stairs. Her mind entered a cloud and she could see her cousin Miguel, age thirteen, staring at her nine-year-old naked body. Raquel shook her head, trying to shake the memory like she had before, but it took over her senses. Miguel had grabbed her shoulder with his left hand, hard and mean, and he used his other hand on her. Where were her parents? How could they let him be alone with her? Raquel suddenly fell into the present and found herself in her bedroom, curled up, sobbing, shaking, trying to breathe.

"Raquel?" Avram called out. Raquel's trance broke and she stopped crying in an instant, almost as if she had pushed the "mute" button on the remote control. She stood up, opened her bedroom door, and went into her bathroom, shutting the door behind her. She curled again into a ball at one end of the dry bathtub and started sobbing again, full force.

CAMERA THREE

Diana watched Avram's muscular neck and back as he walked into the house. She shook her head and smiled. *I'm just a little horny right now,* she justified to herself. *Me and Avram? No way! He's too close a friend.* Diana carried a clean platter to the barbecue, opened its gleaming stainless steel lid, and started salvaging the smoking chicken by maneuvering the clacking tongs to grasp the sizzling pieces of bird. As she filled the platter, she remembered how her father, like most dads, ruled the barbecue. Outdoor cooking was *his* domain. He fumbled at most things in life, like making a steady living or keeping his wife from leaving one early morning, when Diana was fourteen, the day the space shuttle exploded over America. But when he still had a marriage (at least in his mind), he used to stand with one hand on his narrow hip, the other holding tongs like an artist's brush, sunglasses hiding brilliant blue eyes, and explain to his only child the intricacies of barbecuing. He had joked that the secrets of the art really should only be passed on from father to son, but she'd do. This made Diana laugh, understanding the joke, and she felt special.

Diana closed the barbecue, lifted the now-heavy platter, and turned to go back to the card table. But she stopped. She saw something in her peripheral vision. The mountain lion! It stood by the pool's edge, on the other side, not moving, just staring at Diana. The water rippled with the constant breeze that blew through the backyard. She knew that she should be frightened, but she wasn't. Should *it* be frightened of humans? But there they stood, not more than ten yards from each other, neither one moving. She remembered that her father had said that mountain lions and pumas were, in all actuality, the same animal, just different names. But one sounded more dangerous, didn't it? *Which one?* Puma, of course. Puma is a more dangerous name, don't you think, my sweets? And which one was this? A mountain lion? A puma? She had automatically called it a mountain lion when they first saw it. But right now she wanted it to be a puma. It made her feel something. Was it a good feeling? She didn't know. She couldn't name *that*.

LUCKY DOG

Months before Adriana returned to St. Mark's Elementary School, gossip swirled about at PTA meetings, bake sales, and recesses like those dirty little dust twisters that take over downtown L.A.'s streets in the autumn. She had left, suddenly, in the middle of sixth grade, and returned during a heat wave in late October the next school year. The mothers who volunteered to cook hot lunches saw it coming from a mile away.

Look at how Adriana wears her skirts!

She shaves her legs, too!

¡Qué lástima!

Yes, she had sturdy smooth legs and every boy eyed them. Even the priests couldn't help but admire the lively flexing muscles just beneath her short plaid skirt. And then she developed a bosom, to boot! Trouble, trouble, trouble. Too easy to predict, eh? Who couldn't have?

So when people started to notice a tummy on Adriana (not much of one, a mere shadow, really, but on her slim hips, it was quite noticeable), *poof!* she was gone. Sent away to Mexico to stay with relatives.

Money problems, said her mother, Ana. She can help out with her rich tía Isabel and send money to our family here. I'd go instead but who'd raise the other four niños, not to mention mi esposo? You know men! Roberto would let the children run around naked, dirty, and hungry.

What of her studies?

Oh, the nuns are wonderful! They give me the homework and I mail it down to her. Her tía is very educated so she helps Adriana. My sister went to the university!

They knew it was all bullshit. Bullshit, bullshit, bullshit. But they played along with the charade.

She's such a good daughter! You must be very proud.

Oh, yes. Very proud. We are lucky parents.

James didn't care about any of this. Before she failed to come back to school after the Christmas break, Adriana sat across from James (to his left and one desk up, to be exact) in Sister Sharon's sixth grade classroom. From his vantage point, he could rest his tired eyes on the white nape of Adriana's neck. Her short brown curlicue hair, with the help of the white Peter Pan collar of her uniform blouse, framed that little patch of peaceful beauty just for James. There in that safe place, two almond-colored freckles hung just below her curls and above the horizon of her collar like twin dark stars. If he could only kiss her neck, in that spot between the freckles, and breathe in her shampoo-scented hair, he would be a happy boy. So with a Halloween dance looming not more than a week away (planned by his friend Davie Gómez, whose reckless parents never seemed to be around), this was his chance to ask Adriana to come with him.

At morning recess, Davie egged James on. Don't be a pendejo, James! Ask the bitch out! Can't get none unless you ask! Davie dug a bony elbow into James's equally bony ribs.

James winced but he kept his eyes on Adriana, who was playing handball across the schoolyard.

Go! Another jab in the ribs.

Okay, okay!

James jammed his hands into his worn-out corduroys to hide his erection and started his trek to Adriana. As he approached, he admired her tough punches of the large red ball. She seldom lost. A warm Indian summer wind blew through the yard, and the other children's laughs, shouts, and cries merged into a big invisible woolen blanket that seemed to swathe James's entire body. His stomach hurt and he burped up the flavor of his morning café con leche. James finally stood a few feet from the three girls.

Adriana?

She didn't hear him.

Adriana?

She heard him and looked up. The ball bounced past her.

What?

Sonia ran for the ball and Monica stared at James. Monica's mouth hung open like an old sweater.

Adriana repeated: What?

Do you want to come with me to Davie's party? Next week?

Davie's laughter could be heard from across the yard.

Heads up! yelled Sonia. Adriana acted fast and caught the ball.

No, Adriana finally answered. She turned away and hit the ball with a tight little fist. No, I don't.

Maybe if I died right now, she'd feel sorry she said no, James thought. But he didn't die right then. He merely stood there and watched helplessly as Adriana easily beat Monica. James sighed and turned. He could see Davie doubled over, laughing. As he walked back to his friend, he muttered, shit, shit, shit, shit, shit. His erection shrunk and his brain hurt. Shit, shit, shit, shit.

Davie tried to catch his breath. ¡Pinche pendejo! he finally got out.

Fuck you, whispered James as he retook his place near his friend.

Davie wiped tears from his face and let out one more chuckle. The bell rang, making James jump. The nuns signaled with waves of their arms for the children to go back to the schoolhouse.

Race you! yelled Davie as he slapped the back of James's head, making a sound like the butcher, Mr. Ortiz, assaulting his cutting board with a fat salmon. Davie jumped forward and started pumping his thin legs. James narrowed his eyes and took off after him.

As Adriana strolled with her friends, she looked up and watched the boys racing. She smiled and dribbled the ball.

* * *

At the last bell of the day, James fled the school. Luckily, Sister Sharon had not assigned any homework that night, so he was not burdened by books. James simply didn't want to walk home with Davie or anyone else. He headed toward Pico Boulevard instead of taking his usual route on Fifteenth Street. Once on Pico, James breathed freely and he slowed down to enjoy the sights of the busy street. His stomach growled because, in a nauseous fit, he'd thrown away his lunch. He turned and headed east toward Palomera's Books, an ancient bookstore that also sold snacks. The owner, Marta Palomera, wanted to make more money so she had her husband, Pedro, add a glass case for pan dulce, sodas, and candies to attract the schoolchildren. (Also at her behest, her husband added a comic book rack, which was a stroke of brilliance, truth be told.) Pedro disappeared one night six years ago but the glass case and comic books stayed along with Marta.

Being Cubans, she and her husband were oddities in the Mexican neighborhood and were, for many years, viewed with great suspicion. You know Cubanos! They were all rich before Castro. Uppity, uppity, uppity. ¡Ay!

Now people just referred to Marta as pobrecita, not because she was starving but because she was abandoned by her husband. Now, at age fifty-five, how could she ever find a husband? Gracias a Dios she couldn't have children.

James entered the bookstore with a tinkle of the tarnished bell that hung on the door. The delicious musty-sweet odors took over his senses. Marta chatted into her old black rotary telephone receiver in rapid-fire Spanish. She looked up and waved at James. Her after-school assistant, Leonard, a lanky Chinese boy from the nearby high school, sat on a tall stool at the far end of the counter reading *Sports Illustrated*. Several adult patrons browsed about but luckily no one from school was there. James wandered up to the glass case and perused its treasures. His stomach rumbled so loudly that a dapper large man at the SALE! table looked up and frowned. Marta finally finished her conversation, dropped the receiver into its cradle with a loud clack, and maneuvered her still-lithe body to the other side of the glass case.

An oreja and a 7-Up, please.

Well, Jimmy, a hello to you, too.

James blushed. Only she called him Jimmy. And he should have said hello before ordering.

Hello, Mrs. Palomera. He scratched a scab on his sharp elbow. A Tito Puente song, "Lucky Dog," played on a small Sony compact disc player behind the counter. She kept the music low enough not to bother the customers but loud enough to keep herself happy.

Hello, Jimmy. Marta picked up a pair of metal tongs, deliberately and efficiently used them to snatch an ear-shaped piece of pan dulce from the corner of the glass case, and put it into a little paper bag. She handed it to James.

And a Coke?

No. A 7-Up. Please.

She pulled a green and silver can from the other corner of the versatile case and put it on the counter. That'll be $2.75, por favor.

With some effort, James pulled three crumpled dollars from his pocket and laid them near the 7-Up can.

Marta rang the order up and slid a quarter toward the boy. Quiet today, Jimmy. A lot on your mind?

No. Yes. No.

Which is it?

No.

Sure?

Yes. James grabbed the soda. Bye.

Bye, Jimmy.

As he turned to go, the shop door opened with a tinkle and there stood Adriana with two friends.

Shit! James turned back to Marta. In two seconds she figured it out, but she didn't know which of the three giggling girls, who now hovered by the comic books, was the problem.

Leonard! Watch the store.

Leonard's head popped up.

Marta signaled to James with her head. I'm taking this young man to the back to help me pack up those books, okay?

Sure. Leonard returned his gaze to the magazine. Tito Puente started up with "On Broadway."

Marta lifted the counter's wooden panel so that James could follow her to the storage room. He quickly obliged, rushing so fast he beat her there. The area in back was almost as large as the store itself. James stopped in the middle of the room and examined its contents in wonderment: boxes of Coke, 7-Up, and Orange Crush took over one corner, while piles of books and half-emptied boxes took over another. The back wall owned a counter, sink, and small refrigerator. A gurgling Krups coffee maker sat near the sink. Spider plants, burro's tail, and Boston ferns hung like bats from the ceiling, encouraging James to duck, even though there was really no need. A dirty narrow window ran across the back wall above the little kitchen area, allowing a little sunlight to bleed in. A single unshaded one-hundred-watt light bulb hung over the sink.

¿Café? asked Marta as she swished past the engrossed boy. She touched his shoulder on her way to the sink.

James liked the perfume she wore. Sí. Gracias. He usually didn't like to speak Spanish, but it seemed right to do so just then.

She poured coffee into a large white mug that had a dancing Snoopy emblazoned on it. ¿Con leche?

Con crema, por favor.

Marta smiled, opened the refrigerator, and pulled out a little carton of half-and-half. James noticed a wall calendar hanging near the boxes of soda. The calendar was nothing more than a long piece of laminated paper with a vibrant painting of a city's shoreline and all twelve months of the year 1958 lined up in neat little squares below it.

As Marta handed James the mug, he asked, Why do you have that up?

She looked over to the calendar and smiled. James liked the crinkles that formed at her eyes.

That was the last year my parents and I lived in Cuba. Before we had to escape. You know about Castro, don't you, Jimmy? She touched his shoulder again.

Yes. He felt his cheeks grow warm. What a stupid idiot! he thought. Of course that's the year she left! James took a sip of his coffee.

Delicious.

Thank you. It'll go better with your pan dulce. Sit, sit. There's a nice comfortable chair over by the books.

But I thought I was going to help.

Later. Let's talk first. I think I can help.

But help she didn't. In between interruptions from Leonard, who had trouble opening the cash register, Marta attempted to pass on to the befuddled James every ounce of her knowledge concerning all things romantic. He sat in an overstuffed brown leather chair while she walked back and forth in front of him like she was teaching a science or history lesson. Men want this. Women think that. Don't force things. But don't ignore her too much. Marta gesticulated with great ferocity, making her numerous gold bracelets jangle and clink like wild background music.

Sadly, none of it helped James. All the information merely confused him and made him feel small. The only consolation was being able to hide out until Adriana left. That, and getting a chance to enjoy wonderful coffee, sweet bread, and the curves of Marta's breasts that pulled against her almost sheer turquoise blouse. When she ran out of advice, she said, Anything else you want to know, Jimmy?

No. No, thank you.

Sure?

Yes. Thank you. What about the boxes and books?

Marta smiled. No. That's okay. Some other day, Jimmy.

James handed her the empty mug, nodded, and left the bookstore, cradling the now-warm can of 7-Up in his left hand.

* * *

Davie's Halloween party came and went (Adriana didn't even show up), as did All Saints' Day and Thanksgiving. James spent the last day before the Christmas break alternately lost in the lush terrain of Adriana's neck as she worked on a Christmas card and admiring her athletic purposeful movements at the handball wall. Happily, Davie was absent so James could enjoy his thoughts without harassment. Ever since that day Adriana said no to him, he had decided to admire her from afar, despite Marta's advice to the contrary. It was certainly safer that way. And it gave him such joy just to watch Adriana living her life. She looked a bit different recently: a little heavier, clearer skin, fewer smiles. But her beauty only seemed enhanced as far as James was concerned. In the end, however, she lived in her world and he in his. And James came to accept this as their reality on the last day of school before Christmas.

So you can imagine his shock when she spoke to him after the dismissal bell rang and the children burst into a cacophony of ecstatic screams.

Hey, James.

He looked up from his desk and saw Adriana standing above him, hands behind her back, swaying slightly like she was nervous.

Hey.

Wanna walk me home?

James stood and tried to speak but couldn't.

Well?

He coughed. Yeah. Sure.

Come on, then.

And so they headed out together. Sister Sharon smiled and said she hoped they'd have a good holiday. Then she put a hand on Adriana's shoulder and wished her good luck, which confused James. Why did she need luck?

They walked down Fifteenth Street in silence while other children ran by, laughing and horsing around in general. When most of the others had disappeared, James felt ready to ask a question.

Why did Sister Sharon wish you luck?

Without hesitation, Adriana answered: I'm going to Mexico for a few months. Probably won't be back until a month after seventh grade starts.

A restored '67 Thunderbird appeared from around the corner and blasted away their solitude with an old Al Green song. They didn't speak until it had disappeared.

Why are you going?

Have to.

Have to?

Yes.

They had reached Adriana's house. She turned to him. You're a nice boy.

James smiled but he didn't answer.

I wish I had gone with you to Davie's party.

Me, too. James quickly put his hands into his pocket. He looked at her home. It was a duplex, with Adriana's family squeezed into the two-bedroom unit on the right and the Romo family shoehorned in the other. The cement stairs shot up quickly to a large landing that met the two front doors.

James?

He turned. Adriana leaned close to him and lightly kissed his lips. He tried to kiss back but couldn't. She pulled back slowly. Bye, James.

Bye.

Adriana turned and ran up the steps and quickly disappeared into her home. James touched his cracked lips with his right index finger. He closed his eyes and smiled. Shit, he thought. Shit.

That night, as his brother, Marco, twitched and snored in his creaky metal bed across the small bedroom, James drifted in and out of sleep, dreaming that Adriana sat near his feet. She spoke to him and laughed a gentle laugh. And he laughed and listened to her. Finally he fell into a deep sleep with no dreams at all.

* * *

Because of that little kiss, Adriana's ensuing ten-month absence stung James that much less. The rumors, however, entered his soul with a

searing ache so deep that he found it hard to breathe whenever he
heard people speak of her.

Davie was the biggest source of news. Shit, man, she had a boy!
Can you believe it?

No, said James as he tried unsuccessfully to swallow the first bite
of his tuna sandwich. No, I can't believe it.

It's goddamn true!

No.

Yes! Tom told me and his mom knows a family in Mexico that
lives near Adriana's aunt. A baby boy named Jesús! Shit, man! Tom
says the father is José, her older brother!

No!

Their mom caught him on top of her on Halloween! Guess that's
why she couldn't go with you. Had better plans!

James felt sick.

Davie laughed and little white spittle formed at the edges of his
mouth. Notice he ain't around no more? Joined the army. Wouldn't
you?

And so it went for ten months. The stories got wilder and wilder.
The one baby became twins one day, and then triplets the next. And
through it all, James kept the kiss to himself and refused to believe
any of the rumors.

Finally, a month after seventh grade started, there she was, suddenly, appearing at the school gate just as the morning bell rang. Adriana held her books tight across her chest, kept her gaze to the ground,
and worked her way through stares and murmurs right into Sister
Marie's class. She found her desk, carefully put her books down, and
slowly lowered herself into her seat. When James came into the classroom, he saw her and a shock ran through his thin body. Adriana!
She looked the same but different. Older. Thinner. Taller. But it was
her. James smiled but she averted her eyes. He found his desk. Now
her place was behind him and to the right. The second bell rang, and
the children scrambled to their desks as Sister Marie, a large woman
with clear, almost beautiful skin, moved to the front of the classroom. James twisted in his seat and tried to get Adriana's attention.
She looked up and fluttered her eyelashes for a moment, but then
tilted her head down again.

The nun cleared her throat. James turned to the front. Sister Marie began to talk about the children's impending Confirmation. As she explained, once again, how they would soon become soldiers for Jesus, James ever so slowly turned his head toward Adriana. Within a minute, he could make out her face in his fuzzy peripheral vision. She was looking up now, but James couldn't tell if she was gazing at Sister Marie or him. He turned toward the front, closed his eyes, and brought to his mind the back Adriana's neck, the way it looked last year when he sat behind her. In his mind, Adriana's skin looked so soft, so peaceful. James smiled, took a deep breath, and wondered what Adriana would do if he stood up right then, walked over to her, and planted a soft kiss where her hair met the nape of her neck. Would she scrunch up and smile? Would she push her neck into James's lips? Would Adriana say, hi, I missed you? I'm glad I'm home?

YAHRZEIT

Julieta looked into the rearview mirror and saw her son staring back at her from his battered Corolla. She didn't know the young man in the passenger seat, but without a doubt it was Rolando behind the wheel. Julieta's body buzzed with a shock like the first time she took the twins to Disneyland when they were four years old and she turned for but a second to pay for two Mickey Mouse balloons. Within those moments, Mateo had wandered away from his mother and twin brother. Julieta still remembers how her brain kicked into high gear with a jolt of adrenaline. But the ever-vigilant Rolando pointed through a gaggle of teenagers to his brother, who chatted happily with Cinderella. Now, fourteen years later, that same vigilant child sat one car length behind her, eyes bulging in recognition and alarm. Julieta pushed Max away from her.

"Ouch!"

"Sorry," said Julieta, confused by the force with which she had pushed this kind older man away from her.

"I wasn't getting fresh or anything," Max said as he rubbed his left shoulder. "You got quite a right hook there."

"I didn't punch you."

Normally Julieta would have laughed at Max's tendency to talk as if he were some kind of tough guy from an old movie. She knew it was partly an act, partly an honest recognition of his humble beginnings in New York, the sixth of seven children born to Russian immigrants. But under the circumstances, she found no humor in his response. Julieta reminded herself that her conscience was clear. They'd done nothing but enjoy an early dinner together. That was it. But why had she lied to Manuel about her plans for that evening? She certainly had no intention of ruining her marriage by jumping into bed with this gentle older man. Admittedly,

Max was a charmer who made Julieta feel beautiful as he tossed off compliments about her outfits or hair whenever he came into the camera shop. Even Manuel liked Max. He enjoyed the company of this dapper but down-to-earth man—a widower—who knew something about *real* cameras that used *actual* film. Especially one who happily ventured far from his West L.A. home to their little shop a few miles from downtown L.A. "A dying art with all this cockamamie digital stuff," Max had said to Manuel when he came in the first time. From that day on, Manuel enjoyed seeing this retired lawyer who knew quality and decried the loss of things that were just fine as they were, thank you very much. If it ain't broke, why fix it? Of course Manuel stocked all the new digital products, but he kept a corner of one glass case for connoisseurs such as Max, though their numbers dwindled with each passing year.

Julieta returned her eyes to the rearview mirror. No Corolla. No Rolando. Had she really seen him? Or was guilt playing games with her imagination?

"You just passed my street," said Max.

"Darn it!"

"No big deal," he said. "Turn here and we'll sneak up on my house from behind, scare it real good."

Julieta couldn't help herself this time and let out a laugh.

"About that shove, Max," she ventured.

"No, no," said Max, feeling pleased that he could lighten the mood. "It was my fault. I just had such a nice time tonight, I felt close to you. But I was not making a pass." He put his right hand on his heart and added: "Promise."

"I know," Julieta whispered.

They drove in silence until Max said, "That's the old homestead."

"There?"

"Yeah, just pull into the driveway."

Julieta parked but kept her eyes on the house. "Nice."

"Moving soon," said Max as he unbuckled his seat belt.

"No! From this beautiful place?"

"Yep. My daughter thought that I should simplify my life."

Julieta nodded. Max had mentioned his late wife, Ruth, several times but he always pulled back just a bit and then changed the subject when confronted with questions.

"It's good to simplify," she offered, not knowing how far to go with it. "Life gets complicated and then you don't know which way is up."

"Never a truer word spoken, young lady," Max laughed. "You are both wise and beautiful."

Julieta turned to Max. Max smiled. "Time to go," he said. "Got things to do."

Julieta couldn't imagine what Max had planned. All he'd said earlier that day was that he wanted to have an early dinner so he could get back home before dark.

"A girlfriend to call?" she teased but immediately regretted it.

Max seemed to think for a moment. And then: "In a sense."

He reached for Julieta's hand, pulled it gently to his lips, and kissed it softly. Julieta blushed. "Charming evening," he said.

"Yes," said Julieta. "Beautiful evening."

Max bowed just a bit, winked, and got out of the car. Julieta didn't drive away until he was safely in his house.

* * *

Max entered the kitchen and stood for a moment, taking it in. His cleaning woman, Corina, had come by while he was out, leaving everything gleaming, spotless. Not like Ruth had kept it. She'd believed that good cooking required making a mess. The bigger the mess, the better the food. And though Ruth had been a full-time teacher, she'd refused Max's offer to hire someone to help around the house. In retirement, despite becoming somewhat frail, she'd been fully capable of maintaining a relatively clean home. It was only in the last year of Ruth's life, when the chemo sapped her "oomph"—as she had put it—did this stubborn, loving woman relent and allow Max to hire someone. Corina came highly recommended and proved to be a wonder. Her cooking wasn't all that bad, either. And she loved Windex, Pledge, and anything advertised as possessing maniacal scrubbing bubbles. Max liked to joke that Corina was a chemical engineer. Though Ruth complained that her home had been invaded, Max knew she appreciated not having to worry about such things and that Max would, at the very least, have a clean house and hot meals.

But the one thing about Corina that irritated Max was her penchant for putting away things that he'd set out to use. At that moment, he squinted and scanned the kitchen in search of precisely such an item. Where was it? On Monday, he'd dutifully visited the temple's gift shop and purchased a yahrzeit candle. Tomorrow was the third anniversary of Ruth's death and he wanted to light the candle at sunset tonight. Max wasn't particularly observant but it wouldn't seem right not to do this in Ruth's memory and in preparation for his trip to the cemetery tomorrow.

Max went from cabinet to cabinet but couldn't find the candle. Where would I put it if I were Corina? he thought. But this didn't help because he knew there was no way he could ever comprehend how Corina approached her vocation. He looked out the kitchen window. The setting sun threw out spectacular reds and yellows. Ruth would have appreciated it.

"Damn it," he said, ready to give up.

But then Max remembered something. He trotted to the study and searched through his desk. Ah! A Yom HaShoah candle from the Federation of Jewish Men's Clubs. He got it in the mail last year as a simple but thoughtful token for Max's donation. The yellow candle sat in a small tin cup emblazoned with the words THE NEXT GENERATION! above a picture of Jewish boys and girls waving the Israeli flag. The healthy youngsters stood in front of a former concentration camp, a physical reminder of the 6 million who had perished. This will do, he thought. It looked about the same size as the yahrzeit candle and would probably burn for the required twenty-four hours. Max returned to the kitchen, rummaged through what Ruth had dubbed the tchotchke drawer, and found a book of matches. He set the candle on the counter and lit it. Max stood back and watched the flame rise and fall and then rise again with a small crackle. At times he wished that he were more observant so that he'd know from memory what prayer to say. But no matter. As he allowed the flame to mesmerize him, Max let his mind wander with thoughts of Ruth. He remembered how his father also outlived his wife. Samuel had lit a yahrzeit candle for three years but stopped once he remarried. When the fourteen-year-old Max protested, Samuel patiently explained to his son that it would be an insult to his new wife to continue to do so.

"So Mama didn't exist?" Max had argued.

"It's tradition."

"Who says?"

"Rabbi Weiss."

Max couldn't figure how the wisest man he knew could tell his father to do such a mean thing. But in the end he didn't blame his father for following tradition, though the young Max promised himself that if he lived longer than his wife, he'd light a candle each year regardless of what happened in his romantic life.

Max opened the cabinet near the microwave, pulled out a bottle of Glenfiddich and a tumbler, and poured generously. He lifted the glass to the candle. "Here's to you, doll."

Max took a sip. He wished his daughters could be in town for tomorrow but Marcie had just started her first trial as lead counsel and couldn't fly in and out of Boston without begging the judge for a two-day recess. Marcie was no beggar and she'd never do anything to prejudice a client's case. And Rachel's sons both had pink eye and felt absolutely miserable. Leaving them behind in Santa Rosa would require a seventy-mile drive to the nearest airport but first adjusting the hard-fought custody schedule she'd hammered out with her ex. Rachel sadly but forcefully demurred and Max understood. Both his daughters had made it to L.A. on the first anniversary for the unveiling of Ruth's headstone and no one could expect them to get back each year. But tomorrow Max would not be alone. Ruth's brother, Aaron, had promised to come. At times he seemed to take her death harder than Max.

Max finished his drink and gingerly placed the tumbler in the spotless sink. He glanced at the candle one more time before turning off the kitchen light. It was too early to go to bed but Max didn't know what else to do. He didn't feel like reading the novel he'd started. Too depressing. Max wandered about the house, searching for something to do, until he finally ended up in the den. He flipped through various channels for a minute but grew annoyed at how much dreck there was on TV, even though cable gave him endless choices. He finally settled on a John Garfield movie that he'd seen many times before, but at least it was quality all the way. Garfield. Ha! Ruth had liked to remind Max that wonderful actors such as Garfield, Danny Kaye, Edward G. Robinson, and Paul Muni were originally Julius Garfinkle, David Kaminsky, Emmanuel Goldenberg, and Muni Weisenfreund. But the public wouldn't pay for pictures with such Jewish names headlining, so the studios and agents forced "safe" monikers on them. Ruth had gloried in the changing times when it became more acceptable for Jews in show business to be themselves. Art Garfunkel! Barbra Streisand! Steven Spielberg! Though she'd been quite annoyed when she learned that Bob Dylan was born Robert Zimmerman. Of all the people who should have been true to himself! But Ruth didn't care for his music anyway unless sung by someone else like Joan Baez. Now, *she* had a voice.

Max watched as John Garfield got tough with his racketeer brother in glorious black and white. Yes, Max could settle in with a fine movie and then watch the early news. But maybe he was more exhausted than he'd realized: no matter how much Max wanted to stay awake, his eyes fluttered, his breathing slowed. After several valiant attempts to concentrate on the movie, Max gave up and allowed himself to drift slowly into a soft inevitable slumber.

And then there Max sits, in Julieta's Lexus, driving on Wilshire Boulevard, having a grand chat with this lovely woman. But in his dream Max possesses great bravery: he fearlessly leans close to Julieta, knowing that she will not push him away. Max's heart fills with both tranquility and exhilaration. And in his dream there are no messy histories or attachments to worry them, to keep these two healthy good people from enjoying a little private time together. Complications don't exist. As they drive along, the other cars ease by on either side, offering a colorful current through which the Lexus sluices. Max allows his eyes to rest on the smiling Julieta, and then swivels his head to the right to observe the other cars, filled with happy people, and then back again to Julieta. "I think I love you," says Max. "I know I love you," Julieta answers without hesitation. "You're the man of my dreams," she adds with a whisper. "And you're all I've ever wanted," Max smiles. He turns to look at the traffic, feeling proud of his heroic assertion of love. The vibrant red and blue and green and silver cars swim by. A brilliant black night sky shrouds the city; the streetlights offer little halos of light. And then an old black Mercedes comes into view. I know that car, he thinks. Max squints and tries to discern the driver, but the Mercedes is two lanes away and other cars keep blocking his view. Finally the Mercedes changes lanes and pulls even with the Lexus. Max peers into it. Shadow and light take turns filling the black car. Who's driving? Max's heart leaps as he sees that *he* is driving the Mercedes. And Ruth sits in the passenger seat. They're talking, seriously, to each other. Max stares at them, wondering what he and

Ruth are discussing and how he could be in two places at once and how could his beloved dead Ruth be there too. The other Max and the dead Ruth suddenly stop talking. Then she does it: Ruth leans forward and turns her head to the Max in the Lexus. She doesn't frown or scowl or make any face at all. She simply stares at Max, green eyes glittering, catching the moving lights. Nothing more. Max blinks, coughs, tries to remain calm. He turns back to Julieta to see if she's seen the passengers in the Mercedes. But she's smiling, happily oblivious, staring straight ahead as she steers them along Wilshire. Max turns back to the Mercedes. What? He and Ruth no longer sit in the other car. Instead, an older woman now drives all alone. Max doesn't recognize her, though she looks familiar. He squints. Where has he seen her before? Suddenly he realizes that the woman resembles Julieta but older, smaller. And she puffs on a fat hand-rolled cigarette that begins to fill the Mercedes with billows of white smoke. She turns to Max and frowns. She's saying something to him, plump cigarette bobbing up and down with each word. Max rolls down his window. "What are you telling me?" he yells. The woman rolls down her window and the smoke is sucked out by the wind. Max yells again: "What did you say?" The woman answers: "The fact of the matter is, if Saddam Hussein were still in power in Iraq, he would be rolling in petrol dollars. Think of the price of oil today. He would have so much money. And he would be seeing the Iranians interested in a nuclear program, he would be seeing the North Koreans developing a nuclear program, and he'd say, well why shouldn't he? And he would. So we're fortunate that he's gone." Max shakes his head. "Why are you telling me this?" The woman puffs on her cigarette and then continues: "We're fortunate that the Taliban have been thrown out of Afghanistan and that 50 million people have been liberated. The situation in Iraq is difficult and the violent extremists who are trying to hijack *that* faith have killed an awful lot of Muslims in Iraq and elsewhere around the world."

"What?" Max sat up with a start. "What?" he said again.

Max rubbed his eyes and took a deep breath. Donald Rumsfeld stared back at him from the TV screen, making his pronouncements on Iraq. Max fumbled for the remote. Finding it under a pillow, Max aimed it at the TV. "Go to hell," he said as the screen went dark.

The next morning Max walked across the carpet of almost perfect lawn toward Ruth's headstone. Aaron had promised that he'd be there right on time, but of course he was nowhere to be seen. Aaron liked to joke that he ran on Jewish standard time. Max believed that being late was simply rude and a sign of disrespect. Ruth was never late, that's for sure. He figured this explained Aaron's inability to keep a job or remain married—Max lost count of how many wedding presents he and Ruth had purchased for Aaron over the years. His brother-in-law skated along on little more than a deep anchorman's voice, a head full of curly hair, and a bright, easy smile. With a little hard work, he could have run for office, maintained a marriage, fathered children. But such is life. Ruth had adored her baby brother and that's all that mattered.

Max pulled out a fresh white handkerchief and wiped the smooth granite clean around the carved RUTH KLEIN. He stood back and smiled, as if he'd just given Ruth a gentle kiss. They both knew, deep down, that she'd be the first to go. While Max had been born in New York, Ruth spent much of her childhood in the camps. After the war, Ruth was the only survivor from her immediate family: mother, father, two brothers, three sisters—all perished from starvation, abuse, or disease. The gas chamber wasn't needed for Ruth's family. Thank God for her aunt Hannah in Brooklyn who tracked Ruth down with the help of the Central Tracing Bureau and the meticulous lists kept by the Nazis. Otherwise Ruth would have spent the rest of her childhood in a miserable displaced persons camp in Austria. Hannah couldn't have children of her own and had been somewhat jealous of her sister, who'd produced so many back in Poland. But now it was her duty to take in Ruth. Hannah's husband, David, couldn't deny Hannah anything, and if she wanted to adopt this scrawny concentration-camp girl, then that was that. With Ruth came remarkable luck: Hannah eventually got pregnant and brought Aaron into the world to be Ruth's adoring little brother. But even with their own child now, Hannah and David knew that Ruth was special, a smart girl whose only real failing was her health. Asthma. Brittle bones. All caused by malnutrition from years in the camps, said the doctors. And the New York winters didn't help much. When Ruth and Max met during their sophomore year at Brooklyn College, she told him that she dreamed of moving to California. How could he resist? They married after graduation and moved to Los Angeles, where Max began studying law at

USC. Ruth's adopted parents and Aaron eventually followed her out west more because they missed Ruth than because they were searching for paradise. And over the years the sunshine and blue skies did help Ruth, some. But they both knew that Max would someday bury her. It had been preordained by the Nazis.

"Hey, Maxie."

Max looked up at Aaron's silhouette, the morning sun creating a bright aura around his trim outline. Max squinted and tried to focus on his brother-in-law's eyes. Even though Aaron and Ruth were technically first cousins, they shared the same green eyes. These eyes gave Max a strange sort of comfort, almost as if Ruth hid in her brother's mind to steal a peek at her beloved.

"Hi."

Aaron came to Max's side so they both could look down at Ruth's headstone. "She was a peach," he said to Max.

"Yes, she was."

"No one like her. One of a kind."

"Never a truer word spoken."

Aaron shifted from one foot to the other. He cleared his throat as if he needed to make an announcement. After a moment, Aaron said: "I haven't mentioned this to you, Maxie, because, well, for obvious reasons, but it's hard living in my parents' old house, especially with Ruthie gone. I mean, it makes me realize how really alone I am."

Max didn't know what to say so he didn't respond. Maybe Aaron didn't need a response. Maybe he just needed to say it to someone who would understand. So they stood quietly, both listening to the almost-quiet of the cemetery. A few other people loitered nearby, visiting their loved ones. An unseen lawn mower roared in the distance. Aaron sighed, making Max wince at the smell of alcohol. So early to be drinking, even for his brother-in-law. Max looked down and searched for a pebble or small stone. He spotted a nice smooth one—not too big, not too little. He reached down, emitting a grunt, retrieved the stone, and gently placed it on Ruth's headstone. There. Now people will know that Ruth Klein had family who visited, that she had not been forgotten. Aaron let out another sigh. He reached into his jacket pocket and pulled out a blue crumpled Kleenex. He slowly opened it, as if a mouse hid inside, ready to escape. Max wondered what all this was about. Then he saw: Aaron removed a black porous stone from the Kleenex, kissed it, and set it next to the one Max had put on the headstone.

"From the Big Island," said Aaron. "Volcanic rock."

"Ah," said Max with a smile. "She loved Hawai'i."

"Yes."

Max and Aaron admired the small black rock as if they both had created it, molded it by hand, using great artistic skill.

"Aaron?"

"Yes?"

Max coughed, rubbed his chin, and wondered what he was going to say. But then it came out: "I've met someone."

Aaron turned to Max. Max immediately regretted saying anything. And then Aaron did something that surprised Max: He gently punched Max in his right shoulder. "Good for you, Maxie."

"You're not mad?"

Aaron laughed. "Maxie, boy, you're still here on God's good earth. I know you loved Ruthie. You were the best goddamn thing that happened to her, ya know? But you're still breathing," and he waved his hands, palms out, for emphasis.

"But no one could replace Ruth."

"Of course, Maxie."

"But there's a problem."

Aaron grinned. "Hey, they make fine medicines for that."

"No, no, no!" said Max. "Not that."

"I use a little Viagra every so often."

Max grabbed Aaron's shoulders. "No, that's not the problem."

Aaron searched Max's face but he couldn't read an answer there.

Max let his arms fall. "She's married."

Aaron guffawed.

"It's not funny," said Max as he started to walk away.

"Sorry," Aaron said as he followed Max. "It's not funny."

Max stopped and turned to Aaron. "Then why laugh?"

"Because," began Aaron, "I'm usually the one doing stupid things."

"Stupid?"

"Not stupid . . . impulsive, let's say."

Max thought about this. Yes, Aaron was right. He *was* being impulsive. Letting a little friendship turn into love when it really should be enjoyed for what it was.

"Have you done it?" asked Aaron.

"Done what?"

"You know."

Max's face transformed into a horrified mask. "No!"

"Oh," said Aaron. "No harm, no foul."

Max stepped back, rubbed his chin. He'd certainly fantasized many times about making love to Julieta, imagined kissing her, holding her body next to his, whispering into her ear. But to hear Aaron demean such an act was almost too much for Max.

"Look, Maxie, you deserve to be with someone," said Aaron as he drew near. "You're a good guy. A total mensch if there ever was one."

"Thank you," said Max. He realized then that Aaron had meant no harm.

"Hey," said Aaron, perking up. "I have a little joke my buddy Ben told me after shul last week."

"You *still* going to temple?"

"Yeah."

Max blinked but accepted this as true. "Go on."

"Okay, so this old man and woman at a nursing home were sitting in their rocking chairs after lunch."

"Old, like us?"

Aaron laughed. "Old, real old. Like a hundred, okay?"

"Okay, old."

"So the old guy turns to the woman and says: 'I'll give you 50 bucks if you let me have sex with you.'"

Max crossed his arms. "One of *those* jokes."

"Hear me out, you'll like this one."

"I'll be the judge of that."

"So the old woman agrees. They go up to her room and do the dirty deed. Afterward, as they're lying back in bed smoking cigarettes, basking in what they just did, the old guy turns to the woman and says: 'If I knew you were a virgin, I'd have offered you a $100.' The woman turns to the old guy and says: 'If I'd known you could still get it up, I'd have taken off my pantyhose!'"

As the punch line left Aaron's lips, he widened his eyes and grinned in anticipation of Max's response. At first Max didn't flinch. Then, ever so slowly, he smiled and started to shake. Finally, Max couldn't control himself despite the surroundings: he allowed himself to be lost in loud laughter for nearly a minute. Max wiped away tears with his sleeve and then grabbed Aaron's shoulders: "Goddamn you!"

"You're welcome!" said Aaron.

After a moment Max's arms dropped to his sides. "Say, are you doing anything tonight? I mean, for dinner?" Max said. "There's this new place on Wilshire, near the old homestead, got a good review in *Los Angeles Magazine*."

"Ah, Maxie, dinner any other night would be fine but tonight I got this Schwarzenegger fund-raiser thing to go to."

Max stifled a laugh.

"I know, I know," said Aaron as he raised his hands, palms outward, near his chest as if to block a punch. "I'm not the political type."

"What's her name?"

"Yeah, you've got my number, Maxie." Aaron dropped his hands and let them dangle in surrender. "Her name is Robin. She's this environmental lawyer who thinks the Terminator is the best thing since sliced bread. Limiting greenhouse gases, smart energy, yada yada."

"How old?"

Aaron grinned. "Old enough."

"Does she have a last name?"

Aaron hesitated. Finally: "Robles."

"What?"

"Nu?" Aaron stepped back and shook his head. "You, Mr. Liberal, have a problem with me dating a Latina?"

"Ha!"

"What?"

"No, Aaron," Max laughed. "No. The world is just a funny place."

"You bet, Maxie." Aaron threw his arms open and approached Max.

Max preferred not to hug his brother-in-law, but what could he do? He opened his arms and allowed Aaron to pull in tight with a full-body embrace. Despite the drinking, Aaron felt lean, strong.

"Love you, Maxie."

"Me too," said Max. "Me too."

As Max held Aaron, he realized that he could still see Ruth's headstone over Aaron's right shoulder. His own plot—reserved at the same time they bought Ruth's—seemed small, insubstantial. But Max would be there eventually, near his beloved Ruth. He shuddered.

Aaron pulled back and searched Max's eyes. "You okay, Maxie?"

"Oh, sure. You know me. Mr. Tough Guy. You?"

Aaron nodded. He looked at his watch, shook his head. Max nodded back and smiled.

"Gotta go, Maxie. Can I walk you back to your car?"

"Nah, think I'll stay for a bit," said Max, gesturing toward Ruth's headstone.

"Okay, Maxie boy. I understand." Aaron turned and walked away, slowly placing each foot in front of the other as if the ground would open up any second and swallow him if he weren't careful.

Max started toward Ruth's headstone but then stopped after a few steps. Two small birds hopped along the top of the headstone, chirping noisily, heads flicking back and forth. Max wondered if birds could feel happiness, delight, joy. Certainly these seemed bursting with such emotions. Suddenly one of the birds flitted away up into the full green leaves of a nearby tree. The other bird hopped around a bit and came near the pebbles that Max and Aaron had placed on the headstone. It pecked at Aaron's little volcanic rock, gave up, and then tried Max's pebble. Satisfied that there was nothing to eat, the bird hopped one more time, then flapped its wings, brushing against the pebbles. Max let out a little gasp as his fell from the headstone. The bird flew up into the tree and joined its companion. Max walked to the headstone, picked up the pebble, and returned it to its rightful place.

"You take care, doll," he said. "I'll see you soon."

Max turned and tried to get his bearings. Where did he park his car? He squinted and shaded his eyes. "There it is," he said softly after a few moments.

Max made his way to the parking lot. Before getting into his car, he looked back. The small birds had abandoned the tree and again danced on Ruth's headstone. They chirped excitedly.

"Hope you're having fun," said Max as he opened his car door and settled in. "Sing your hearts out."

NEW MEXICO

When Pilar Villa disembarked at the Albuquerque airport, south-western style smothered her like an Indian blanket. Just a few hours earlier, she'd stood at the Burbank boarding gate clutching in one hand an ancient blue backpack filled with maps, guidebooks, and a fresh new sketchbook, and in the other hand a forest-green plastic boarding pass. She'd stood amid mostly elderly men and women dressed in baggy unisex summer wear. They were giddy with Las Vegas dreams and possessed no understanding of why anyone would skip Sin City and continue on to New Mexico. Pilar had scanned the crowd and noticed a few brown faces, most of whom, she correctly predicted, would not get off in Vegas but continue with her to Albuquerque. In truth, all she'd wanted right then was to get settled into a narrow seat and read the Auto Club book on New Mexico while sipping a cold $4 can of Heineken. As she'd waited to board, her eyes eventually wandered past the crowd to the far wall where Jerry Seinfeld, Jay Leno, and the entire cast of *Friends* offered Pilar two-dimensional grins as happy reminders that TV's fantasies really didn't come out of Hollywood but were manufactured right there in the San Fernando Valley.

But now the uneventful flight was over and Pilar stood in a world of southwestern chic with walls, ceilings, and snack shops painted in the soft New Mexican colors of peaches, tans, and teals. Even the seating looked like New Mexico's famous mesas: brown leather-like square cushions sat comfortably in straight-lined wooden frames. Potted cacti stood at attention at regular intervals and seemed to point her to baggage claim. Pilar felt as though she had just entered a large southwestern-style restaurant in Santa Monica or elsewhere in upscale West Los Angeles. In fact, it all reminded her of the last night she saw Eduardo almost a month ago. He had chosen the place to celebrate his finally making partner. It was a new yuppie Mexican eatery near his Century City law office which, he had heard, served great turkey tamales and duck tostadas.

"Turkey?" Pilar had asked, looking into the receiver like she had just been told Elvis had been found taking a nice long bath in the La Brea Tar Pits.

"Yes."

"Duck?"

"Yes, mi amor." Eduardo's good mood couldn't be spoiled by such questioning. "Why can't we improve on tradition?"

"Beef, yes. Pork, of course. Chicken, without a doubt." Her litany of acceptable Mexican food ingredients had been met with what sounded like a good-hearted chuckle. "Well, it's to celebrate your wonderful news," she finally relented. "So how can I complain? We can meet there. ¿Sí?"

As Pilar slowly walked toward baggage claim, remembering their last dinner together, she was struck out of her trance by a bizarre sight: two full-sized quarter horses standing proudly just to the right of the escalator, roped-off and shining under the glare of six ceiling lights. She approached slowly as if they would bolt at any sudden movement. One stood facing east, the other west. Pilar smiled for the first time in a month as she absorbed the whimsy of the fiberglass equines, each painted differently. Her eyes first gravitated to the horse that almost glowed with metallic silver paint and resembled a mad scientist's successful attempt to merge the beast with a '57 Cadillac. An early-model car's taillight fin rose from the creature's spine, while the same car's grillwork protected the horse's chest like so much Detroit armor. The other horse was nothing more than a powerful blast of color: the artist had splashed reds, blues, oranges, and greens here and there in an orgy of Jackson Pollock exuberance.

Pilar leaned forward to read the informational card. *Like our angels,* Pilar thought. Los Angeles had its painted angels—a project to celebrate the spirit of the city—and New Mexico had its painted ponies. She read that more than a hundred fiberglass quarter horses dotted the state's major towns and cities, each painted by a different New Mexican artist, and each to be sold, eventually, to support various charities. Pilar looked up again and reached for her sketchbook but abandoned the idea. Instead, she tried to imprint the horses onto her memory before continuing to baggage claim.

* * *

Pilar had planned on giving herself exactly one week in New Mexico, even though her mother suggested a trip twice as long.

"Mi cielo," her mother had said, "there's so much to see there and your brother-in-law has cousins on one of the reservations." She paused before continuing, "Besides, you need time to heal."

But no. Pilar had decided that seven days would be enough, and cousins-by-marriage were not on the itinerary. Three days before she flew out of California, she unfolded her Auto Club map so that the geometric state covered most her dining table. She peered at New Mexico's blue and red circulatory system which, compared to the morass of Los Angeles freeways, seemed beautifully simple, logical, and inviting. Placing the flat tip of an orange highlighter on Albuquerque, Pilar deliberately traveled east on the I-40 to Cliffs Corners, and then south on the 285 through Vaughn, Roswell, and Artesia, finally settling in Carlsbad, not far from the Texas border. She took a deep breath as if she had just jogged these many miles and then restarted her highlighter back up the 285, retracing her route until she hit Cliffs Corners again. Here, rather than switching to the I-40 west, Pilar continued up to Santa Fe, then Taos, and back down to Santa Fe with a slight detour along the Turquoise Trail before ending in Albuquerque. This was the route, the plan, the brilliant excursion Pilar and Eduardo had planned by reading tour books, maps, and even a Willa Cather novel. But they had never committed it to paper. Now, within a minute's time, Pilar had completed the task but she didn't revel in her solo accomplishment.

* * *

The large smiling young man behind the Hertz counter offered Pilar a free upgrade from a Taurus to a Monte Carlo. She had little reason to refuse. The man punched a few words into his computer, waited for the new contract to spit out, and then ripped the long yellow paper out of the printer with an adroit and elegant flourish that surprised Pilar. After he showed her where to initial and then sign, the man said, "Just go through those doors to parking space number 116."

When Pilar found the car, her heart sank. It resembled a huge black battleship while she was used to her little but dependable Toyota. She approached it the way the Crocodile Hunter approaches wild and deadly prey. Once inside, Pilar took fifteen minutes just to understand the car's controls—lights, seat adjustment, air-conditioning, and radio—before she felt secure enough to leave the parking lot. The sky glowed an impossible blue and she remembered when Eduardo had explained the science of color to her: what made the heavens blue, gray, or black, why the ocean can, at times, glisten a wild orange based on the simple physics of geography, seaweed, and currents. She thought this was funny considering the fact that she was the artist and he the lawyer. Well, an aspiring artist, at least, with an MFA under her belt and a day job at the Museum of Contemporary Art's gift shop. Eduardo always said that her day would come. And she believed him because he had never lied to her.

* * *

After allowing herself a full day to enjoy Old Town Albuquerque, Pilar left the city early the next morning to start her drive to Carlsbad. Compared to the experience on L.A.'s congested freeways, the drive was easy, though hot and not rife with excitement or wonder. She stopped in desolate Vaughn to stretch and then again in Roswell, where the streetlights sported slanted, teardrop alien eyes just to remind tourists why the town was worth visiting. But she wanted to arrive in Carlsbad by dinner and get an early start the next morning at the caverns. She thought that she could do some sketches, something worthwhile, once in Carlsbad. Eduardo had enticed her with his uncle's spectacular photographs of the caverns. "You can't go to New Mexico without seeing them" was Eduardo's mantra.

Pilar rolled into Carlsbad just before 6:00 and checked in at the hotel. After a long bath, she decided to skip dinner altogether and get to bed early. She towel dried her short, thick hair, put on a baggy ZYZZYVA T-shirt, and slid beneath the cool over-bleached sheets. Pilar chose to sleep on the left side of the mammoth bed more out of habit than reason. She smashed her pillow into a ball and lay on her side facing the empty expanse of mattress. Pilar was asleep within minutes.

The next morning she awoke sprawled across the bed, face buried deep into the mattress. Her neck ached and her left hand felt as though it were being pricked with a million small needles. *Where am I?* she thought. A relentlessly bright sun invaded where the curtains didn't quite meet and forced Pilar into the waking world. She slowly got her bearings. *New Mexico. Carlsbad. Alone.* Her stomach then released a tumultuous rumble, and images of a hot breakfast began to invade her thoughts.

The woman at the front desk directed Pilar to a Denny's within walking distance, but she drove instead. She quickly nestled into an aquamarine vinyl booth, and a waitress just as quickly appeared at her table.

"Coffee, dear?" She smiled, exposing yellowed teeth that seemed to be held in place precariously by sunken black gums. Stringy blond hair hung unceremoniously from her head like tinsel on a late-January Christmas tree. She was probably only in her twenties and Pilar wondered what kind of life she had led to make her look so much older.

"Yes," answered Pilar. "Thank you."

The waitress didn't move but held her pencil and pad before her as if she were ready to take dictation from a studio head or Bill Gates. Pilar noticed elaborate and indecipherable writing covering the back of the waitress's hands. She became so entranced by the fleshy hieroglyphics that she almost jumped when the waitress offered, "I can take your order, too, if you're ready, that is." This time Pilar discerned a Texas accent and remembered Carlsbad's location on the Auto Club map.

"Yes," Pilar finally answered. The waitress lifted her pencil higher. "Short stack, no butter, and orange juice."

The waitress wrote this down. "Any bacon? Sausage?"

Pilar pondered the question as she would a semi-difficult math problem. "Bacon," she decided. "Yes, bacon, thank you."

The waitress's smile broadened, as if Pilar had given her a present. "It'll be up in a jiffy, dear." She turned with a squeak of her shoes and disappeared into the kitchen.

Pilar had left her backpack in the car, so she needed reading material. Her eyes eventually rested on a shiny metal rack that held glossy real estate magazines. Pilar sprang from her booth and retrieved a copy of *Enchanted Homes,* which boasted the famous New Mexico skyline on its cover with promises of *Cabins, Condos, Ranches and More!* in and around Taos, Angel Fire, and Red River. When her breakfast arrived, Pilar was already immersed in Old Taos charm: pueblo-style homes with kiva fireplaces, thick adobe walls, traditional viga/latilla ceilings, and *Views, Views, Views!* She enjoyed her thick sweet pancakes with dreams of living in an enchanted New Mexican home.

* * *

With the now well-thumbed *Enchanted Homes* tucked safely in her backpack for future dreaming, Pilar arrived at the large government-built and -owned structure just outside the caverns. Unlike the Denny's, the large room of displays, tour schedules, and ticket windows bustled with tourists of all colors speaking English, German, Japanese, Spanish, and other familiar but not quite nameable tongues.

As she headed toward the ticket line, she saw another one of her equine friends. It stood off to the side, away from the crowd, enjoying its relative solitude. Pilar changed course and walked over to the horse. As she approached, she noticed that this one was covered with oversized multicolored insects: mosquitoes, beetles, praying mantises, dragonflies. Without thinking, Pilar reached into her backpack and pulled out a pencil and sketchbook. In deft, fluid strokes, she captured the powerful contours of the frozen beast. She smiled as she noticed that the sculpture was dubbed *Horse and Buggy* by its creator.

As Pilar penciled in the detail—some shading here, a butterfly there—she felt more alive than she had in a month. She suddenly realized that she had not picked up a sketchbook in all that time. She smoothed the lines with her thumb, rounded the horse's rump, added depth to the animal's muscular neck. The noisy crowd faded from Pilar's senses as she brought *Horse and Buggy* to life on paper. She marveled at her ability to capture the creature's essence so quickly. But she was trained to do so. Years of honing her innate skills. Now she happily used her talents to render other artists' creations.

And so it would be: as she continued her trip, back up through Roswell and over to Santa Fe and then Taos and finally returning to Albuquerque, Pilar searched out the painted ponies and, page by page, filled her sketchbook with dappled, rhinestoned, and dazzling creatures, each with its own special personality.

Many years from now, Pilar will join the art department at UCLA, marry a fellow instructor, buy a three-bedroom house in the Fairfax District, and have a daughter named Isabel. When Isabel is five, she will stumble upon Pilar's many sketches of wild, strange horses and ask about them. Pilar will sit down with Isabel and tell her about that remarkable trip to New Mexico and the whimsical painted ponies that appeared almost wherever she turned. She will thumb through her sketchbook and tell Isabel funny little stories about each horse and how she felt when she drew the pictures. But Pilar won't tell her daughter that she went there because a nice man she knew couldn't, even though he had planned to. That this nice man was handsome and smart and had a great future ahead of him but that a drunk driver took all that away one night. That Pilar had promised herself to make the trip, in honor of this nice man, and learn the splendor of New Mexico on her own. And she wouldn't tell her daughter that sometimes, when it is late and she is tired, she wonders what life would be like if that nice man had not died. Would they have married? Where would they have made their home? Taos? Los Angeles? Any children? But Pilar will quickly shake such thoughts away as she remembers the wonderful life she now has with the two people she loves most in this world.

EL PADRE

Father James Cortés placed the compact disc into one of the five circular cradles of his Yamaha player. With a click and a whir of the internal mechanism, a steady piano rhythm commenced, backed by some kind of brass instrument—was it a flügelhorn?—that lay the carpet for the Beach Boys' malleable harmonies. Though he and his grammar school classmates had danced to Marvin Gaye, the Jackson Five, and Carlos Santana, once Father Cortés left most of friends behind and entered a prestigious, mostly white Jesuit high school, the sounds of Led Zeppelin, the Rolling Stones, and the Beach Boys became the background music for his Southern California adolescence.

Now a fit and trim man of forty-five, he listened to all types of music, the music of his congregation. Jazz, salsa, rap, old school, rock, pop, smooth jazz, world music, everything. But at times of personal turmoil, he wanted to fall into the comfort and sublime production of the post–surf sound Beach Boys. "God Only Knows" bathed Father Cortés in nostalgic days of Friday Mass at the campus chapel, Saturday night football games, and brilliant introductions to Latin, ancient cultures, and religious thought of the twentieth century. He couldn't explain why this particular group consoled him. Perhaps the melancholy undertones masked by the joyous perfect melding of voices spoke to the priest, reached him on some subliminal level. Maybe Brian Wilson's melodies acted as healing fetishes like the ones used by the Sonoran Desert's Pima and Papago Indians, who believed that pernicious entities, mostly animals, caused life's numerous ills. They simulated the offending creatures in miniature wooden charms to be pressed upon the afflicted areas of the patient's body. He remembered that the Native people relied on the figure of a snake to cure stomach ailments and a horned lizard for foot sores, while feverish babies required a gila monster. Not too different from praying to St. Anthony of Padua when you've misplaced something, or St. Jude Thaddeus when facing a lost cause, Father Cortés thought. It's all essentially the same.

He reached for a plaid shirt that his mother had bought him two years ago, the last gift she would give her only son before succumbing to ovarian cancer. Though his mother understood that, at least technically, her son had taken a vow of poverty, Father Cortés acquired over the years a useful and wide array of birthday gifts, courtesy of the late Guadalupe Canción Cortés. The priest cherished the CD player. His "civvies" were a close second because he refused to dress as a priest when he worked the soup kitchen on Saturday mornings. Father Cortés buttoned his shirt and tucked its long tails into his crisp khakis. "Sail on, Sailor" started up and he closed his eyes and took a deep breath. He started to sway to the song's rhythm and tried to slow down his heartbeat, elevated since the alarm went off at 6:00 a.m.

"It will be okay," he whispered. His eyes opened as the song ended. "It will be okay."

* * *

The old wood-framed house creaked with the other nuns' morning rituals of bringing to life the new day. Sister Antonia's roommate, Sister Olivia, made her usual racket just below in the kitchen, but the end result would be a fine filling breakfast of buckwheat pancakes, honeydew melon, and scrambled eggs. As Sister Antonia dressed, she tried to give her attention to a special report on the California recall election that emanated from Sister Olivia's clock/radio. Such a waste of money, she thought. Could the Terminator really replace Governor Davis? All of that money could be used to feed hungry families. "Such a waste," the nun finally said aloud as she zipped her capri pants. Saturday meant work at the soup kitchen and civilian dress. Freedom. As former governor Pete Wilson spoke of the need for change, Sister Antonia slipped her little feet into Keds sneakers and stood quickly. Too quickly. She wobbled on the pads of her feet and fell backward onto her bed. As the nun wiped perspiration from her upper lip, a loud rap on the door brought her to her senses.

"Breakfast," said a husky German-accented voice through the thick wood.

"Coming," said Sister Antonia. The voice could only be Sister Gertrude, whose apparent goal in life was to make certain this small community of nuns ate their three squares a day.

"Lazybones," laughed the voice. "There won't be anything left if you don't hurry."

"Coming," she answered again. "I'll be right there."

Sister Antonia took a deep breath. Pete Wilson's voice still filled her small bedroom. Bastard, she thought as she reached over and clicked off the radio. The nun shook her head in disgust as she remembered Wilson's campaign to pass Proposition 187 and stomp on the already suffering undocumented immigrants. People like her maternal grandparents who made their way from central Mexico to San Diego when Eisenhower was president. People who had no choice but to leave their home to make money just to live at poverty's edge in a strange city. She would always be embarrassed that this pinched man, this selfish, vicious politician, had been mayor of her beloved San Diego.

Sister Antonia stood, slowly this time, and straightened her cotton blouse. "Time to eat," she said to herself as if to encourage her feet to move. "Time to eat."

* * *

Mrs. Estrada's large beefy back met Father Cortés as he entered the kitchen. The July sun invaded the small but neat kitchen and reflected off Mrs. Estrada's white cotton blouse, making her glow like a full moon. She turned and offered a smile that reminded the priest of a succulent slice of sandía. She held a sizzling skillet filled precariously with a high mound of chorizo con huevos.

"¡Buenos días!" Mrs. Estrada said. "¿Tiene Ud. hambre?"

So formal, thought Father Cortés. So old country. "No, thanks. Just coffee and toast will be fine."

Mrs. Estrada's smile slipped away as if she had just learned that her ten-year-old Siamese cat, El Cucuy, had been run over by an SUV.

The priest sighed. He worked hard to keep both his weight and cholesterol in check. But Mrs. Estrada was a godsend compared to the brusque and slovenly Mrs. Ballesteros.

"Okay, just a little," he offered. "But you must promise me to take the rest home to your family."

His housekeeper's smile reappeared, and she jumped into action preparing a plate and pouring a large mug of coffee. "You have a big day ahead helping those people," she said as she served Father Cortés, who had already settled into his chair and was reaching for the newspaper.

"Yes," said the priest. "A big day."

* * *

"Pass the melon, please."

Sister Antonia looked up from her untouched plate and searched for the source of the request. She couldn't focus on any of the faces. In defeat, the nun finally asked, "Who needed melon?"

Sister Olivia leaned playfully into her. "Over here, silly. How could you not recognize your own roommate?"

"Sorry," said Sister Antonia as she reached for the large platter of sliced melon.

The other nuns chatted away about their work at the hospital. Sister Olivia tilted her small head toward her friend. "Are you getting the flu?"

Sister Antonia scooped up a forkful of scrambled eggs. "I'm fine. Just a little tired." She brought the eggs to her mouth and chewed. The nun knew that an empty stomach simply aggravated her nausea.

"Sure?"

Sister Antonia swallowed and took a deep breath. "I'm sure," she said through a forced smile. "I'm peachy."

* * *

As his used but trustworthy Honda Odyssey exited the freeway, Father Cortés spun the radio dial, searching for something other than commercials. The priest rebuked himself for leaving his CD case in his bedroom. He finally settled on a public radio station as Nina Simone began what he believed to be the definitive version of "Strange Fruit." The priest took the first right toward the soup kitchen and could see men, women, and too many children lining the sidewalk for breakfast. He parked and, after many hellos, holas, and hiyas to the now-familiar desperate faces, Father Cortés entered the kitchen.

"We'll be open in five minutes," he mouthed, holding up five fingers for emphasis as he closed the glass door behind him with a loud metallic squeak.

Inside, the priest witnessed the well-orchestrated work of the high school boys and girls under the guidance of Sister Antonia. The nun wore a long-sleeved white cotton blouse that disappeared smoothly into a pair of green Old Navy capri pants, revealing a few inches of smooth brown calf and ankle. Her little feet sat sockless in slightly worn canvass sneakers. Such an outfit would normally not raise an eyebrow. But on Sister Antonia's delicate, refined, long-legged physique, the ensemble put Father Cortés in mind of a young Audrey Hepburn with Fred Astaire in *Funny Face*.

They worked side by side for almost two hours, setting up, cooking, and serving the homeless. Except for a few directions given to the high school volunteers, the priest and nun spoke little, exchanging no more than a half dozen words with each other. The priest's mind wandered repeatedly to the thought he'd carried for a week now. A week since Sister Antonia had told him she was pregnant with his child. What would they do? Leave their respective vocations? No. That would not happen. Not if Father Cortés had any say in it. And why wouldn't he? He was the man, after all. There was no choice. There was only one choice. No baby. Period. Pure and simple. God is loving. He would forgive, wouldn't he? How could he not? Even St. Thomas Aquinas argued that abortion was not a sin if done before "quickening," before the awakening of the fetus, before a woman could tell that there was a life growing inside her. But the Church had said no, we can't afford to lose one soul. It was Aquinas, wasn't it? Or was it St. Thomas More? Father Cortés couldn't quite remember, though he could picture the classroom, his instructor Father Williams, and even the faces of the young men who sat attentively, respectfully in the other chairs.

"All done here," said Sister Antonia.

Father Cortés looked up from the pot he had been washing for too long.

"Looks clean to me," she smiled.

The priest turned off the water and reached for a towel. "Yes, clean."

"I need to get back."

Father Cortés put the pot on the counter and carefully hung up the towel. "Well," he said, "I have a surprise for you."

Sister Antonia smiled like a high school girl. "What?"

The priest reached into his shirt pocket and pulled out a small envelope. "Here, open this."

The nun looked as radiant as he'd ever seen her. Why wasn't she panicked like he was? What was she thinking about this? About the situation?

"Tickets to the Old Globe!" she almost screamed. "*Julius Caesar!*"

"Tonight," said Father Cortés. He felt triumphant for a moment.

"Tonight?"

"Yes."

Sister Antonia looked down at herself. "But I'm not dressed for the theater."

"Don't worry," said the priest as he put his hand on the nun's shoulder. "It's very casual. Everything from Dockers to shorts."

"But Sister Gertrude won't let me."

Father Cortés let out a little laugh. "Took care of it. I told her that we had a lot to do for the kitchen."

The nun blushed. "Okay," she said. "This is wonderful."

"Nothing, really," said the priest. "Just a little treat."

* * *

Parking in Balboa Park was a pain and Father Cortés found himself wishing ill on every vehicle that took a space before he could. Finally, after going up and down several aisles, he spotted a burnt orange PT Cruiser pulling out clumsily just a few yards ahead. Ah! That space was his.

"Success!" said Sister Antonia.

"Yes," he answered. "Let's run. We have only a half hour to cram some food down our throats."

The Old Globe food court bustled with casually dressed Shakespeare lovers. Father Cortés ordered two large coffees and turkey croissant sandwiches. They ate quickly, in silence, glancing occasionally at each other only to look away. Things were different. How could they not be? Eventually the priest let his eyes rest on this beautiful woman. The woman he loved. Maybe they could start a life together. Somehow. Somewhere. But each time this possibility slipped into his mind, Father Cortés realized that it was pure fantasy. His emotions talking, nothing more. He would not let twenty years of priesthood be flushed away so easily. He would not become a scandal, the one his parishioners would whisper about for years to come. No. Father Cortés had worked too hard for what he had.

The theater's electronic bells roused them from their silence. The priest and nun stood, careful not to touch, and joined the stream of bodies leading toward the entrance. The now-cooling air felt good on Father Cortés's face, and he was pleased that the play would take place on the outdoor festival stage. They found their seats. The priest scanned the stage: an apocalyptic setting meant to convey some horrific period in the not-so-distant future. He glanced at Sister Antonia, whose wide eyes also scanned the stage. She was greatly anticipating hearing Shakespeare's words. The priest smiled and flipped through the program. Though he had no doubt that Robert Gammell would make a very fine Julius Caesar, Father Cortés had a few misgivings about Robert Foxworth's Brutus. The priest had trouble envisioning Foxworth as anyone but the noble Chase Gioberti battling his venal aunt, Angela Channing, for several years in the nighttime soap opera *Falcon Crest*. But Father Cortés would suspend all judgment and just enjoy the play.

And this is when it happened, when the priest took a path that he had hoped never to take, never envisioned that he could follow. The play had started and the actors strutted and declaimed and gesticulated. The cool air, the bright klieg lights, the audience all conspired to shut down Father Cortés's senses. He no longer sat there next to his lover. Sister Antonia was now his enemy, the person who could do more harm to him than anyone else. And she had no right to have such power over the priest. The nun was nothing more than a silly girl, an immature, gullible little thing. But in her failings, she possessed the ability to bring this fine man down. All it took from the nun was one phone call to the right person in the archdiocese. Or perhaps a reporter. Father Cortés's stomach flipped and a cold veneer of perspiration spread over his face, arms, back. The actors spoke gibberish. He could sit there no longer.

"I'll be back," the priest whispered.

Sister Antonia looked up, startled. "Oh?" she said softly, trying not to disturb anyone.

Father Cortés didn't answer. He stood and stepped over the nun's legs and was gone in a moment. Sister Antonia returned her gaze to the actors. The clarity of the cool night air imbued the stage with a sharpness that almost overwhelmed the nun's senses. She closed her eyes; the actors' words became muffled, far away. Sister Antonia rubbed her small tummy and took in a long, slow breath. This is the beginning, she thought. This is what God wants for me. For us. This can't be wrong. This can't be sinful. And Sister Antonia knew without a doubt that her baby would be beautiful and healthy and brilliant. She had no doubt whatsoever.

A commotion among the actors made the nun's eyes suddenly pop open. The men crouched over Caesar's lifeless body, bathing their hands in the dead man's blood.

"Sorry," whispered Father Cortés as he settled back into his seat. "Too much coffee."

Sister Antonia nodded but kept her eyes on the actors as they raised their bloody hands for all to behold. "It's okay," she whispered back. "It's okay."

* * *

"I can't see it," said Sister Antonia. "I don't remember where we parked."

Father Cortés patted her shoulder, the first time he had intentionally touched this woman the entire evening. The crowd jostled them and the nighttime air was that much cooler now that it was later. "Don't worry," he said. "I remember."

The priest guided the nun down three aisles and there sat the old blue van. The nun greeted it with an effusive "Ah!"

Father Cortés added: "Parish luxury. Nothing but the best."

As they approached the passenger side, they noticed that a Volvo had been parked too close to the van. Behind the Volvo, a young woman struggled to fold a stroller with her right hand as she clutched the hand of her toddler—a chubby-cheeked girl—with her left. Before either the priest or nun could jump in to assist, she'd successfully collapsed the stroller and swung it expertly into her open trunk. The toddler let out a squeal of delight at her mother's deftness.

"¡Brava!" said Sister Antonia.

The woman and toddler looked up and smiled in unison. Then the mother nodded a good-bye, put the girl into her little cocoon-like car seat in the back, strapped her in, and got behind the wheel. As she pulled out slowly, the nun smiled broadly, caught up in the simple joy of this mother and child. She looked up to share her smile with

Father Cortés, but he was not smiling. He averted his eyes toward the night sky. "Clear night," he said.

Sister Antonia studied his face. Her smile disappeared. "Let's go," she said. "It's getting cold."

* * *

He loved the quiet of Mrs. Estrada's day off each Monday. Father Cortés could eat as lightly as he wished, take care of important calls, be independent. Today the priest needed to do research. He clicked on the Google bookmark and typed in: "Los Angeles abortion clinics." It had to be done away from San Diego. In a bigger city where it was easy to disappear, not be noticed. The search engine brought up only four hits, one of which was an anti-abortion organization. *Abortion.* He hated that word. So ugly. An easy word for the Church to spit out with disdain. The word itself sounded evil. But it was a necessary one. An option that was the lesser of two evils. The baby could not come into this world. What good could come of that? Such a birth would lead to nothing but a lifetime of shame and eventual failure. And at what other cost? The congregation would certainly lose Father Cortés. The Church could not let him keep his flock, even with the extreme shortage of priests, particularly Spanish-speaking clergy, to fill the still-thriving parishes. And what of Sister Antonia? She would lose everything too. She couldn't possibly understand the implications of her decision. The nun was still a silly girl in so many ways. She needed Father Cortés to make the decision. The only decision.

In truth, if one really thought about it, there were an infinite number of options. Father Cortés remembered the Borges short story "The Library of Babel," where the great writer once again wrestled with metaphor to explore the complex reality of infinity. This nun and this priest had infinite options, like the hexagonal galleries of Borges's metaphorical library. So many permutations. The nun could run off to Mexico and have her baby there and never return. Not a bad option. Or she could go along with an abortion. Imperfect but cleaner. No baby to come back to the United States as an adult searching for his or her father. Or they could leave their vocations and marry. No. Takes two to tango. No way, not if the priest had any say in it. Or worse yet, she could have her baby and announce to the world the sordid circumstances. So many ways this thing could go.

If he had the inclination, Father Cortés could spin out dozens and dozens of roads they could take together or separately and still come up with new ideas, some outrageous and improbable, but all possible in the physical world.

The priest would sweet-talk her. Take her to dinner. Share a little wine. Let her know he did indeed care. But then he'd turn serious. Frank. Totally honest. He'd lay out the options and show through pure logic that there was really only one option. She would be hurt at first. Scared. *Isn't it a sin?* she'd ask him. *It is, isn't it?* she'd cry. And he'd give a little history lesson. St. Thomas Aquinas and all that. Yes, it was Aquinas, not More. Thomistic ethics. And St. Augustine was of the same mind, too. Right? Abortion as a sin was a relatively new concept. Nowhere in the Bible. He would review some of his old history books. He had to win this one through rigorous logic. Abortion was not a sin in and of itself. It was a valid option. The only option. The priest needed to lay out his arguments to the nun. Sister Antonia would be doing her rounds ministering at the hospital today. Father Cortés would surprise her, take her to dinner. It would all work out.

The priest prepared both physically and mentally for the evening. He had a light lunch, pulled the appropriate books from his library, refreshed his memory on the subject, practiced his little speech. After a few hours, he went for a good hard run, then ended his preparation with a scalding shower and close shave. He then made reservations at Sister Antonia's favorite Italian restaurant. As he drove to the hospital just before sunset, the Beach Boys' harmonies of "God Only Knows" filled his van. He felt good, right on course. The priest eased into a parking space not to far from the hospital entrance.

As he approached the information desk, he recognized Mrs. Stahl, a handsome, efficient woman who dispensed information better than anyone else who staffed that desk. She looked up and nodded at the priest. "Father, how are you?"

"Fine," he said. "You look lovely today."

Mrs. Stahl blushed. Father Cortés was one of a few men who could do this to her. If she were Catholic, she'd no doubt attend each and every Mass he said. "How may I help you today?" she asked.

"I have a meeting, dinner meeting, planned with Sister Antonia," he said carefully. "She's on today, isn't she?"

With these words, Mrs. Stahl's smile disappeared. "She was supposed to be on."

Father Cortés leaned into the hard edge of the wooden counter.
"What do you mean?"

"Something is happening with her," she almost whispered.

"What?" He clutched the counter to steady himself. "What?" he
asked again.

Mrs. Stahl looked around. She then leaned toward the priest.
"They can't find her."

This was excruciating. "What do you mean?" He bit down hard
on each word.

"She's up and left," she said. "Gone. No trace whatsoever."

"Who told you this?"

"Sister Gertrude. She's in a total panic. All the nuns are." And then
Mrs. Stahl added the kicker: "They've called the police."

Father Cortés fell back on his heels and pulled away from the
counter. "Thank you," he said as he walked away.

"Are you okay, Father?" asked Mrs. Stahl as the priest moved
toward the sliding glass doors. "Are you okay?"

The priest reached the van and took a deep breath. What was Sister
Antonia up to? What the hell was she doing? The air grew cool as the
sun began to disappear. Four small birds played happily in a puddle
by the van's front left tire. He took another deep breath and wiped
his forehead with his jacket sleeve. Father Cortés knew exactly what
the nun was up to, only he didn't know where—Mexico probably, to
have that baby. The priest had no power to do anything about it. He
shook his head and let out a little laugh. And so the words finally left
his lips: "Silly girl," he said. "Silly little girl."

KIND OF BLUE

"So what?" says René. He adds a shrug for emphasis.

Silence. René just stares at me. And then another "So what?" It's not really a question. It's a statement. A declaration. A dare.

René wipes his nose on his torn shirtsleeve. He gets most of the blood and snot that had been seeping slowly from his nostrils off his upper lip. René holds his arm in front of him and examines the sleeve. His dark skin peeks out from the torn blue cotton. He blinks and then lets out a muffled laugh, as if he has just discovered 5 bucks in his pocket.

I can't stand seeing René's eyes when he gets like this so I turn and look over toward his apartment's kitchen window, which now has most of its glass piled up in jagged shards inside the sink and a few pieces on the floor. Big Man lays right there, on some of the broken glass. He's in a heap, like he's drunk or something. But he's not.

"So what?" René says again.

He follows my eyes over to Big Man. "Fuck that pendejo," says René. "He tried to kill me, that fucker. You saw."

"But . . ." I start to answer.

"But the fuck what?"

I look down at my feet, tired of looking at Big Man, who really isn't very big. Maybe five-five, if that. Muy flaco, también. Skin and bones.

"Never mind," I say. "Forget about it."

"Damn straight," says René, victorious. "Damn straight."

* * *

René gave us all names. His own little group, his followers. Branded us like cows with stupid little names.

René named Humberto "Big Man." Funny because he's so small. René made himself laugh with that one.

Big Man's little sister Sylvia is "Slinky" because she's kind of sexy in a weird way. Goth. Pierced left eyebrow, left nostril, and left cheek. She gives René blow jobs but they don't fuck. René says he has too much respect for Sylvia to stick her. Even though he doesn't—or didn't—think much of her brother. Sylvia turned fifteen last week. Big Man and me and René finish high school this year. Well, at least I will.

Anyway, René named me "Freddie Freeloader," which I hate. Kind of a fucked-up name, you know? It's just because of that time I bummed some mota off of René behind the dumpster at our high school. It was this one hot day during our Ancient Cultures class, which we cut at least twice a week. Just that one time I didn't have any weed on me. But then, right there, after passing over the joint real nice, he calls me Freddie Freeloader through tight lips, trying to keep the smoke in his lungs, but then he starts to laugh and then he chokes, tears running down his face, totally cracking himself up. After he calms down, René looks up at me and says, "You're Freddie Freeloader, Alfredo." He adds: "From now on." And it's stuck with me for almost four years.

René isn't called anything but his own baptism name. Nobody dares call him something else. Not me. Not nobody.

* * *

Blue in green. Or is it green in blue? Anyway, that's Sylvia's eyes. They kind of glow with the two colors mixed in. Because her skin is real dark and her long hair shines black, Sylvia's eyes are the first thing you notice about her. They make her beautiful. At least, that's what I think. But whenever I start daydreaming about those eyes, that skin . . . my mind wanders to what I know she does to René and I feel sick. I don't understand it. It's fucked up. And it's going to get more fucked up when Sylvia finds out her brother's dead.

* * *

"All Blues." That's the name I'd give René if I could. He'd probably kick my ass if I tried so I never even *thought* about saying it to his face. He always wears this long-sleeved blue shirt tucked into blue Dickies, the real loose kind. René even likes to put on these blue Chuck Taylors. Maybe he'd laugh, take it in stride, not care if I called him All Blues. But I doubt it. I mean, I try to act tough, but I'm nothing like René. Look at Humberto. Dead. In two seconds, before Humberto could even open the window and sneak in, René hears something, jumps up from the couch where we had been smoking and watching some stupid shit on TV in the other room, and runs into the kitchen before I know what's happening. That's the funny thing about René: he can be all fucked up on mota but he never gets fuzzy or out of control. He stays alert, like a fox. Or a snake. Or a rat.

Anyway, before I even realize he's run out of the room, I hear a grunt and then all this glass breaking. I freak out at this point and get to the kitchen as fast as I can, tripping over my untied shoes. And there I see Humberto on the floor, not moving, with broken glass all over the place. René is hovering over the body, his shirtsleeve torn and bloody, looking up at me and smiling.

* * *

"Flamenco Sketches," whispers Sylvia. "That's what I call them."

She hands me one drawing and then another. I don't know why Sylvia calls her pictures Flamenco Sketches. I don't see any Spanish dancers. Just black circles, going round and round and round from the outside edges to the center. But I don't criticize her. I just look at each one and nod like I really like the drawings. I don't know why she brought them here, of all places, but she has a right to do what she wants. Especially right now.

The church is crowded, people are crying, the priest is saying something over Humberto's coffin, which is closed. His mom's a mess, collapsed down into herself, weeping but not making a sound except for a moan that scares me. Sylvia finally puts the drawings down on the pew, leans her head into my shoulder, closes her eyes. I was surprised she wanted me to sit next to her with the family, but René was nowhere to be found so I guess she needs me. They don't blame him, not really, because I told everyone it was an accident. I had to.

I look around, see all of these people I've known since I was little. And then I see him, René, off at the side of the church, by the statue of St. Thomas. You know, doubting Thomas, the one who didn't believe Jesus had come back from the dead. René turns his head just enough to stare back at me. And then he does it. He smiles. Just a little. With *that* look in his eyes. The same look I saw the night Humberto died. And I swear René starts to laugh, real quiet, but it's still a laugh. I turn away, feeling like I can't breathe, and then kiss the top of Sylvia's head. Her hair is so soft and smells good. "It's okay," I whisper. "It's okay."

THE LOST SOUL OF
HUMBERTO REYES

Early one Tuesday morning, Isabel Camacho signed for a package
and observed that the return address belonged to her ex-lover, Humberto Reyes. She assumed Humberto had sent yet another exotic
trinket he had purchased on one of his many excursions to foreign
lands. For despite ending their three-decade romance two years ago,
Humberto still adored Isabel and could not help remembering her
when he wandered through distant mercados, bazaars, and souks.
Isabel found this particular habit of Humberto's somewhat annoy-
ing, though also a tad flattering.

Isabel placed the package on her fireplace mantel and proceeded
to forget about it for a full day. The next morning, as she drank her
first of what would eventually be three cups of very strong black
Cuban coffee (which she preferred despite being Mexican), Isabel
saw the package sitting quietly across the room. She sighed, wondered what Humberto had found for her this time, and brought the
package to the dining room table so that she could continue drinking her coffee.

After she carefully removed the thick brown paper of the type
that Humberto always used to wrap gift boxes, Isabel lifted the note
inside and read. Such notes usually told the story of how Humberto
had stumbled upon the contents of the box, related in a way that
conveyed pure unadorned luck combined with incredible cunning
and genius. But not this time. Isabel read the note. And she read it
again. She blinked, coughed, looked at the package and then back
to the note, which she read a third time. In his elegant hand Humberto had written:

Mi amor, I hope this finds you well. I returned from New Zealand three days ago, but by the time you receive this I will be in transit to a place I would rather not disclose, at least not at this time. While I am away (which should be no longer than a week), I ask you to protect what I have placed into this box. What is it? Well, to be blunt (something I attempt to avoid in my daily interactions, as you know), I have put my soul into this box for safekeeping. Why? I am afraid that I will lose it during my travels. I will explain more fully when (and if) I return. Con abrazos, Humberto.

Isabel opened the box and sure enough there was her ex-lover's soul, resting on a bed of purple velvet. She had expected something a bit larger, perhaps more Byzantine in appearance. But there it sat, a soul nonetheless. Isabel closed the box and shook her head. "Damn him," she whispered. "Damn him."

Seven days later Humberto appeared on Isabel's doorstep. To her eye, he looked ten, maybe fifteen years younger. Humberto had lost weight but not in a sickly manner, in a way that made him look vigorous, youthful. Isabel let him in and poured two small glasses of sweet wine. After a bit of small talk and cheerful laughter, Humberto suddenly grew serious. He sat up in his chair and leaned toward Isabel. "May I have my soul back?"

Isabel took a sip of wine and looked away. "What do you mean?" she asked, keeping her eyes trained on the crackling flames in the fireplace.

Humberto let out a sound that was not quite human, a cross between a hum and a scream. He collected himself and asked again: "May I have my soul back?"

Isabel did not answer and kept her eyes on the blazing logs.

Finally, after what seemed years to Humberto, Isabel answered: "Isn't the fire lovely? It has never looked more beautiful."

DIPLOPIA

The classroom's florescent lights and afternoon sun seemed to converge directly at Alisa's eyes. She knew that her headache would quickly morph into a full-blown migraine and she needed to do something soon, otherwise her twenty-seven fourth graders would be grossly entertained by their teacher's violent vomiting into the nearest receptacle. Alisa wanted nothing more than to close her eyes and rest in a quiet room. Just for a minute or two.

"Skylar," she said to a red-headed boy in the front row.

"Yes, Ms. Varela," said Skylar in a voice that was almost too eager for Alisa to take, but she needed him desperately at that moment.

Alisa pulled a paperback book from her desk drawer. "I have to make a phone call. Would you mind reading from the *Trumpet of the Swan* for a few minutes?"

Skylar wriggled in his seat. "To the class?" he asked. The other students giggled.

"Yes," she said. "To the class." Alisa opened the book and handed it to the boy. "We're at chapter 15. You can sit at my desk."

Skylar couldn't believe his luck. He leapt to his feet and was at Alisa's chair before she could get to the door.

"Behave, children," Alisa said as she left, feeling unable to control her now-convulsing stomach. She barely made it to the faculty bathroom.

* * *

Today was going to be the day Alisa reentered her life. Dr. Ramos had been very clear about it: in a day or two after the surgery, Alisa could jump right into the things she always enjoyed doing, observing only a few precautions. The doctor told his anxious patient to rest her eyes when they got tired, use the antibiotic drops three times a day, and not to lift heavy objects for about a week or so. But it had already been ten days since the surgery and she could barely drag herself to work. The whites of Alisa's eyes were awash in blood, much to the entertainment of her students, and the stitches pulled and irritated every second she was awake. The constant low-grade fever didn't help matters much. Yes, the surgery had apparently restored Alisa's "ocular alignment," but they wouldn't know for sure until more time had passed.

"This is usually done on infants," Dr. Ramos had said. Alisa remembered how the doctor's head was simply too big for his almost petite body. But his face was like that of a TV doctor: empathy almost bled from his pores, his temples sported just the right amount of gray, and he had perfected looking over his black-rimmed reading glasses in such a way that Alisa could only feel safe, protected.

"And?" she had responded.

"And so we have to be careful with adults. But I see no reason for you to restrict your activities other than not lifting heavy objects for one or two weeks." At this point, Dr. Ramos had lowered his head, lifted his eyebrows, and peered kindly over his reading glasses. "All will be fine."

But there was still no explanation as to why Alisa's left eye had decided to turn in toward her nose after the retinal surgery two years ago. "The strambismus is not related to the retinal repair, as far as I can tell," Dr. Ramos had said. "You just had a propensity for it, let us say."

The only comfort was that Alisa knew she had to have the surgery to reverse the diplopia. There was no other option. The double vision had intruded more and more into her life, and driving became a fretful activity. Twice already she had to pull over to rest her eyes before getting back into city traffic. And little activities sometimes became difficult. More than once when a cashier held out change Alisa had trouble putting her hand in the right place to receive the money. She remembered how one cashier looked at her as though alcohol or illicit drugs were the culprit.

Friday, after class, Alisa had planned a wonderful day with Emilio and Greg, her favorite couple. First they were going to browse at the Alexander Book Company and then wander over to Dolby Chadwick on Post to look at some new Kanevsky paintings. And the Meyerovich Gallery was within walking distance from there. Then maybe a nice dinner on the Embarcadero. A perfect afternoon and evening with two good friends. But as she pressed the cool wet washcloth on her eyes and enjoyed the near silence of the faculty lounge, Alisa couldn't imagine looking at anything, let alone books and paintings. Keeping her eyes covered, she reached into her purse, found her cell phone, and speed-dialed Emilio.

"Talk to me," came his voice, too loud but very welcome to her ears.

"I feel really crappy," Alisa barely got out.

"Mija," said Emilio in a softer voice. "Do you need me to get you to the doctor's?"

Always available for me, Alisa thought. Always there.

"No," she almost whispered. "No. But I think I need to cancel. Sorry."

Alisa could hear workers banging away at something in the background. Emilio was supervising a remodel that was proving to be as painful as it was lucrative. But in this economy, he said, he couldn't complain. A remodel in San Francisco meant money. Good money.

"No, mija, you can't cancel completely. We can do something else. Something easy on the eyes."

"Like what?"

"You can watch me and Greg make out."

Alisa laughed. "Oh, then I'd just get hot and bothered and then what would I do?"

"Hey, I'm just your friend," said Emilio over the ever-growing construction din. "I don't mind getting your motor running, but you need to find your own action, mija."

"I feel like I'm living an R-rated version of *Will and Grace*."

"You are, mija. But without the residuals."

* * *

Whenever Alisa entered the world of Emilio and Greg, she felt intensely inadequate and quite impoverished. True, she owned her own home while her friends merely leased. But Alisa's house was nothing more than an unoriginal cracker box in Daley City, inherited from her mother and father, while the boys lived in the city itself. Emilio and Greg existed in style, the kind Alisa only saw in home-furnishing magazines and made her drool and feel as envious as she could ever feel about anything. Alisa still furnished her home like a dorm room, relying heavily on IKEA or, if she splurged, Pottery Barn. The boys' apartment, on the other hand, not only had a view of the bay, but looked as though it was lifted from the pages of *Metropolitan Home*. Their Paola Lenti chaise cost more than her entire bedroom set, mattress included. But she couldn't complain. They were the happiest people she knew, and Alisa felt free and at home in the boys' apartment.

"Sweet Jesus!" said Greg as he opened the door. "You look like something from an old Vincent Price movie."

"I need a drink," said Alisa as she hugged Greg. "And thank you for making a girl feel so special."

"I'm sorry. Emilio said you looked pretty bad but I had no idea."

Alisa pulled back. "You just keep on charming me, don't you?"

Greg closed the door. "I'm an idiot."

"Yes."

"Drink?"

"Just like I asked."

Greg took Alisa's jacket and ushered her in. "We'll begin with martinis and then move to wine with dinner."

"Heaven. Where's Emilio?"

"In the kitchen, of course. Where I like my men."

"Pregnant and barefoot."

Greg laughed as he walked to the bar. "At least barefoot. Go say hi to him."

"Need drink now."

"Need drink now?"

"Must have drink."

"You sound like Superman under the influence of kryptonite."

"Sí."

Greg mixed the martini and poured a generous amount in a chilled glass. "Olive?"

"Two."

"That's my girl."

He handed Alisa the drink and then narrowed his eyes.

"What now?" said Alisa.

"You don't really look that bad."

"Thanks."

"What is it? Something about you?"

Alisa took a sip of her martini and let out a little *ah*. "Well, for starters, I'm not wearing eye makeup."

"Yes! That's it!"

"And to top it off, I'm not wearing my contacts."

"Right."

"So I'm four-eyed tonight just for you."

"Cute glasses, though." Greg poured himself a drink and tasted it carefully. "Perfect."

"Yes, wonderful bartender. I need to give you a big tip."

As the words left her lips, two arms slid around her waist. Greg smiled as Emilio pulled Alisa in tight from behind. "Mija," he whispered into her ear. "How are you?"

Alisa closed her eyes and enjoyed the hug. "I feel like crap, sweetie," she said. "Really lousy."

Emilio kissed Alisa's hair. "Dinner is ready," he said.

"And I look like a goon."

Emilio turned Alisa around. "Not so bad."

"Yeah, right."

"Let's eat," said Emilio. "Some good food, some nice wine, and you'll be good as new."

Alisa put her head on Emilio's chest. "Oh, sweetie, I love you so much."

"And I love you."

Greg took another sip of his martini. "Maybe I should leave you two alone," he laughed.

"Come on," said Emilio. "Vamos a comer."

* * *

Alisa was not surprised that the food was perfect, as per usual with the boys. And the wine followed the martini with ease. Emilio and Greg chatted, laughed, teased, and smiled. Alisa needed this support. The surgery, far from pleasant, had triggered something in her that she had never before felt: an acknowledgment that she was nothing more than human and that someday she would notice that her body, bit by bit, needed repair. Until one morning she would look in the mirror and see a very old woman staring back. And this made Alisa shiver. But she dared not mention it to these two friends who had seen more than their share of young men, and a few women, get sick, wither, and die too early. She needed to buck up. It could be worse. A few decades ago she would have been blind in one eye with a retina that could not be repaired. Alisa was ahead of the game. She would heal in due time. Though here she was almost thirty, married once for only a year to a very vicious man and divorced before she turned twenty-one, she still was relatively young with a chance at happiness. But her time on earth was slipping away, disappearing with each new crop of students, each parent-teacher meeting with people who didn't realize how lucky they were to have a child.

"Oh!" said Emilio. "Listen!"

They all stopped chatting and simultaneously tilted their heads up to hear the song that had just come on the radio.

"Who is that?" said Greg.

"How could you not know?" said Emilio.

"Sorry."

"No sex for you tonight."

Alisa laughed. "Yikes! I'd hate to find out how you punish Greg for bigger infractions."

"Oh," said Greg. "Emilio has a whole chart he follows."

"God, this is a great song," said Emilio.

Alisa took a sip of wine. "Tower of Power," she said as she started to sway to the melody.

"Yes!" said Emilio.

"'You're Still a Young Man,'" she concluded with a triumphant nod.

"Sí, mija," said Emilio. "You win. You get sex tonight!"

"Oh, goody," said Alisa.

Greg let out a snort. "I should test you on house music and see how you do."

Alisa touched her forehead and closed her eyes.

"What is it?" said Emilio. "Too much wine?"

"Too much Emilio?" asked Greg.

Alisa took a big breath, almost gulping air down. "No. My migraine is coming back. I don't feel so great. Maybe alcohol was not the best idea."

"Need to barf?" asked Emilio.

"I hope not."

"Lie down?" asked Greg.

"Please. I'm so sorry. I'm such a dope."

Emilio stood up and put his hands on Alisa's shoulders. "No, mija. Don't worry. Come with me."

* * *

Alisa slept through the night in her friends' guest room. She tumbled in and out of dreams that were not as vivid as her dreams usually were. Alisa's dreams this night were muffled, blurry, black-and-white, with no sound. It was as if her now limited sense of sight dulled even her sleep vision. She could sense her mother, that was certain, and a little of her father. But one perception was clear: she felt very alone. How she had ended up this way seemed to be the theme of her dreams this night. Yes, her parents had both died, first Alisa's father and then, more recently her mother. Alisa's husband was forced to stay away by the justice system. And her female friends had married one by one and started spitting out children which, of course, made socializing with them that much more difficult. Even when some of her friends divorced, they had a baby or two to stave off loneliness. At least that's what it looked like to Alisa. Relief from these dreams finally came with the smell of coffee and the glare of morning sun.

"Mija," said Emilio as he kissed Alisa's forehead. "How do you feel?"

She kept her eyes closed and reached for Emilio's unshaven face. "Sandpaper."

"Sí, mija. Just got up and made breakfast. Have some coffee." He guided Alisa's hand to the warm mug. "Have a sip."

She obeyed and let out the deep sigh that comes with the morning's first taste of coffee.

Alisa slowly opened her eyes and then blinked several times. She tried to focus on the mug, which had a photograph of a sleek Weimaraner emblazoned across it in honor of Emilio's late dog, Inca.

"You've expected too much of yourself," said Emilio. "You're only human, you know."

Once Alisa focused on the perfect gray canine face, she turned to Emilio. She blinked hard again because this shift of subject proved to be difficult to process. She closed her eyes for a second, breathed in the coffee's aroma, and then opened her eyes very cautiously as if they would roll out of her head if she weren't careful.

"Are you all right?" asked Emilio.

Alisa blinked one more time. The two Emilios slowly came together into one. The one she knew so well. The one who was her best friend. The one she loved more than anyone in her life.

"Sí, mi cielo," Alisa said. "I'm all right."

Emilio caressed her cheek and smiled. "Sure?"

Alisa took another sip of coffee and looked away. "Of course," she said. "I've never been better."

AN INTERVIEW WITH LOVE

: Comfy?

: Oh, yes.

: Shall we begin?

: I want whatever makes you happy.

: Beginning would make me happy. I've had a long day.

: I am all yours. Shoot.

: Okay, great. How old are you?

: Really? We're going there? I am falling out of the mood, fast.

: Sorry. I just like getting some of the basics out of the way.

: Okay, I will go with the flow, as we used to say. I am as old as human life itself.

: You definitely don't look your age.

: You charmer, you. Have we met before?

: (*clears throat*) Okay, let's get to the meaty questions.

: (*leans forward*) As I said, I'm all yours.

: What is your biggest accomplishment?

: Just one?

: Well, name a few.

: (*leans back, thinks*) Let's see—I am responsible for a few wars. Wait, who's going to read this?

: We have a wide audience.

: You're being coy.

: I'm being honest. Back to the subject. You're responsible for a few wars?

: That sounds harsh when you say it.

: Anything else besides wars?

: Of course! Without me, most novels, short stories, poems, and plays would not have been written.

: I could see that.

: As you should.

: Anything else you would take credit for?

: Half the population.

: Only half?

: I am not needed for procreation. Half. Maybe a little less than half.

: If you could go back in time and change one thing, what would you do?

: (*sips water, thinks*) That's a tough one.

: Take your time.

: I got it!

: Yes?

: I would have gotten into the stock market decades ago.

: What?

: Have you seen the Dow Jones? My goodness. I really blew that one.

: I expected something a bit deeper, you know, a bit more . . .

: What?

: Romantic.

: Ha! Do I look like a pendejo?

: Well . . .

: Watch it . . .

: This interview is not going the way I thought it would.

: You've seen too many movies. Love is not what you expect.

: What are you, then?

: What do you mean?

: How would you define yourself?

: Love is a familiar. Love is a devil. There is no evil angel but love.

: (*sighs*)

: What?

: Shakespeare. Really?

: Oh, you've heard that before.

: I was an English major.

: Well, it's pretty good, no?

: Of course it's good. It's the Bard.

: (*lifts glass of water*) To the Bard!

: But is it true?

: Oh, yes. (*yawns*)

: Do you want to continue this tomorrow?

: If you don't mind. I didn't sleep very well last night.

: Okay, let's pick up tomorrow, say 9:00 a.m.

: Yes, that works. But . . .

: What?

: I have one question for you.

: Okay, I guess that's fair. What is it?

: Do you validate?

MILES

"Están más cerca mis dientes que mis parientes," my father says as he grips the steering wheel of his ancient rattling Plymouth Fury Gran Coupe, knuckles white in contrast to his hairy brown fingers. He shouldn't be driving these days because of his eyes, but this time he insisted, like a grizzly bear deciding that I will be its dinner. If grizzlies are carnivores, that is, because I don't really know what they eat. Likely omnivores, I guess. The point is, when my father decides something, even at sixty-seven years of age, you can't argue.

"What?" I ask. "What about your teeth?" My Spanish sucks, big-time.

He coughs, irritated with me, and translates: "My teeth are closer to me than my relatives."

Oh, I think. Yeah. I get it now. We're off to see his cousin Leonardo. I call him Leo. For reasons beyond me, Pop hates Leo, who made it big in the garment district on Los Angeles Street downtown. Selling to the Mexicans Leo called "mojados" or "wetbacks," even though he himself snuck across the border forty years ago, dragged along by his poor mother, Alicia, when he was only ten. But Leo has a house—a mansion, really—in Hancock Park (Tip of the Cock, as he says) just from making and selling clothes to Mexicans. Pop, on the other hand, did a lot of things in his lifetime, but the last twenty before retiring two years ago he spent driving a bus for the Rapid Transit District, or the Metro, or whatever the hell they call it now. But this isn't why Pop can't stand Leo. Something else happened between them long ago, but I was never told what. They probably don't even remember. Anyhow, we're off to see Leo because he invited us, his closest relatives in this country, to celebrate his daughter's acceptance to USC dental school. Alma, that's her name. And if we weren't related, I'd be after her sweet tight ass faster than you could say, "Go, Trojans!"

"The pendejo just wants to show off his pinche new car," Pop says as he turns left on Olympic without so much as a signal or acknowledgment of the oncoming traffic. "Otherwise he'd think of an excuse to not invite us."

I close my eyes. The car stinks of Pop's rancid off-brand cigars. Even White Owls would be better. Luckily he didn't light one before leaving, otherwise I think I would have puked back at Pico and Western. I tip my head out the window and let the warm mid-morning air hit my face like so much cotton candy, thick and almost sickening in its own way. But it helps, a little. I open my eyes and watch the palm trees whiz by, the neighborhoods improving with every mile, less and less graffiti on the walls and sides of houses, lawns greener and greener and more sculpted.

We live pretty simply compared to Leo and his daughter. Back in the '60s, Pop bought this two-story wood-framed house near downtown. It probably was a middle-class neighborhood in the 1920s, though it's hard to imagine with all the gang activity and crap. But it's home. Pop and Mom raised six kids there, me being the youngest and least motivated. At twenty-two, I still live with Pop (Mom died four years ago—goddamn breast cancer), taking a few units in art now and again at Cal State Los Angeles. I sell shoes at the Robinsons-May to maintain *my* junker of a car, a '77 mustard-yellow Mustang. On the other hand, Alma, who is only six months younger than me, has her own apartment in the Fairfax District and is going to be a dentist. I have little doubt that Pop's particularly gruff demeanor this morning is caused by my impending embarrassment when Leo toasts Alma in front of all her college friends and us. Pop could brag about my sisters, all pretty successful, living in other states, and all married except for Ernestine who, Pop doesn't yet realize, likes girls way more than guys. He could pull out pictures of his five grandchildren, too, just to emphasize that Leo's only child is far from bringing such joy to Leo. But he won't do any of that because that would be insulting to me. Pop loves me too much to do that. In truth, I couldn't give a rat's ass about any of it. I just want to arrive there in one piece, get quietly drunk on Leo's excellent booze, and have dirty little daydreams about Alma's silky chestnut skin rubbing up on mine. I'm a simple man with simple needs.

We finally get there, more or less on time, and I wonder aloud if Pop drove the bus that way.

He pushes his thick black rimmed glasses up his nose and turns to me, owl-eyed and unsmiling. "My driving paid for our mortgage, your and your sisters' schooling, and everything else. Don't forget that."

Oh, shit. It's going to be one of those visits. If he's this rough on me, wait until Leo says one wrong thing. My strategy will be to get to the bar and stay there.

We get out of the car and amble up that long walkway to Leo's humble abode and ring the doorbell. We hear laughter, music, and all kinds of fun coming through the recently painted Spanish missionary exterior. I look over to Pop. He stands there, perfect posture, hawk-like nose pointed up, ready for battle. This is going to be bad. I can hear Leo's voice, loud and in command, getting closer. The door opens slowly, clearly for our benefit, and there stands Leo, resplendent in a powder-blue jumpsuit, the kind they used to wear in the '70s, Rolex glistening in the sunlight, holding a drink in one hand, his arm around the waist of some pretty young thing (probably a friend of Alma's). He flashes these huge white teeth at us. He kind of reminds me Ricardo Montalban, but with a bit of a paunch.

"¡Mi familia!" he yells a bit too loudly. "Come in, come in!"

Leo lets go of his lovely companion so that he can slap my back. This makes me trip a little on the threshold, and now I'm thinking that it might be fun to watch Pop go after him. He then grabs Pop's hand and shakes it so hard it's all a blur. Some of Leo's drink spills on Pop's new brown Hush Puppies.

Pop takes a deep breath. "Hola, Leonardo," Pop says so softly you can barely hear him.

"¡Vamos! Let's get drinks in your hands!" Leo almost screams.

Now he's talking. I turn and look around. Guys and girls are everywhere, some I recognize as longtime friends of Alma's, others strangers. Some sweet ass, too. Goddamn if Alma doesn't attract some real babes as friends. Dave Brubeck's "Blue Rondo a La Turk" is blasting, clearly Leo's choice—loves American jazz—and everyone seems to be having a great time, though I'm sure, judging by the looks of the crowd, they would have preferred listening to something more

MILES

along the lines of Phish, Linkin Park, or perhaps Quetzal. I spy the bar which, of course, has a rented bartender standing there, flawlessly attired in a little white jacket and black bow tie, blond hair in perfect ringlets, well-trimmed goatee accenting his faultlessly chiseled chin. Ten to one odds he's not really a bartender but an actor with one or two commercials to his credit. I fight my way through beautiful, young, and well-educated people and get a nice spot right behind this huge white guy wearing nothing but Tommy Hilfiger from head to toe. He turns.

"Zeus!" he yells as he punches me hard in my right shoulder. It hurts. I suddenly recognize him.

"Josh," I mutter as I rub some feeling back into my shoulder. Josh played football for UCLA and has been Alma's friend since their freshman year. He likes to call me "Zeus" because my name is Jesús and I think, being a born-again Christian and all, he'd prefer to mangle my name to sound like a Greek god rather than Our Savior. I think he's had a crush on Alma all these years, but the idea of bringing a brown girl home to meet the ol' parents, Mr. and Mrs. Tilghman of Pacific Palisades, probably gives him nightmares.

"How the heck are you, Zeus?" The bartender hands him a Dr. Pepper still in the can, the way Josh likes it. Josh shoves a couple bucks in the tips glass.

"Fine, fine."

"Whatcha doin' these days?"

"A gin and tonic, please," I say. "First things first, Joshie boy."

"Oh, sorry." He waits until the bartender gives me the drink. I don't tip him.

"Come on, let's talk," Josh says as he pulls me away from the crowded bar. "Got some good news."

Just then, Miles Davis's "Freddie Freeloader" comes on. Leo's CD player is clearly set on "random play." I actually like his taste in music, but I'd never admit that to Pop.

"Got into biz school. Brown." Josh flashes a grin and then takes a long swig of his Dr. Pepper. It's difficult not to like Josh. He's such an innocent guy and he treats everyone so well. They're going to eat him alive in grad school.

"Congratulations!" and I smile, grab his hand, and shake it the way Leo did to Pop a few minutes ago.

170

Our conversation suddenly comes to a halt because we realize that Alma's standing there, smiling, hands clasped before her like she's about to pray or something, and she screams, "Jesús!" She throws her arms around me and I almost spill my drink. She hugs me tightly and I bury my face in her thick hair. It tickles and smells so good and clean, like apricot shampoo. My free hand reaches around her tiny muscular waist and the silk dress she's wearing feels so promising under my fingertips. I begin to get hard so I pull back. Unfortunately, it's the kind of hard-on that feels so good, it makes your whole body tingle. God, I need a date.

"Alma!" I say. "You look beautiful!" And she does.

"We'll talk later, Zeus," smiles Josh, and he wanders off to let me and Alma catch up.

"You stranger!" says Alma, silly grin on her face. "Where have you been hiding?" She grabs my free hand and squeezes.

"Oh, doing this and that," I say, feeling totally lame.

"Still doing those beautiful drawings?"

Ah! Alma always loved my artwork. Of all my family members, Mom and Pop included, she was the only one who encouraged me. Alma thought I could make it as an artist.

"Still taking a few classes, building a portfolio." This isn't a lie, but I am far from methodical about the process. I know that to get into a good MFA program, my portfolio has to be stellar and a bit edgy, but I'm a bit of a traditionalist when it comes to art. Tradition isn't in vogue, unfortunately. Anyway, I have this dream of getting into UC Irvine, but I'll probably be elected president or pope before that happens.

"You have to draw me sometime," and she squeezes my hand even harder, which makes me get harder.

"But you're going to dental school," I say as I shift around trying to hide my erection.

"Silly! I'll still be in L.A.!"

How did I get so stupid? Of course she'll still be in town. And what am I afraid of? We're not even first cousins, for Chrissakes! But I shouldn't mistake Alma's affection for anything but a lifelong friendship. Before I can answer her, I hear Pop's voice above the din of the partygoers. Shit! It's starting so soon. Alma and I turn and see Pop and Leo standing nose to nose, which is kind of funny because

Pop towers over Leo by about six inches. Pop holds an old album that looks so large and ancient next to the neatly stacked CDs in the oak entertainment center. As we get closer, I see the old bulldog face of José Alfredo Jiménez, one of the great old Mexican singers of Pop's generation, smiling from the album cover. Pop has discovered Leo's secret stash of Latin music.

"*They* don't want to hear this old shit!" Leo growls at Pop.

"How do you know?" Pop growls back. "There are plenty of Mexicans here. Including *you*."

A few of the kids start to stare at them. Alma slides up close to Leo and gives him a big hug from his left side. "This is a wonderful party, Pops!"

Leo's face softens and he offers up a wan little smile. "Thank you, mija. I'm happy *someone* appreciates me."

Leo can be so pathetic sometimes, especially around this time of year. Leo's wife, Luna, ran off to Mexico City with his head designer (or knock-off artist, if truth be told) three years ago this month.

Pop, unfortunately, is undeterred. "Let me just play one song, Leonardo. Will that kill you?" As he says this, Pop pokes Leo's unprotected right side with the album corner.

Stupidly, I intervene. "Pop, we can listen to it at home. Not here."

Oops. What a shithead I can be. Pop's eyes widen even more. But before he can say anything else, Alma releases Leo, grabs the album, and in one fluid movement takes the record out of its sleeve. "Which side, Enrique?" she asks.

Pop's eyelids come down a bit, and a little smile appears on his face. "Lado dos, por favor."

"Side 2 it is," says Alma.

She flips open the Denon turntable, gently positions the black vinyl record, and pushes a couple of buttons. The stereo suddenly fills the living room with the macho strains of "El Rey." Pop closes his eyes and hums along. Leo looks around to see the reaction of the guests. He notices that the Latinos in the room are smiling, recognizing the song. The others don't seem to mind. Leo lets out a sigh of relief.

Well, the party goes on pretty well after that. They play more old records. Leo even puts on Celia Cruz just before we get ready to go.

As we say our good-byes, Alma pulls me aside. "Jesús," she whispers.

"I meant it when I said that you could draw me. I'd love it." She squeezes my hand.

"Okay."

"When?"

"Well," I stammer. She's being very pushy about this. "I've just started sharing a studio with five other artists. Kind of expensive, but Pop thinks it'll help me focus. It's downtown, a loft. Maybe next Friday."

"How about dinner? I could bring something. And then you could start."

I think for a moment. She's now rubbing my hand with both of hers. Her large brown eyes swallow me. "Perfect. Wear something nice. For the picture."

Alma pulls me close and whispers into my ear, "I want to pose nude."

I suddenly shudder under the weight of Pop's big hand on my shoulder. "Mijo, time to go," he says. "Give your cousin a kiss and let's go."

I blush six shades of red. "Yeah, Pop." kiss Alma on her cheek. She smiles. I smile.

Leo comes up to me. "Jesús! Thank you for coming!" he says and shakes my hand. "You're getting so handsome, like your father."

Pop laughs. We walk out. The evening air is warm, the sweet smell of Leo's lush garden filling our nostrils. We hop in the car and Pop starts it up with a roar. I notice he's humming something as we lurch forward. I don't recognize it, not exactly. It's a little familiar. "What's that song?" I ask.

He smiles. "Oh, it's a little song I heard tonight. By that Negrito."

"Who?"

"Davis. You know. Miles Davis."

We drive home without talking, Pop's humming filling the void.

THE ANNOTATED OBITUARY OF ALEJANDRA LÓPEZ DE LA CALLE

ALEJANDRA LÓPEZ DE LA CALLE, UNAPOLOGETICALLY POLITICAL
PLAYWRIGHT, IS DEAD AT EIGHTY-TWO AFTER FALL[1]

The iconoclast's experimental plays were rooted in controversial
political views[2] and blunt cultural commentary[3] that yielded
uneven[4] though revolutionary live performances.[5]

by Lucy Broderick[6]

Los Angeles—Alejandra López de la Calle, an influential experimental playwright whose works focused less on traditional theatrical ele-
ments like plot and dialogue than on the socioeconomic sensitivities
of her audiences,[7] died on Wednesday at her home in Los Angeles,
California, where she had taught for decades at the University of
Southern California. She was eighty-two. Her son, Armando Blancarte López, said the playwright succumbed to complications after
a fall in her home.

Born on April 8, 1940, in the now-shuttered Temple Community Hospital near downtown Los Angeles, Ms. López was the only
daughter of Hortencia López de la Calle,[8] an unmarried Mexican
immigrant who had arrived in the United States three years earlier from Ocotlán, a city in Jalisco, Mexico. In one of her last interviews, Ms. López responded sharply to a question about any regret
she may have harbored in not knowing the identity of her biological father: "I care more about a dog's flatulence than I do about who
that man might have been!"[9]

Over a sixty-two-year career in which she wrote nearly one

hundred plays, Ms. López sought to reflect[10] the Chicana's urban experience unadulterated by the traditions of what she termed "White, male-centered" theater. Most of her work appeared in small and Latinx-led theaters in cities such as Los Angeles, Austin, Chicago, and Tucson, and perhaps for that reason she never reached the pinnacles of acclaim that other, less daring playwrights attained and whose plays appeared on Broadway and were adapted for the screen. Ironically, many of those more successful, non-Latinx playwrights cited Ms. López as a major inspiration for their own writing careers.[11]

Among Ms. López's most frequently produced plays were those known informally as her Los Angeles Trilogy: *The House on Ardmore Avenue* (1981), *A Blue Death at the Observatory* (1990), and *No Hay Rosas Sin Espinas* (2012). One of her more "conventional" plays, *Six Steps to Redemption* (2006), was optioned by a major studio a decade ago, but discussions for development came to an abrupt halt after Ms. López objected when the studio suggested Ron Howard as director.[12]

"She was able to get the heart of what it means to be a Chicana," the playwright Luisa Camacho said in an interview. "She was a writer who spoke to the values of her cultural and gender-informed experiences. She was also a mentor and friend. It's a shame she never received the accolades she deserved."[13]

"Of course Chicana writers can write for all audiences," she told the *Los Angeles Times* in 1999. "But I don't need to. I write for Chicanas because I am Chicana. If anyone else wants to go along for the ride, that's fine. Otherwise, I don't really care who 'gets' my plays. ¿Entiendes?"[14]

Ms. López's mother, who worked as a seamstress in the garment district, settled with the future playwright in a small apartment in Harvard Heights, in what was then, before gentrification, a predominantly immigrant community adjacent to Koreatown. Ms. López attended the local Catholic schools for twelve years before enrolling in California State University, Los Angeles, where she majored in English literature. It is during her time in college that Ms. López met her future husband, the late Rolando Blancarte, a biology major who eventually became a dentist.[15]

The couple settled in Boyle Heights as Mr. Blancarte started his dental clinic while Ms. López worked variously as a secretary, receptionist, waitress, and any other employment that allowed her to take evening courses in playwriting at Los Angeles City College. It was during this time that the playwright wrote several early works, including her acclaimed one-woman play, *Confessions of a Chicana Parochial School Girl* (1967), which established her underground[16] reputation as a daring new voice in Los Angeles's burgeoning small-theater world.

The couple had one only[17] child, but their partnership was fruitful: Ms. López became a prolific playwright while her husband transformed his dental practice into a thriving community clinic. Mr. Blancarte once said of their respective professions: "I fix our people's teeth while Alejandra feeds their souls."[18] Mr. Blancarte predeceased Ms. López by ten years.

Theater critic Bernard M. Hurley offered this assessment upon learning of Ms. López's passing: "She was a remarkable voice who never compromised her art for commerce as she limned the lives of Hispanic[19] girls and women through powerful kinetic plays. Perhaps that is why Alejandra López de la Calle is not a household name. And that, in my humble estimation, is a true tragedy."[20]

1. For my final exam, I have selected the "annotation" project, in which we are tasked with annotating a published obituary so as to examine, explore, and expose the vagaries of biography vis-à-vis the lives of BIPOC creatives. For this project, I chose the obituary of the playwright Alejandra López de la Calle (she/her/hers), who died last year. I will interrogate the chasm between the public recognition (i.e., acceptable) "truth" of a public figure's legacy and a deeper examination of that truth based on independent research I conducted on the subject.

2. López's "controversial political views"—based on her numerous public statements as well as the themes explored in the vast majority of her plays—consisted of being against, on the one hand: (1) the Vietnam War; (2) racism; (3) sexism; (4) police brutality; (5) all forms of segregation; and (6) the "diminution of non–western European cultural aesthetics." On the other hand, López supported: (1) equal rights for all; (2) freedom of expression; (3) a woman's right to choose whether to carry a pregnancy to term; (4) universal healthcare; and (5) clean energy.

3. Ibid.

4. While I could not review all of the playwright's work for this assignment, I did read a sampling of her plays in each decade of her career from the 1960s to the present. Rather than uneven, the quality, themes, and forms of López's plays remained consistently mature, sophisticated, and developed. Perhaps the unevenness perceived by critics was due to López's refusal to recycle narratives and structures while addressing her central concern and theme: the life of the Chicana in an urban landscape.

5. Unfortunately, the only video recordings of her live performances consist of three Zoom readings—available on YouTube—of plays in progress recorded during the pandemic. Thus, all earlier plays are documented only through reviews, interviews, and still photography.

6. Some controversy arose on social media regarding the assignment of Lucy Broderick to write this obituary based on her prior coverage of other BIPOC creatives that betrayed a lack of understanding of or experience with basic historical and societal influences on such creatives such as systemic racism, Latinx colorism, gentrification, the various civil rights movements, anti-immigrant government policies, etc.

7. This description of López's work is lifted directly, word for word and without attribution, from Christina J. Escondido's essay published on May 25, 2018, in the online journal *La Bloga*, which is a well-regarded independent website dedicated to the coverage of Latinx literature and the arts. Escondido is a playwright and educator who collaborated with López on at least four productions.

8. López's mother was an excellent student and completed two years' worth of education at the University of Guadalajara. Unfortunately, once she was in the United States, her immigration status and economic pressures resulted in employment that was not commensurate with her education. Though this was never confirmed by the playwright, there is circumstantial evidence in López's plays that her mother escaped an abusive relationship. She introduced the future playwright to the works of Juana Inés de la Cruz, Octavio Paz, and Rosario Castellanos, among others. The playwright often credited her mother with nurturing her literary aspirations.

9. There appears to be no record of such an interview. This alleged quotation first appeared in a blog post published on September 24, 2003, written by Beatrice Ammonds, who was a college student at the time. The quotation appeared in numerous articles thereafter. The most puzzling aspect of this alleged quotation is that López often expressed regret that she never knew her biological father, and such regret served as the inspiration for her early well-received one-act play, *The Education of a Chicana* (1969).

10. Perhaps "successfully reflected" would be more accurate than "sought to reflect."

11. This phenomenon is all too common in the literary arts generally, not simply playwriting. See, e.g., Olivas, Daniel. "Yes, Latinx writers are angry about *American Dirt*—and we will not be silent." *Guardian,* January 30, 2020. The 2020 release of the novel *American Dirt* by Jeanine Cummins resulted in one of the biggest literary controversies in Latinx literature due to the non-Latina author being paid a seven-figure advance for a book that many Latinx writers—including most notably Myriam Gurba—considered nothing more than "trauma porn" filled with bigoted tropes and ham-handed storytelling.

12. The playwright's objections went far beyond Ron Howard, whose movies López actually praised in several interviews. The primary conflict appears to have been the studio's suggestion that López rewrite the ending of the play so that is was not "such a downer" (the phrasing of one studio executive in an email to the

playwright). López replied: "I like downers." Development discussions broke off shortly thereafter.

13. Camacho is one of many young playwrights whom López mentored throughout the decades.

14. López apparently subscribed to this philosophy throughout her career. In a 1972 interview with a college newspaper, she phrased it another way: "White, straight, male playwrights write for white, straight, male audiences about matters of interest to them. But those plays are considered 'universal' in theme. Why aren't the matters that interest Chicanas considered universal as well? I suppose we should ask the white, straight, male play critics that question."

15. Her husband's profession made its way into only one of López's works, a ten-minute comedic piece titled *I Married My Dentist . . . And So Should You* (1983). Nonetheless, López credited her husband's "normal, boring" profession as the "perfect foundation" for her creative life. Her husband allegedly did not read his wife's plays but rather waited to see them performed. López found this liberating and often criticized writers who forced their significant others to serve as their beta readers. "My husband doesn't ask me to review his patients' dental x-rays before he drills. Why should I require him to read every precious little draft of mine? I am not that needy, and I respect his time too much."

16. I question the use of the term *underground*. The small theaters that produced López's plays in readings and on the stage were indeed small, but nothing about them was "underground" in any sense of the word. They were mostly BIPOC owned and operated, which may appear to some as "underground."

17. I have no explanation for the author's use of the modifying "only" other than a bias toward more traditional family structures.

18. López once quipped: "Of all the dentists I've known, my husband is the most poetic."

19. López eschewed the word *Hispanic* as "nothing more than a government-created, sanitized, and exceedingly tedious categorization for the census."

20. While Hurley's sentiment is apt, it is somewhat ironic because the critic never gave López a positive review. Indeed, of the sixteen reviews Hurley wrote of the playwright's work, only one could be considered somewhat "positive"—and that is a generous characterization. Hurley seems to have been distressed by López's centering of the Chicana in the narrative of virtually every play. In one review (of López's 1992 *Brown Woman's Blues*), Hurley exclaimed: "Are there no white people in the playwright's world?" To which López responded in an interview: "No. Why should there be?"

NEW YEAR

"She doesn't have to know, right?"

Claudio held the receiver hard against his left ear as he caressed the granite by the kitchen sink with his right hand. His fingers were still moist with perspiration from his workout. Claudio rubbed the smooth cool granite, which was interrupted periodically and randomly with miniature canyons that dipped down far enough to avoid the polisher's tool. His eyes traveled over its dappled black and tan surface, following an imaginary line from his fingertips to the bone-white lip of the porcelain Kohler sink. Claudio remembered choosing the granite with his wife several years ago after the Northridge quake. They were forced to live in "corporate" housing for three long hot summer months courtesy of their Aetna policy. Their contractor had visited them at their temporary home schlepping six different granite samples. He laid the small chunks of stone on the orange carpeting like they were diminutive Monets. His name was Lionel—a former soap opera actor, or so he said—who had decided on a complete change of lifestyle seven years earlier immediately after he and his second wife split up. An attorney in Claudio's office swore by him. Lionel's black curly hair and sharp tanned features looked too planned and he dressed better than any of the other contractors they had interviewed. He proved to have a great eye for design but, as Claudio and Lois eventually learned, he stumbled a bit in the execution. Lionel stood by the granite samples, one hand on his hip, the other at his chin, and he hummed a nervous little tune.

"Well," Lionel had said after the silence got to him, "which will it be?" Luckily, Claudio and Lois had similar aesthetic sensibilities so they chose the same sample, almost simultaneously both pointing with their right index fingers. Lionel exclaimed in an overly dramatic voice, "Lovely! I would have chosen the same piece."

Claudio quickly switched the receiver to his right ear, pushing it even harder against his head. "I mean, look, she shouldn't have to know. Right? I mean, where does it get any of us? It isn't really necessary, is it?"

As the woman's voice started again, he looked out the kitchen window. The cawing grew louder and harsher. Claudio never saw the bird but he knew it was a crow because his father had identified its call when they first moved out to the west end of the San Fernando Valley ten years ago. The whole family had come over for a housewarming. "Mijo," his father had said. "Sounds like you got a big ol' crow living in one of those trees in back. They're such noisy and mean birds." His father took a sip from his can of Coors and added: "I hate crows."

"Me too, Pop," Claudio had answered, though he had never really thought about it before. Now, ten years after his father's pronouncement and his unthinking agreement, he did indeed hate crows. Especially the one who wouldn't shut up just then.

The woman's voice stopped. Claudio said, "Okay, then. We're in agreement." After a pause, a few more words, and then a curt goodbye, he hung up, letting out a long breath of air. "Goddamn her," he said softly, almost gently. He headed to the refrigerator and scanned the bottom shelf. He stood there mesmerized by the bottles and cans of Snapple, diet Coke, and various fruit juices in small rectangular boxes that his son loved. Claudio suddenly felt dizzy from dehydration. He grabbed a Snapple Peach Tea.

* * *

Earlier that morning, Claudio woke at 6:00, thanks to the obnoxious shrill buzz of his combination telephone, AM/FM radio, and alarm clock, the Chronomatic-300 sold under the Radio Shack label. Lois had bought it for Claudio's thirty-eighth birthday last year. It was a thoughtful and useful gift, but he grew to hate that damn buzzer. Lois, already showered, stood in front of her sink with a white towel wrapped around her head, making her look like the strolling Turk on the Hills Brothers coffee can. She wore her delicate floral cotton robe and brushed her teeth with a Braun electric toothbrush.

Claudio sat up at the edge of their bed and rubbed his face while listening to the soft hum of the Braun. "Morning," he said.

Lois didn't turn around but answered with a muffled noise and a nod of her head. She turned off the toothbrush and spat into the sink. "Morning, sweetheart." Lois then turned and looked in the general direction of her husband, but because she didn't have her contacts in yet, all she saw was a blur.

It was Friday and that meant that Claudio could work at home. A couple of years ago they had purchased a computer, laser printer, and fax machine so that Claudio could telecommute at least once a week because his normal commute to downtown was pretty god-awful. So was Lois's but her office didn't believe in telecommuting. But because Claudio worked for the government, his employer had an institutional bias in favor of parent-friendly flexible work hours and anti-smog programs. So if he didn't have to be in court on Friday, he could work on his briefs in peace and quiet at home, checking his voicemail every so often when he needed a break from the computer.

Claudio went to his son's room but he wasn't there. He then heard muffled voices from the downstairs TV so he walked to the staircase. As he went down, the sounds of *Scooby Doo* became clearer. Before going to the den, he headed out to the driveway to get the *Los Angeles Times*. It was chilly and a bit foggy. The week and a half between Rosh Hashanah and Yom Kippur had been particularly difficult this year. Claudio reached down and grabbed the paper. As he stood up, he saw his neighbor across the street bend to get her paper. She was wearing a short nightshirt that exposed plump and very white legs. What was her name? She'd given birth to a baby girl a month ago and she complained that she would never get her figure back. Claudio waved and she looked up, clearly embarrassed by her outfit. She waved without a smile and scurried back into her house, her fleshy bare feet slapping on the dew-covered cement.

Claudio headed to the den to check on his son. Jonathan still wore his Goosebumps glow-in-the-dark pajamas and was, as usual, doing several things at once: as he looked up to the TV every so often to keep track of Scooby Doo's exploits hunting ghosts, he was using his kid's scissors to cut an old T-shirt to make a cape for his new Spider-Man that his Grandma had bought him and, every few minutes, he reached over to his box of apple juice perched on several books on the floor and took a drink from a tiny straw.

"Morning, mijo," Claudio said.

Jonathan just stared at the TV.

"I said, good morning, Jon." Claudio grew annoyed Still, Jonathan didn't answer. Finally Claudio put himself between the TV and Jonathan and said again: "Good morning, I said."

This broke Jonathan's trance and he looked up to his father. "Good morning, Papá."

Claudio bent down and kissed his son's hair. It smelled like blueberries from Aussie Land Blue Mountain Shampoo. Jonathan's hair was soft, straight, and dark blond like Lois's but his skin resembled Claudio's and had an olive glow about it. He had long dark eyelashes like his father.

"Jon, I'm making Pop Tarts for you. What kind do you want?"

After a moment of contemplation, Jonathan said, "One strawberry and one cinnamon. And cut them up in funny pieces."

"And?"

Jonathan looked puzzled. "That's all. And milk too."

Claudio looked at his son and said again: "And?"

Finally, Jonathan got it. "And thank you, Papá."

Having obtained the answer he wanted, Claudio walked to the kitchen and got his son's breakfast ready, getting the coffee going too. Lois came down to the kitchen, pulled a bowl out of the cabinet, and poured some Quaker Oats granola. She opened the refrigerator and said, "Honey, you gotta get some milk tonight. We're almost out."

* * *

Their routine that morning was well set. They ate breakfast, each glued to their respective portions of the newspaper: Lois read the movie reviews in the Calendar section, Jonathan earnestly worked through the funnies, and Claudio scanned the front page. After putting her bowl and coffee mug into the sink, Lois went upstairs, and set out their son's clothes for the day, and then went to finish doing her hair. Claudio made Jonathan's lunch and then went up to put on some sweats, a ragged Stanford T-shirt, and his cross-trainers while their son got dressed, made his bed, and then brushed his teeth with a miniature version of his mother's Braun electric toothbrush. Lois kissed them good-bye and left first. Within ten minutes—at exactly 7:45—Claudio loaded his son and his son's Star Wars backpack into their Honda Accord and headed toward school. They chatted about silly things and listened to "The Wave"—the local soft-jazz station—during the seven-minute drive.

As they entered the school's driveway, the teachers signaled the cars to keep on moving after dropping off the children. Jonathan pointed to one of the teachers and said, "She's Mrs. Horowitz. I hate her. She has really bad breath and she breathes on all the children."

"Maybe she's a nice person with bad breath," said Claudio, trying not to laugh. He made it his quest to teach his son that you have to look deeper into people to really know them. "Maybe she doesn't know that she needs to brush more. Or maybe she needs to floss."

"Oh, she knows she has bad breath. She's mean so she doesn't care."

When Claudio could stop safely, he unlocked the doors with the master switch and said, "I love you." Jonathan said, "I love you too," and got out of the car, dragging his backpack behind him. Claudio locked the doors and headed to the exit as he changed the radio station to hear the news on NPR. There was something about the ethnic Albanians. Claudio didn't understand what was going on over there, even though he knew that he should care more. But he decided that he simply couldn't listen to that story right then so he pushed the button preset for KUSC. Ah, Bach. The Goldberg Variations.

Claudio drove north on Shoup and then turned right on Sherman Way. He aimed his car toward the Spectrum Club for his usual half hour on the recumbent stationary bicycle and half hour with the weight machines. As he turned into the parking lot, he tried to decide whether to bring the paperback edition of *Bless Me, Ultima* or the latest *Ploughshares* to read while pedaling. Claudio always kept books and literary journals stashed in the armrest and glove compartments so that he never lacked reading material. He decided on Anaya's book. When he majored in English back in the late '70s, Chicano writers weren't studied the way they were now. So last year Claudio had made a list of classic Chicano authors to read, like Anaya, Morales and Rechy, and then he added the "newer" ones like Cisneros, Soto, and Villaseñor.

He slid his car into a spot, turned off the motor, pulled the paperback out of the armrest compartment, and stuffed it into his gym bag.

Claudio got out, locked his car, and walked slowly to the entrance of the club. He felt stiff. At the front desk, he handed his membership card to a young woman who wore a gleaming white uniform Polo shirt with a large nametag that said DONNA. She smiled, exposing large and very straight white teeth that matched her shirt. Donna stared at Claudio with translucent blue eyes.

"Got your braces off," said Claudio, realizing that she wanted him to notice. A tall skinny young man, another gym employee, leaned against the wall near Donna and glowered.

Donna smiled even wider. "Yes," and she looked down at his membership card, "Claudio." Donna swiped the membership card through a narrow plastic trough and the computer let out a little beep. She then leaned forward on the counter and brought her face closer to Claudio's. She smelled like almonds and honey. "I was totally sick of them but now, you know, it was totally worth it."

Claudio smiled. "Yes. You look nice."

Donna bounced a little on her toes and tossed her blond hair away from her face. "Have a good workout, Claudio," and she handed the card back to him, letting it linger in Claudio's palm before releasing it.

"Thank you." Claudio headed to the locker room to dump his bag and glasses before going to the weight room. At this hour there wasn't much of a crowd. Claudio shuffled by a large older man who stood naked, hands on his hips and legs spread in a pyramid like Balzac, while an electric wall dryer blew his sparse stringy white hair into a frenzy. The man's belly hung so low that his private parts were not visible. Claudio quickly averted his eyes, found a locker at the far end of the room, and put his bag and glasses away. He snapped shut the lock, looped the key on his right shoelace, and trotted to the weight room, taking a roundabout route to avoid Balzac. Once out of the locker room, Claudio slowed and walked the long hallway of racquetball courts, his head hanging down.

He came to several older men and women who were laughing. "Beat the shit out of those two little punks," snorted a man who looked like the Monopoly man but without the top hat and tails. "Didn't know who he was messin' with," and he shook his fists from side to side like a bear showing his strength.

"Yes, sweetheart," said the woman sitting next to the Monopoly man. "We showed him and his girlfriend, right, honey?"

"What do you mean 'we,' white woman?" her husband answered, and their two friends burst out laughing.

Claudio tried to pass them but they were blocking the way. "Excuse me," he said, still holding his head down.

"Sorry," said the Monopoly man. "Didn't see you with your head down so low. Cheer up. Can't be that bad, can it?"

Claudio looked up and smiled a small smile in appeasement just so he could pass without getting into a conversation. He'd learned that the retired people who used the gym loved to talk it up with anyone because they didn't have to get to work. Claudio smelled stale perspiration and some kind of medicated ointment.

"Now that's better," said the Monopoly man's wife, and they let Claudio pass.

In a few moments he got to the safety of the weight room, grabbed a little towel from a plastic shelf, and wandered over to the stationary bicycles. Since the remodeling after the Spectrum Club bought out Racquetball World, everything was newer but in a different place. Claudio liked the greater variety of weight machines but hated learning a new floor design. He looked at the six stationary bikes. The one to the far left by the StairMasters was occupied by a stroke victim and his trainer. The stroke victim looked as though his body had once been a magnificent specimen of strength and agility. Now his left side dragged and he used a cane. The trainer said, "Good, Howie, good! You're moving way better this morning! Pedal, pedal, pedal!" The trainer was probably a sophomore or junior in college. His flat-top made him look like a Marine, and he had a serpent tattoo on his right forearm. Howie pedaled slowly, staring up at one of the five large TV screens that hung suspended from the ceiling. He didn't acknowledge his trainer's presence and wore what appeared to be a sneer on his face, though the expression could have been the result of the stroke. When the trainer wasn't around, Howie liked to flirt with the young women.

Claudio approached the bicycles. A very thin woman pedaled on the one to the far right. Large splashes of perspiration covered three of the four unoccupied bicycles. Claudio chose the dry one near the thin woman. He adjusted the seat, chose the program, set it for thirty minutes, opened his paperback, and started pedaling.

After a few minutes Claudio felt the thin woman staring at him, but he kept his eyes on his book. Finally the woman said, "Excuse me." Claudio turned. "Yes?"

"Could you do something about that noise?" Claudio noticed that the young woman was so thin and white that he could see what appeared to be most of her circulatory system throughout her face, neck, and shoulders like algae-filled canals. She reminded him of those pictures of Auschwitz and he wondered if she had cancer or an eating disorder. Perspiration rained from her face and arms. Claudio worried that there'd soon be nothing left but her tiny tank top, shorts, and Nikes sitting in a pool of liquid.

"What noise?" said Claudio.

She shifted in her seat and looked annoyed. "Your shoe. The plastic tip on your shoelace keeps hitting your bike as you pedal and it makes a noise."

Claudio hadn't noticed the sound before the woman mentioned it. "And?" he asked, betraying a less than charitable tone.

"Can you please stop it?"

Claudio took a deep breath and tried not to get angry. "Okay." He stopped pedaling, double knotted the offending shoelace, and started pedaling again. No more noise.

"Thanks," she said with a smile.

"Don't mention it," Claudio answered and he tried to find his place in the book.

***

After working out, Claudio came home and was walking slowly into the den from the garage when he heard the phone ringing. He hurried to get to it before the answering machine picked up.

"Hello," he said still out of breath from his workout.

"Oh, hi. It's Dr. Kayess." She had a heavy and deep voice, punctuated with an Israeli accent, that didn't match her petite body and elegant face. She couldn't have been more than thirty years old, but she sounded much older.

"Hello, doctor. A belated Happy New Year." Claudio tore a sheet from the roll of Scott towels that stood on the counter and wiped his forehead. Though he had converted from Catholicism ten years ago, he still felt ill at ease with the Jewish calendar and didn't want to sound foolish.

"L'Shona Tova," she answered half-heartedly.

The crow started to caw and Claudio looked out the window, vainly trying to spot it. "Do you have any news?" he asked as he pushed to one side several of the plastic vertical blinds.

"Yes," she started. "Yes, the tests came back. Should I call your wife at work?"

Claudio sighed. "No, she said that you could tell me if you called here."

On Rosh Hashanah Lois miscarried for the fifth time. Each time she had carried for only eight or nine weeks. Getting pregnant wasn't an issue. Keeping it became the battle. Dr. Kayess and her older partner, Dr. Mizrahi, had run every imaginable test on Lois *and* Claudio, but they produced no answers. The team had come very highly recommended from two moms at their son's school who had tried to have babies for years but couldn't get pregnant until they went to these doctors. Dr. Mizrahi was about fifty, trim and dapper, with a medical degree from UCLA and a very kind demeanor. Dr. Kayess had studied at Harvard but, because of her youth, she still had not mastered the nuances of the doctor-patient relationship. Lois's miscarriages stymied both doctors. But this time they had some fetal tissue from the DNC and ran some tests. Was there an anomaly in the DNA? Maybe they would have some answers.

"Well, the tissue came back normal."

"Oh," Claudio said as he threw the sopping paper towel in the trash can under the sink. "Anything else?"

"Yes. Though she was only eight weeks along, we know that it was a girl."

Claudio suddenly stiffened his back as he looked up to the ceiling. It was as though an unseen attacker had shoved a long knife between his shoulder blades and held it there just for emphasis. He took a deep breath, trying not to raise his voice. "She doesn't have to know, right?"

There was silence on the other end. Dr. Kayess stumbled on her words. "I'm so—so—sorry."

"I mean, look, she shouldn't have to know. Right? I mean, where does it get any of us? It isn't really necessary, is it?" He looked down to the piles of medical bills and insurance statements that covered a full third of the kitchen counter.

"You mean the gender, right?" she said.

"It would be devastating. We've been hoping for a girl. We even know that we'd name her Rachel. There's no reason for her to know that we lost a girl. Unless that's part of what you need to tell her for a complete consultation."

There was silence. Finally she said, "She doesn't have to know. I'm very sorry. Have her call me so that we can set up an appointment and we can talk about your options."

Claudio said, "Okay, then. We're in agreement."

"Yes." Her voice sounded very small, as though she felt stupid and inexperienced.

"Thank you, doctor," Claudio said and hung up. He sighed and wondered if he had done the right thing. Claudio sighed again, closed his eyes, and counted to ten to calm himself. Since the doctor had agreed that the baby's sex was not relevant to the miscarriage, there was no need to share this news with Lois. So Claudio must have been right. But a voice in his head questioned this logic. Of course she has the right to know, the voice said.

The crow's sharp squawking grew louder and he looked out the window again, searching for it. The morning fog had already burned off, and the bright sun blinded him momentarily. The fig and lemon trees displayed deep green leaves, though one of the six cypresses that lined the back wall was dying from some kind of orange fungus. They had to get a tree doctor out there sometime. Claudio finally gave up, resigned to the fact that he would never see the creature that tormented him. He moved his hand from the vertical blinds and they waved back and forth, making a hollow clacking sound. Claudio slowly walked over to the refrigerator to get something to drink.

NACHO

For Gabino Iglesias

The truth is, Abundio Abarca de Jesús had grown accustomed to the lump on his neck. The mass sat just below his right ear but did not cause any pain or discomfort. Three months earlier, on November 1, his birthday, Abundio had noticed a small, barely perceptible nodule when he slathered on Barbasol shaving cream. Abundio remembered how intriguing he found this new feature—if that was the correct word for it—and eventually anticipated the slow but certain growth he perceived each morning as he commenced his daily ablutions.

When he finally mentioned it to his mother during their once-weekly phone calls, Amaranta Guadalupe de Jesús had exclaimed: "Mijo, you must see the doctor about it!" Since his father had succumbed to lung cancer six years ago, Abundio knew what his mother feared. So he agreed to mention it to his doctor during an upcoming annual checkup. "I promise to show it to the doc, Mamá." And his mother knew that her son's promise was as good as gold.

* * *

Dr. Yesenia Reyes pressed and prodded Abundio's lump as she hummed an indistinct melody that must have sounded quite lovely in her mind's ear but did nothing but annoy her patient, who sat uncomfortably in a backless rough paper robe without anything to shield his skin from the over-active air-conditioning system other than his boxers and argyle socks. Finally she pulled back, looked up into Abundio's wide eyes, and said: "I suspect it's not malignant. But let's do a biopsy to make certain, okay? We can do it here, now."

"Now?"

"Why wait?"

Abundio and Dr. Reyes stared at each other in silence, each waiting for the other to buckle. Abundio lost that battle, as he always did with his doctor.

"Good. Let's get you prepped."

Four days later Abundio received a phone message from Dr. Reyes. He had missed her call because he had taken a wonderful afternoon nap that day, and in order to get the most out of this special time of peace, he had turned off his cell phone. This is what the message said: "Good news. Not cancer. It's what we call a benign lipoma. Nothing to worry about. We can remove it, and you will be as good as new, save for a tiny scar. I have an opening next Thursday. Call my assistant, and we'll take that baby out of you."

Abundio played the message three times, and each time he listened to it he grew a little sadder. He let his mother know, and she was relieved. "¡Maravilloso!" she exclaimed. And then she added: "Is the doctor single?" Abundio ignored this last question and directed his mother to other news about his job, which was not exciting but worked as a perfect deflection. "I got a great annual performance review, Mamá," he said.

"Por supuesto," his mother responded. "They are lucky to have my son!"

* * *

The benign lipoma floated in a small jar that Abundio had set on his nightstand when he came back from the doctor's office. At first, when Dr. Reyes had asked him if he would like to bring it home, Abundio had laughed, thinking this was nothing more than obtuse doctor humor. But Dr. Reyes did not smile and waited for a response to her question. So Abundio said: "Sure."

* * *

Abundio did not like the clinical, somewhat impersonal term of *benign lipoma,* so he renamed the mass of tissue something a bit more friendly: Nacho.

Each night before Abundio turned off his nightstand lamp, he would tap the top of the jar three times and say: "Good night, Nacho."

Sometimes Abundio would add: "Sleep tight, and may you have pleasant dreams."

* * *

Not surprisingly, Abundio's kind and thoughtful care of Nacho did not escape Nacho's notice. Over the course of a week Nacho's once pinkish pallor ignited into a vibrant burgundy. Nacho's fleshy mass responded as well, growing just a bit each night while they both slept.

One morning Abundio realized that Nacho was bulging within the tight confines of the little jar, so Abundio retrieved from the attic an old fishbowl that had once served as a lovely home to three guppies he had named Nina, Pinta, and Santa María, but all three were now long deceased and buried at sea with a flush of a low-flow toilet. The fishbowl now had a new purpose. Nacho seemed quite content in his new abode and continued to flourish.

Eventually Nacho outgrew the fishbowl in a somewhat remarkable and astonishing manner. This is what happened one Sunday night: Abundio plumped up his pillow, turned to the fishbowl, tapped it three times, and said, "Good night, Nacho. Sleep tight, and may you have pleasant dreams." Abundio then turned off the lamp on his nightstand, snuggled into his plump pillow, and fell into a deep sleep. The next morning, as he slowly awoke, he sensed someone standing over him. Abundio opened his eyes and above him was Nacho, no shorter than five feet, eight inches, leaning down to examine Abundio. But since Nacho had no eyes, Abundio was not certain what Nacho perceived.

"Good morning," said Abundio.

Nacho pulled back and stood erect. "Good morning," said Nacho.

At the sound of Nacho's greeting, Abundio thought, *Nacho's voice is much deeper than I would have expected.* And then he wondered, *How does Nacho speak without a mouth?* Many other questions came into his mind, but Abundio decided that they could be saved for later.

"Would you like some breakfast?" asked Abundio.

"Oh, that would be delightful," said Nacho.

Abundio put on a robe and trundled into the kitchen, with Nacho following close behind. He prepared a large pot of coffee and chilaquiles as Nacho sat patiently at the kitchen table. The two new roommates ate their delicious breakfast in contented silence. Nacho eventually drank the last bit of coffee that had cooled at the bottom of his cup.

"Would you like more?" asked Abundio.

"Oh, yes," said Nacho. "You make the best coffee."

This warmed Abundio because no one had ever complimented his coffee before. He poured another cup for Nacho.

"Mil gracias," said Abundio. "I am glad you like it."

"Por nada," said Nacho. "And these chilaquiles are to die for!"

Abundio grinned.

They eventually set up a simple but workable living arrangement. Nacho slept on the living room's foldout couch and Abundio kept his bedroom to himself. Abundio cooked their meals while Nacho eventually got the hang of cleaning house, which he did when Abundio was away at work during the day. On weekends they stayed in, watching movies on the flatscreen, reading magazines and books, playing board games. At first Abundio missed Nacho's nightstand presence, but over time they fell into a placid and fulfilling routine.

* * *

Abundio eventually told his mother about Nacho. When he'd given her as many details as he could think of, she remained silent.

"Mamá, are you still there?"

"Sí, mijo."

"Well?"

"Mijo, I have never heard of such a thing before," his mother ventured. "But you live in a big city, and I know many strange things happen in such big places."

"Strange?"

"Mijo, isn't it strange?" she pressed her son.

"Mamá, what is strange for one person might be very normal for someone else."

"Pues, mijo, most people make friends at school or the office or even at Mass," she said slowly, sensing that perhaps she was pushing her only son a bit too far.

"But this is different, Mamá . . ."

"Sí, diferente, mijo . . ."

"I don't have time to make friends, so I feel lucky I have Nacho."

"Pero, mijo, it is not normal."

"And what is normal?" said Abundio, attempting to control his temper and the conversation.

"Pues, normal is what you see on TV . . ."

"Your telenovelas are normal, Mamá?" said Abundio with a snicker.

"Ay, mijo, never mind," she said, surrendering. "It is your life. And I am sorry."

"Sorry for what, Mamá?"

"I am sorry your father and I could never give you a brother or sister . . ."

"Mamá, don't . . ."

"We tried, but it was not in God's plan."

And with that, mother and son said their good-byes and ended the conversation.

Eventually during their weekly phone calls, she would ask Abundio about Nacho, and he inevitably would tell some funny story about what Nacho had done or said. His mother could not help but chuckle at these stories, and in the end she was happy her son had a new friend, and she never again questioned Abundio about it.

Then one day everything changed.

On a Wednesday Abundio came home from work and could not find Nacho. He searched each room of the house—he even spied into the attic with a flashlight—but Nacho was not to be found. Abundio started to panic. Should he call the police and report a missing . . . missing . . . a missing what? No, the police must not get involved. So Abundio heated some leftovers, quickly ate his dinner, skipped desert, and then made a large pot of coffee to keep him fortified as he waited at the kitchen table for Nacho to return from who-knows-where.

After three hours of waiting—and four and a half cups of coffee—Abundio heard the front door open, then shut. Abundio decided to play it cool and to wait for Nacho to come into the kitchen. After a few moments of silence, Nacho slowly sauntered into the room, deliberately retrieved a cup from the cabinet, and poured the last of the coffee. He took a sip, let out an almost imperceptible burp, and sat down across from Abundio.

"So," said Abundio, unable to stop himself from inquiring. "Where were you?"

Silence.

Then Nacho said: "I went to Lake Balboa."

"In Encino?"

"Yes."

"It must be twenty miles away from here."

Silence.

Then, in almost a whisper, Nacho said: "Why didn't you tell me?"

"Tell you what?"

"How beautiful it all is?"

"How beautiful what all is?"

Nacho leaned forward. "All of it."

Abundio was at a loss. He had no idea where this conversation was headed.

Nacho answered: "The strong tree branches that seem to be reaching for the clouds. The rippling lake water with all types of ducks and geese paddling wildly. The people—children, adults, grandparents—of all shapes and sizes and colors speaking a multitude of languages. And the music coming from small portable speakers. I heard Vicente Fernández's buttery baritone for the first time!"

"Ah, yes, my mother called him Chente. She loves his music. Which song was playing?"

"'Tu Camino y el Mío.'"

"My mother's favorite," said Abundio. "It's such a sad song."

"Yes, it made me cry," said Nacho. "Such heartbreak."

"Yes, such heartbreak."

They sat in silence, wrestling with their own thoughts.

Finally Nacho said: "Why do you think the man doesn't open the letter?"

"The letter?"

"You know, in the song," said Nacho, leaning in toward Abundio. "The man finds a letter written by his love, but he doesn't open it. He just drinks wine and somehow he knows he's lost her. But we don't really know for sure, right?"

"Well," ventured Abundio, "I guess sometimes we just *know.*"

They sat in silence, each pondering the lyrics of Fernández's musical lament.

"It's so sad he passed away," Abundio finally offered.

"What?" said Nacho. "Who passed away?"

"Vicente Fernández. My mother said that she thought he'd live forever."

NACHO

"So sad."

"Yes."

After a few moments Nacho observed: "But in truth, Vicente Fernández lives forever through his music."

"You are quite a philosopher."

Nacho raised his coffee cup: "To Vicente Fernández."

Abundio raised his coffee cup: "Vicente Fernández."

Nacho added: "¡Presente!"

Abundio echoed: "¡Presente!"

With that, Nacho stood and said: "Time for bed."

Within ten minutes both were in their separate sleeping quarters, snoring softly in unison.

* * *

The next morning Abundio awoke as the morning sun came through his window. He felt refreshed, at peace, knowing that Nacho was safe at home. He got out of bed and went into his bathroom. As Abundio slathered on Barbasol shaving cream, he gently fingered the raised scar on his neck just below his right ear. Abundio smiled. After shaving and showering, he walked through the living room and saw that Nacho had already closed the foldout couch and neatened up. Then the wonderful aromas of coffee and chilaquiles wafted into Abundio's nostrils. This was new! Nacho had never made breakfast—or any other meal—before. Abundio sauntered into the kitchen to welcome the new day.

Abundio beheld a perfectly set kitchen table: a full coffee pot, a skillet brimming with steaming chilaquiles set carefully on a trivet, cloth napkins, a small vase with a single pink rose in the middle.

But something was very wrong.

Nacho was nowhere to be seen.

And Abundio suddenly noticed that there was only one place setting.

Abundio broke into a cold sweat. He scanned the modest kitchen for clues. Then he saw it: a small white piece of paper folded neatly leaning against the gleaming toaster. On the paper was the name "Abundio" written in lovely cursive writing.

Abundio crept up to the note, snatched it, and held the paper, wondering what he should do. He held it for seven seconds before deciding that he should open it. And as he read and reread the note—also written in a beautiful cursive hand—the reality of Abundio's new situation slowly sunk into his consciousness. He let the note fall from his fingers, and it floated gently to the tiled floor. Abundio crouched to retrieve it, but then felt himself falling onto his knees. The note looked blurry, and Abundio realized that his eyes brimmed with hot tears.

Abundio's body crumpled, and he shook and trembled. He could feel his chest heave without control. And at that moment Abundio realized that his life had changed forever.

PERMISSIONS AND
SOURCE ACKNOWLEDGMENTS

"Kind of Blue": First published in *Antique Children* (2009). From *The King of Lighting Fixtures: Stories* (The University of Arizona Press, Tucson, AZ, 2017). © 2017 by Daniel A. Olivas. Reprinted by permission of The University of Arizona Press.

"The Lost Soul of Humberto Reyes": From *The King of Lighting Fixtures: Stories* (The University of Arizona Press, Tucson, AZ, 2017). © 2017 by Daniel A. Olivas. Reprinted by permission of The University of Arizona Press.

"Diplopia": From *Anywhere but L.A.: Stories* (Bilingual Press/Editorial Bilingüe, Arizona State University, Tempe, AZ, 2009). © 2009 by Bilingual Press/Editorial Bilingüe. Reprinted by permission of Bilingual Press/Editorial Bilingüe.

"Miles": First published in *linnean street* (2000). From *Assumption and Other Stories* (Bilingual Press/Editorial Bilingüe, Arizona State University, Tempe, AZ, 2003). © 2003 by Bilingual Press/Editorial Bilingüe. Reprinted by permission of Bilingual Press/Editorial Bilingüe.

"The Annotated Obituary of Alejandra López de la Calle": First published in *NonBinary Review*. © 2022 by Daniel A. Olivas. Reprinted by permission of the author.

"New Year": First published in *Chiricú* (2002). From *Assumption and Other Stories* (Bilingual Press/Editorial Bilingüe, Arizona State University, Tempe, AZ, 2003). © 2003 by Bilingual Press/Editorial Bilingüe. Reprinted by permission of Bilingual Press/Editorial Bilingüe.

"Nacho": First published in *The Rumpus* (2022). © 2022 by Daniel A. Olivas. Reprinted by permission of the author.

PERMISSIONS AND SOURCE ACKNOWLEDGMENTS